THE BRAND OF BROTHERHOOD

T.D. ZUMMACK

THE BRAND OF BROTHERHOOD
ENDLESS SKY
BOOKS
T.D. ZUMMACK

THE BRAND OF BROTHERHOOD

Published by
Endless Sky Books
Regina, Saskatchewan, Canada
www.endless-sky-books.com

All characters and events in this book are fictitious.
Any resemblance to persons living or dead is coincidental.

Print ISBN: 978-1-989398-78-4
Ebook ISBN: 978-1-989398-79-1

Cover design by getcovers.com

*Dedicated to Miranda, Justin, Jacob, Marlee, Kail,
and Anthony. Keep chasing your dreams.
Run as long and as far as you have to in order to catch them.
Don't let anyone tell you to stop.*

CHAPTER 1

The 1860s had not been good to the Warner family. William Warner had gone off to fight for the Union during the Civil War. He had left behind a wife and two young sons, one four and one two, as well as a prosperous little grocery business in Boston. Once the war had ended, he had found himself somewhat disenchanted with the country and the government as an institution in general. He did what a great number of citizens were doing: he packed up his family and headed west in 1865 for the wide-open space of the western frontier.

He was a bit of a gentleman—a dandy, some of the rougher men had called him—and had very little experience to employ toward survival in the harsh west. It had been a struggle every step of the way. The west proved wilder than the stories he had heard, but he wasn't a quitter, and slowly he gathered the skills needed for him and his family to build a life. They settled in a town called Ash Hollow in the Nebraska territory and proceeded to try to farm to build their legacy.

It wasn't the prosperous start he had hoped for. Drought had plagued the land for the last two seasons. The ground had been baked hard by hours of hot sunshine, and what water there was had been dammed up and diverted to the land of the large cattle ranchers in the area. Outlaws roamed free, thieving and killing with little regard for what law enforcement there was, and Indian war parties crisscrossed the area frequently.

During this time, William had learned how to shoot and how to ride, as well as how to read sign and track a little. As his boys grew—by then, Colt was ten and Brick was eight—he tried to pass on every new skill he learned to them. Both had learned quickly.

His wife, Margaret, had been a rock through it all, never once complaining, doing her best to make the most of a bad situation and be the good wife and mother she was expected to be. He loved her dearly for it. While other women were parked in a sitting room drinking tea and wasting the day away, his Margaret was out there working the field with him every day.

Her fair complexion had become darkened by endless days in the sun, her long, curly red hair looking like a tongue of flame extending off a lighted match. She had lost weight—they all had—but she still kept her girlish figure. She had been a beautiful woman back home, the toast of Boston, with countless suitors, and even now, under these harshest of conditions, she remained stunning. They were truly partners, and William thanked the Lord every day for bringing her into his life. They struggled together as a family to build the life they wanted, even as the drought wore on for another season and the lawlessness became worse. All of them being together was what mattered.

William continued to try to farm and loved his wife and children that much harder every day. He was doing this for them, trying to give them a future, but there were obstacles at every turn. What little livestock they'd had died under the harsh conditions, and with no crops to harvest, they were forced to butcher their last cow in order to eat over the winter. No crops meant no money, and no livestock meant nothing to sell. They were broke. He had taken a loan from the bank the previous spring and now had no way to pay it back. They were threatening to take his farm.

Life was beating him down at every turn—and then came the final blow, the last obstacle, one he could not overcome, could not live with. In the spring of 1869, his beloved Margaret, mother to his children and love of his life, became ill from cholera and passed away. It was the thirteenth of March, the darkest day of William's life.

Colt remembered the day, too. He was twelve, and Brick was ten. He remembered how hard it was to put the shovel into the frozen ground to dig his mother's grave. He remembered the awful sound of the cold steel hitting the frigid soil. They had only been able to chip away a shallow plot and were then forced to pile rocks on top to cover the body and protect it from animals. It had been hard work, made even more painstaking by doing it while his eyes were filled with tears.

Colt and Brick watched their father's struggles and helped out where they could, but it was never enough. They were witness to his slow descent from a once proud and confident man to someone who had been drummed into submission by relentless strife and turmoil. His mother had been the rock of the family, always there to prop up his dad and never allowing her boys to give up hope. When she became ill, he watched his father sink even faster, spending most nights looking for hope at the bottom of a bottle, and when she passed, Colt watched the light in his father's eyes dim and his posture decline. He looked like he was a balloon, and someone had let out the air.

Colt was worried. What was going to happen to them? Who would look after the family?

He took the role upon himself. He would look after Brick during the day, make the meals, teach him to read the way his mother had taught him, and then, at night, he would take care of his father and make sure he made it to bed safely.

His father still wore a gun belt, although Colt didn't know why since he never used a gun anymore. Colt took the gun out each night and carefully cleaned it before he went to bed. After all, you never knew when it might be needed. He was growing up fast, but then most boys did in the west. It was a necessity if you wanted to survive.

Life was tough and getting tougher. It was another drought-filled summer. Working the field all day under the glare of the hot sun, trying to push the plow through the hard ground, trying to plant seeds in soil with the composition of three-day-old oatmeal, and then praying for just a little bit of rain, any moisture at all, was enough to break a man's spirit and his body. The three of them worked the farm the best they could all season, but there were no animals left to put to work, and what little crop did grow wasn't enough to even try and sell.

A herd of bison roamed lazily past the farm one day, and William managed to hunt a little one. He showed the boys how to butcher the animal, and they were able to eat some that night, make jerky with most of it, and still have some left for a few more meals later on. They weren't living high on the hog, but they were living.

Then came the second day that Colt would never forget. It was late in August when his father burst through the door of the cabin and announced that the three of them were moving. "Pack your bags, lads! We are heading west!"

Colt couldn't believe what he had heard. "What? Where are we going, Pa?"

"Sacramento, Colt, my boy!"

"Where's that?"

"It's in California, right next to the ocean."

"What's California?" asked Brick, wide-eyed at the news.

"California is a place where it's warm all the time. No more harsh winter winds and waist-deep snow for us. It's booming, boys! They're finding gold out there, there're ships to work on, there's rich ranch land, there's an honest job for any man that wants one." William was twitching with so much excitement that Colt thought he was going to start dancing.

"How we gonna get there, Pa?"

"The Union Pacific has finished their railroad; we're going to catch a train, and it will take us right into Sacramento."

"We get to ride a train!" screamed Brick.

"We sure do, son." William picked him up and twirled him around in the air. "Things are going to get better now, boys; they surely will."

Colt spoke up. "But we ain't got no money, Pa. How we gonna ride the train?"

"You leave that to your old dad, son. I'll get us on that train."

It was such exciting news that Colt wanted to believe it was true. He hadn't seen his father this lively in a long time. The light had come back in his eyes, and he almost looked a little taller.

California sounded good. He had been young when his family left Boston, and he could barely remember the ocean. No more winter sounded great, as well. In fact, it all sounded too good to be true, but for one night, Colt allowed himself to be excited, and he fell asleep with thoughts of California in his dreams. Maybe they could have a better life after all; maybe his father would turn things around.

He wished his mom were there.

CHAPTER 2

The next morning, the trio packed what few belongings they had into the wagon of a kindly neighbour who had agreed to take them to Ogallala, where they would catch the train. It was a day's ride to the town normally, but their horse was older and needed more stops in order to make the trek, so it was stretched to a day and then some. The ride was uneventful, which was unusual for the territory at that time. There were always war parties about, but Colt was glad to have not seen any.

As the daylight turned into the darkness of the night, Colt sat beside his father, while Brick slept in a corner of the wagon, and stared at the millions of stars glittering above their heads while William spoke of his grand plans for when they reached Sacramento. A full moon hung high in the sky and lit the prairie in front of them like someone was holding a kerosene lantern just ahead. It was a warm night with barely a breeze. The whole world seemed peaceful and quiet. It was in moments like this when you could feel the majesty and the beauty of this harsh, unforgiving land.

"It's going to be all right, Colt. I'll get a job working a ranch or maybe get some money and stake a gold claim. After I've saved some cash, I can open a grocery store, like we had in Boston, and become a businessman."

"What about me and Brick? What're we gonna do?"

"Well, we'll get you boys in school, where you can get to learning. Knowledge is power, Colt. The more a man knows, the better equipped he is to handle any situation that life may bring him. I've tried to teach you boys what I can about survival, give you the physical tools you need; now it's time for you and your brother to get the book smarts to go with it. A man that can think first . . . well, that's a dangerous man. Any fool can draw a gun. It takes a smart man to think of a reason not to."

After that, they sat in silence. Colt had never felt closer to his father than he did that night. He would remember it for the rest of his life.

The slow rise of the sun the next morning brought the town of Ogallala into the light. A typical western town, it popped up out of the open prairie like an arrow jutting from its heart. Wooden buildings lined both sides of a muddy, makeshift street, and as they slowly drove their wagon down the main street, Colt and Brick took it all in. It was larger than Ash Hollow, with some of the buildings being two or three stories high.

The boys squinted as the climbing sun reflected off the windows with a searing glare. There were very few people awake yet, and the town was eerily quiet, only the squeaking and creaking of their wagon as it rolled along putting sound in their ears. Then, off in the distance, there was a volley of gunshots and then another.

The horse kept plodding, and they made their way through

town to the train yard on the far side. William had the neighbor pull the wagon to a stop to survey the scene, and it was then that Colt realized his father's plan might not have been altogether that well thought out.

William asked to have the wagon slowly moved into the train yard and parked it alongside a supply shed, out of sight of the station. He carefully lifted Brick out of the wagon while Colt climbed down from the bench. As his father pressed them up against the side of the building and peered around the corner, Colt realized that the plan was to sneak aboard the train.

He joined his father and sneakily glanced out towards the track. He could see a train, the locomotive slowly and lazily puffing smoke as it got warmed up and ready to make its journey. Looking closer, Colt realized there were no passenger cars on the train, only boxcars for cargo. "How we gonna go, Dad?" he whispered. "There ain't no passenger cars on the train."

There were gunshots in the distance again, followed by some men whoopin' and hollerin'.

William turned and bent down on one knee to speak to his boys. "All right, boys, when I say 'go,' you are gonna light out and run as fast as you can for that last boxcar. When you get there, you crawl underneath and stay hidden there until I tell you to come out. Understood?"

They nodded.

"Good. Okay. Get ready, and . . . go!"

The boys ran as fast as they could while each was carrying his own bag. About halfway to the boxcar, Brick tripped and fell into the dirt, raising a huge cloud of dust. Colt looked back at him in a panic, ran to his brother, picked both him and his bag off the ground, and carried Brick's bag as well as his own as they continued to run toward the boxcar.

They got to their destination, and each boy deftly slipped under the boxcar without much sound at all. William joined them a moment later. "You boys sit tight. I'm gonna take a quick look and be right back."

The boys lay quietly in the dirt until their father returned. "The cars are all full, boys; there's no room for the three of us," he reported.

"What are we gonna do, Dad?"

William thought for a minute and then stood up and drew his gun. He waited and, when he heard the next volley of gunshots in the distance, fired his gun at the lock on the boxcar door. The lock fell to the ground. He slid open the door. "All right, Brick, come here." Brick crawled out, Colt close behind. William lifted Brick into the boxcar. "You climb up them boxes, boy, and squeeze yourself into that far corner back there, as far back as you can, and you lie flat, you understand?"

"Yes, Pa." Brick scurried up and tried to squeeze as far back as he could.

"Good boy. Okay, Colt, you're next. Let's go."

Colt climbed up the boxes and tried to squeeze in with his brother. There was barely enough room for Colt, who was big for his age. There was no way his dad would fit up there with them.

William threw the supply bags up to the boys. "You boys hold onto these and keep hidden the best you can." He removed his gun and holster from his belt and threw them up to Colt, as well. "Keep it safe, Colt. Never let anyone take your gun from you. You remember that."

"What are you gonna do, Pa?" As he asked, Colt heard the whistle blow. The train was gearing up to head out.

"Don't worry about me. I'll do something."

William Warner closed the door on his boys. Colt could

hear his father rustling about outside. Suddenly, with a violent jerk, the train started to pull ahead. Colt tried to peer out between the slats of the boxcar but couldn't see his father anywhere.

The train was picking up speed now. "Pa! Pa!" Colt tried to yell over the noise of the train as it rolled down the tracks.

Out of nowhere, fingers appeared through one of the openings between slats, and there was his father, hanging onto the back of the train. "Pa! You're here!"

"Hush up, Colt and help me with this." William passed one end of his empty gun belt through the slats. Colt grabbed it and held on tight. "Good job, son; now grab this end." He passed the other end around his body and through the slats again.

William tried to wedge the toe of his boots farther into one of the slats to give himself a stronger perch. The train was rocking side to side as it sped along the tracks, and it was clearly getting harder for him to keep his grip. "Pull them together and do up the belt, son."

Colt tried to pull the ends together, but he was on his stomach, reaching his arms down into a tiny crack of space between the boxes and the walls of the car, and couldn't manipulate his fingers as well as he would have liked. The belt wasn't long enough. He couldn't get the ends together.

"It ain't long enough, Pa! They won't go together!" Colt tried to yell over the noise.

"Damn! Well, see if you can find something to tie them together, maybe. And look fast, Colt, it's getting harder to hold on out here!"

Colt and Brick both tried to look around the car, but it was dark except for tiny rays of early morning light peeking through the slats. There wasn't much to see, just rows of wooden crates.

Colt had an idea; he maneuvered his hands around his own waist and removed his belt from his pants. He reached down into the sliver of space again and hooked the two belts together. He pulled as tight as he could muster and locked the clasp. William Warner, for all intents and purposes, was now tied to the train.

The train rumbled its way down its route all morning. They had started their journey, but it wasn't easy travelling. The hot sun beat down on them for hours, and it sapped the strength of William, exposed to it directly the whole time. It wasn't any easier for the boys as the inside of the boxcar was like an oven, the heat almost unbearable. They were squeezed into a tight space and sweating profusely. They had some water in the supply bags, but they were going to use that up quickly if the heat continued like this. Brick was crying that he was thirsty, but Colt rationed the water carefully.

It was an excruciating journey for all of them, fraught with danger as the train had to stop every ten miles for water, and every stop increased the possibility that William would be discovered, but at least they were on their way.

The train kept rolling slowly into the afternoon. The sun was at its highest now, pounding them with its heat.

There was jerky in the bag, and Colt gave some to Brick. He peered through the slats to see his father sweating profusely, his face looking worn, burned by the sun. His eyes were closed, and his body rocked side to side gently with the motion of the train. "Dad?"

William opened his eyes slightly. Colt passed a piece of the jerky through the slats. William took it and managed a little smile. "Thanks, son."

The train chugged on and on. The gentle swaying and the monotonous sound of the wheels, not to mention the excruciating heat, made the boys lethargic, and they slept for the better part of the afternoon. It was late evening when they finally awoke because the train was slowing.

Colt awoke with a start and banged his head on the roof of the boxcar. He checked on Brick and gave him a shake. Brick moaned and started to rub his eyes. Colt's throat was on fire, and his mouth felt like he had eaten a wool sweater. He took a small sip of water and gave Brick one, too. He looked out to check on his father and saw him still holding on but asleep or unconscious.

As the train came to a stop, Colt tried to awaken his father. "Pa! Pa, what do we do now? Is this Sacramento?"

William opened his eyes and looked around. "It's not Sacramento, Colt. Loosen the belt; let me down." Colt undid the belt and watched as his father fell to the ground in a heap.

William finally stirred and then got himself up on all fours. He looked around carefully, then crawled to a large water trough that stood beside the tracks in front of the water tower. He scooped some water in his hands and drank. Then he lifted himself up and dropped his entire body into the trough with a loud splash. He lay there so long Colt was afraid he would drown, but finally, he sat up, wiped the water from his eyes, and pushed his hair back out of his face before locating his hat and putting it on. He took another careful look around and must not have seen anybody because he came back to the boxcar and opened the door. "Come on down, boys, let's stretch our legs a little."

Both boys crawled down and struggled a bit to stand until the circulation returned to their legs. Brick was crying.

"What's the matter, boy?" asked William.

"I wet my britches, Pa. I didn't mean to, but I couldn't wait no more."

"It's all right, Brick. The rules don't always apply, depending on your situation. A man does what he has to in order to survive, and if it comes down to you living or dying, well, then, I reckon there are worse things than wet britches. Nothing to be ashamed of."

The boys washed their faces in the trough, too. William then grabbed the chain and lowered the spout of the water tower so they could refill their canteens with fresh water. They ate some more of the jerky and then saw some lanterns at the front of the train. "Time to get back in, boys, and don't make a sound." They hustled back into their hiding spot, and William closed the door. He ran into the bushes just as two men approached the boxcar.

"Where's the lock on this one?" one of them asked.

"Don't know. Everything in there?"

The first man slid the door open, and the boys squeezed as far back as they could, holding their breath. They could see the lantern light casting different shadows as the man swung it back and forth, but he never climbed into the car. After what felt like an eternity, they heard the first man say, "Looks like it. Don't see nothing wrong."

"Maybe it fell off during the run. Just put another one on and hurry up. We have to attach another coal car yet before we're finished. They hear that bad weather is coming, and they want to go as far as they can in one shot, try and outrun it. And I want to get back to the bunkhouse— we're having stew for supper tonight."

Colt heard the door close, and the metallic click of a new lock being placed on it. After the men had gone, William re-emerged.

"You boys all right?" he whispered.

"We're all right, Pa, but they locked us in," Colt replied.

"It's all right, son. We'll figure it out tomorrow. You and your brother get some sleep."

The boys tried to make the best of the wooden boxes and get some shut eye. The cool breeze was a welcome relief from the heat of the day, and it felt nice as Colt lay in the car, staring at the ceiling.

He felt a nudge at his side, and Brick whispered, "Good night, Colt."

"Good night, Brick."

"Colt?'

"Yeah?"

"I'm a little scared. I wish Ma was here."

"Me too, Brick, me too. Get some sleep. It'll be all right."

Colt lay there staring into the darkness, thinking about his mother. The last sound he remembered before falling asleep was that of his father trying to get comfortable underneath the boxcar.

Chapter 3

The boys were awakened the next morning by the sound of the crew preparing the train to leave again. Colt's body was stiff from sleeping on the hard, wooden crates, and he moved slowly as he tried to face the back of the car. He peered out of the slats to try to see his father, but he was nowhere to be found. "Pa? Pa?"

"Shh!" Colt heard the sound from the bushes. His father must be hiding there until it was time to go.

After a few minutes, the boys heard the lonely whistle sound and then felt the familiar buck as the train started moving. Just as they were picking up speed, William's fingers appeared in the slats again, and they repeated the routine from yesterday morning. Once again, the three were on their way.

Once they were up to speed, the gentle rocking started again, and the boys passed the time by telling stories, each one saying what he hoped Sacramento would be like. It was another blistering day, and they rationed their water and jerky accordingly. Colt couldn't wait for this part of the journey to be over: that boxcar was an oven on wheels. He felt even worse for Pa, who looked so weak in the sun it was like if it wasn't for the belt holding him on, he would have fallen off miles ago. It was the worst Colt had seen him look since his ma had died.

It was late in the afternoon that second day when their arduous journey took a turn for the worse. There was a distinct drop in temperature as clouds filled the sky and blocked out the sun. Peering through the slats, Colts could see the day was now a dreary, hazy grey, not bright and vibrant as it had been to that point. "What's happening, Pa? What's going on?"

"It looks like we're heading into the mountains, boys. We could be getting an early winter storm. You two find something to keep warm with."

"What about you?"

"Don't worry about me; I'll be okay. You make sure your little brother is taken care of."

"Okay, Pa. I will."

The train climbed gradually higher up the Laramie Range of mountains. Colt could see that it had started to snow, and the temperature was still dropping. The train was moving slower, and the boys had nothing to wrap around themselves. Brick had started to cry again as he got cold, and Colt hugged him tightly so they could share body heat.

The snow fell more heavily, and the train just crept its way down the track. Evans Pass was supposed to be the easy way through the range, which was why the track was built there, but the heavy snow was causing problems for the locomotive. It took many more hours for the train to get through the pass than it would normally have, and the boys fell asleep, still hugging one another in an attempt to stay warm. It was dark by the time the snow stopped falling and the train had cleared the pass.

Colt awoke with a violent shudder. He was so cold he

could barely unwrap himself from Brick. In the process, he woke Brick, who weakly opened his eyes. "Colt, my foot hurts. Something's wrong."

Colt looked at Brick's feet and could see that his right foot had been pressed against the wall of the car. He didn't know how long it had been that way, but there was frost gathering on Brick's boot. He did his best to gently pull the foot away from the wall and then placed some of the supply bags over top of it in an attempt to warm it up.

"It's okay, Brick, you're just cold. We'll feel better when we get warm."

He turned his attention to his father. William's chin was resting on his chest, and Colt could see the amount of snow that had gathered on his hat. "Pa? Pa? You awake?"

There was no response from William. Colt tapped his father's fingers to try to wake him. They were cold to the touch.

The train bumped and jostled a little at that point, and William's head fell back. His eyes were closed, there was frost gathering on his cheeks, and his lips were blue. In his already weakened state, William Warner had frozen to death.

Colt wanted to scream, but he remembered Brick behind him and stifled it. What would they do? Who was going to look after them?

Colt felt a tap on his shoulder, and Brick asked, "Is Pa okay, Colt? Did he wake up?"

Colt thought for a second and then decided to answer honestly. "No, Brick. Pa's dead."

Brick stared at his brother wide-eyed as tears started to run down his cheeks.

"You can't cry, Brick. Not now. The tears will freeze, and you'll get frostbite."

Colt didn't know what to do. He wanted to cry right along with Brick, wanted to scream and yell and hug his father, but more than anything, he wanted off that damn train. The two boys lay hugging one another in silence as the train continued along.

It was another two hours before the train finally pulled into its final stop for the day at Laramie. The boys were stiff and cold and barely conscious when they saw lanterns moving around in the darkness outside. "Oh, my Lord! This man is froze! Hey! Over here!"

"Don't touch him! That's our Pa!" Colt yelled from inside the train.

"Who's that? Who's in there?"

"Me and my brother, that's who! He's our pa. You leave him alone!"

"Oh, Jesus, there's kids in there. Somebody get the keys."

A crowd of men had gathered by the time the door was opened and Colt and Brick were helped down. A tall man with a large belly, wearing a vest and trousers and looking very important, grabbed Colt by the shoulder.

"What are you doing in there? How'd you get in there?" He had black, slicked-back hair, a waxed mustache on a pie-shaped face, and large jowls that shook a little when he talked.

"Our Pa put us there. We're going to Sacramento." Colt wriggled his shoulder away from the man.

"Sacramento? Ha! I don't think so. I don't allow stow-aways on my railroad.". The man grabbed Colt by the shoulder again. "Go get the sheriff. I'll make sure these little urchins and their frozen father don't go anywhere except jail and the graveyard."

"Don't touch him!" Colt wriggled free again and pulled his father's gun from his waistband. "Don't nobody touch him or us again! Just leave us alone! We don't want no trouble." Colt was pointing the gun wildly at the crowd and fighting back tears as Brick hid behind him.

"Okay, okay. Just calm down now, son." This was a new voice. The crowd parted, and a tall, thin man with broad shoulders came forward. He had a strong jawline and a square chin, and even in the poor lantern light, Colt could see kindness in his eyes. "Just take it easy. We don't want anybody getting hurt. Do we, now, Mr. Robillier?"

The man in the vest answered. "Listen here, Mr. Borden! These boys are stowaways, and I won't have it. God only knows what they stole while they were in there. And now, to pull a gun? I'm going to make an example of them."

"You'll do no such thing. These boys just did what their father asked, and I think he paid the price." He pointed at William Warner, still hanging on the train. "Some of you boys get a blanket or something, and let's cut the poor man down. And be careful; his boys have been through enough." He knelt in front of Colt. "I'm Jim Borden. You boys will come with me. What's your name?"

"I'm Colt Warner, and this here is Brick." Brick hobbled out from behind Colt on his sore right foot.

"That looks like it hurts, son. What say we get you two over to Doc, and he checks you out?"

"What about our Pa?"

"The undertaker will come and get him. He'll treat him right. How 'bout you give me that gun, and we get going?" He reached out his hand.

"Pa said you never give no man your gun." Colt put the gun back in his waistband.

"All right, Colt. Your pa was a smart man."

The man in the vest spoke again, "Mr. Borden, I must insist that the sheriff . . ."

Borden gave the man a cold stare that stopped him mid-sentence and left his mouth hanging open. "The boys will be at Doc's," he said. "If the sheriff wants to find them, you send him there to speak to me. Any issue with that?"

The man in the vest stood silent.

"Let's go, Colt. There's a wagon right over here we can use."

"Who was that man?" asked Colt as he climbed aboard the wagon.

"That was Mr. Patrick Robillier. He's a representative for Union Pacific and thinks he's a lot more important than he is."

"If he's an important man, why was he scared of you?"

"No real reason. Mr. Robillier is a blowhard Colt, and sometimes with a blowhard, if you blow back harder, they'll fold." He paused for a second. "Sometimes."

They arrived at the doctor's house, and Jim knocked on the door. It was very late by now, and the doc answered in his night clothes, fumbling for his glasses. "What can I do for you, Mr. Borden?"

"These two boys just came off the Union Pacific, Doc. It was mighty cold on that train; their father froze to death, and the little one looks like he's injured his foot. Can you check 'em out?"

"Sure, sure. Of course." He stepped aside so they could enter. "Put the little one on the table, and let's have a look." Doc was gingerly looking at Brick's right boot. "Off the train, you say? I thought they weren't taking passengers yet?"

"They weren't. The boys just hitched a ride in a boxcar."

Colt relayed the whole story as Doc cut away Brick's boot and sock. His little toe and part of the side of his foot were black like tar. "This isn't good, not good at all," Doc said. "He's got severe frostbite here. We're going to have to remove the dead parts."

"Remove my toe? Colt, don't let 'em take my toe!" Brick was terrified.

"They got to Brick, or it'll get worse, and they'll take your whole foot." Colt was crying. "It's okay; it's just the little one. All you ever do is stub that one anyway." He tried to laugh a little.

"Colt, no!" Brick pleaded.

Jim ushered Colt out of the room as the doctor prepared for the operation. "I'm sorry, Brick," Colt said as he left the room.

EXHAUSTED AND WARM AT LAST, Colt fell asleep in the parlor. He was awakened by Jim. "Colt? Brick is okay. The doctor's done."

"Can I see him?"

"He's sleeping right now, but sure."

They walked into the other room. Brick was still on the table, fast asleep. His right foot was wrapped in a bandage, and there was some blood showing through from the still-leaking wound.

"Why don't you come to my place and get some sleep, Colt?" Jim asked. "Brick's gonna be out for a while; there's nothing for you to do here."

"I'm gonna stay here, Mr. Borden. Brick will be scared when he wakes up. He'll need me."

Jim looked at Doc.

"It's fine, Mr. Borden," Doc said. "I'll keep them here for the night."

"Okay, Colt. I'll come by and check on you in the morning." Jim turned to go.

"Mr. Borden?"

He turned back. "Yeah, Colt?"

"Thank you for everything you did tonight."

"You're welcome, Colt. And call me Jim."

Jim walked out the door into the night, and Colt turned his attention back to Brick, asleep on the table. He had promised his dad that he would look after his brother, and Brick was already wounded and lying on a doctor's table. He was failing already. How were they ever going to make it to California?

He made up his mind. They were still going to Sacramento. That was where their father had wanted them, and that was where they were going to be. He just had to figure out how to get there.

He fell asleep in a chair with the thoughts of a plan still swirling in his head.

CHAPTER 4

The sun shining through a crack in the curtains awakened him. He squinted in the bright light, then stretched and rubbed the sleep out of his eyes.

He looked at the table. Brick was gone. Panic hit him, and he yelled, "Brick? Brick, where are you?"

"I'm right here, Colt." Brick came around the corner with Doc right behind him. Brick was using a crutch to walk. "The doc gave me this crutch, Colt. He says I'll only need it for a few days. Isn't it neat?"

Colt was glad that Brick was in good spirits despite everything that had happened. "Looks good, Brick. You had me worried."

"He'll only need the crutch for a bit, but I'm afraid that he'll walk with a hitch in his stride for the rest of his life," Doc informed Colt.

Colt was about to say something when there was a knock on the door. Jim Borden had come to check on the two boys to make sure they were handling things all right.

"Good morning, Doc. Colt, Brick, how're you two doing?"

"We're doing all right, Mr. Borden. Thanks again for last night."

"Look at this neat crutch, Mr. Borden!"

"Brick, I told Colt, and now I'm telling you, call me Jim. And Colt, there's no need to thank me. I just lent a hand where I could."

"Well, thank you anyway," Colt said. "Can I ask you a question?"

"Go ahead, son."

"What happened to our father?"

"The undertaker has him, Colt. It was figured that you boys didn't have any money for a burial, so the town is covering the cost, and he's getting buried on Boot Hill. They're trying to dig the hole right now, but this snow is causing some issues. They'll get him buried later today, and then I'll take you boys to say your respects."

Colt liked Jim. He had a tone in his voice that was calming for him, he didn't treat Colt like he was a kid, and so far, he'd always been honest with the boys.

They ate breakfast at Doc's place. "What's your plan now, Colt?" Jim asked as they ate. "Are you interested in a job here in Laramie? I know some men that may be able to help."

"No, sir. We are going to Sacramento."

"How're you gonna do that? You ain't got no money or horses."

"I don't know, but that's where we're going. Pa wanted us there, and that's where we're gonna be."

"Let me ask around and see what I can find for you. You boys mind a travel partner?"

"Thank you, but we don't need one. We can look after ourselves."

"Oh, I know it, Colt. I was just thinking that Sacramento sounded pretty good, and I got nothing keeping me here. Thought I might like some company with me."

"Well, I guess it sounds pretty good, then."

After Colt had spoken, Jim got up and left Doc's place. "You boys sure are lucky that Jim Borden has taken a liking to you," said Doc. "There are worse travel companions you could have, that's for sure."

"How do you mean?"

"You boys don't know Jim Borden? He used to be a gunfighter. Good one, too. I guess 'used to' is the wrong term since I'm sure he could probably still skin a weapon faster than most men. That's the thing about gunfighters, once you're one, you're always one. The only time you're not one is if you're dead."

"He's killed men?" Colt asked.

"How many?" Brick asked excitedly

"Oh, I'm not sure of the exact number, but it's a good many. He's got a reputation in almost every town in these parts. I've known him five years, and he's a good man, a solid, stand-up guy, not like some of those other gunfighters with cold reputations. He's a killer, all right, but he tries to avoid it as much as he can."

Colt was shook. Jim, a real-life gunfighter? He had read dime novels about some of the west's best but had never met one in person.

He thought back to the previous night and the way Mr. Robillier had backed down when pressed by Jim. It made sense now. Mr. Robillier was no gun hand.

The brothers were hungry, so they spent the better part of

the morning eating Doc's food and listening to the stories he told of the colorful history of Laramie. Jim showed up just before lunch and told the boys that he had secured transportation for the three of them.

"The train's not taking passengers officially yet, but Mr. Robillier has a personal car that he's attaching to the train so that he can get west, and he has agreed to let us travel with him."

"Really? I thought he didn't like us?"

"It took a little coaxing, but he came around. He really is a reasonable man when he wants to be." Jim smiled a little.

Brick was excited. "You mean we get to sit in chairs and look out the windows and stuff?"

"Sure do, Brick. All the way to California."

"Did you hear that, Colt? On the train like fancy people."

"Sounds like fun, Brick. It'll be a good trip. Thanks, Jim."

"Get your stuff together. We leave in about an hour."

The boys packed quickly, and then Jim followed through on his promise and took the boys to see their father's gravesite. As they rode through town, the boys' jaws were agape. Laramie was even larger than Ogallala and was a bustling town. There were people walking everywhere, piano sounds coming from every second building, and the noise from the crowd was a slow, steady rumble that didn't stop for a second the entire time they rode through.

The boys had never seen anything like it. The crowd was a mix of cattle hands, card sharps, businessmen, ladies, and whores. They mingled with one another, each chasing their own agenda. Brick sat wide-eyed in the wagon with a smile as big as the Laramie Mountains on his face, fascinated by the scene. Colt sat next to Jim, "It's amazing. Look at all these people. What are they all doing?"

"Some have business, some want to drink and gamble, others have nothing to do and just want to be part of the scene."

Colt had a question to ask. "Jim? Is Mr. Robillier helping us because he's scared of you?"

"What makes you think he would be scared of me?"

"Doc told us you're a gunfighter, said you were real good."

"*Used* to be a gunfighter, Colt."

"Doc says the only way you used to be a gunfighter is if you're dead."

"Doc talks too much."

"Did you kill people?" Brick blurted out.

"Some."

"That's neat," said Brick.

"It's not neat, Brick. Taking a man's life is serious business, and it's something you should do only when you have no other choice. It changes a man, changes his soul. You should know how to use a gun, it's a tool like any other, but only draw on another man as a last resort."

"So, Mr. Robillier?"

"Yes, he's scared."

The trio arrived at the cemetery, and Jim led them to their father's grave. Colt looked around and felt ashamed. His father deserved more than a simple white cross that didn't even have his name on it. He had been a hard worker, a good husband, and a good father. He'd had his demons, but he'd also had good intentions.

The boys said their goodbyes, and while Brick wiped the tears from his eyes, Colt put his hand on the paltry wooden cross and made a promise to his father that one day he would come back and give him a proper headstone. With that, he turned and walked back to the wagon, taking his place on the seat. "Let's go."

Jim helped Brick into the back and then climbed aboard himself. They sat in silence as they rode to the railyard. Once there, Jim spoke to a man and told him to make sure that the horse and wagon got returned to Doc's place. Then they grabbed their things and climbed the ladder to Mr. Robillier's personal car.

Jim knocked once and then opened the door to the car. Mr. Robillier was sitting in the middle of the car in a large leather chair. When he saw the boys, Colt could swear he made an expression like he had just smelled the business end of a horse. This was a man that Colt did not like.

The car was something the boys could have only imagined. Part of it had been walled off to make a sleeping quarter for Mr. Robillier. There were more leather chairs, artwork on some of the walls, and fancy tablecloths and silverware. It was better furnished than all the houses back in Ash Hollow. Colt couldn't believe one man could have this much money.

"Mr. Borden! Welcome aboard. It is quite fortuitous to have a man such as yourself along for this journey; it is my understanding that the territory can be quite dangerous. And the children! I imagine this trip will be quite educational for them as well. What luck!" Colt could feel the sarcasm dripping from every word.

"Well, it was mighty generous of you to allow us to tag along. We won't be a problem, I promise you that. You won't even know we're here."

Colt could tell Jim was laying it on just as thick as Mr. Robillier. It made him smile a little.

"Nonsense, nonsense. What kind of representative of Union Pacific would I be if I didn't help the less fortunate when the chance presented itself? Please, make yourselves comfortable."

Brick hopped into a chair next to a window and stared out excitedly. It had been hard to see from inside the boxcar, and he didn't want to miss anything. Again, the boys heard the familiar whistle announcing that the train was getting ready to leave, followed by the same lurch forward, and they were on their way.

They slowly rolled out of Laramie into the empty wilderness of the Wyoming territory. Colt settled into a chair and stared aimlessly out the window. So much had happened over the last few days, and he hadn't had time to process it. He looked out over the landscape as the train rolled down the track and tried to figure out their future. What were they going to do? He was glad Jim had come with them; it gave him some comfort.

Mr. Robillier started to talk again. "We'll only go as far as Green River today, Mr. Borden. We'll spend the night there and then start out early in the morning, get a full day's travel in."

"That sounds just fine, Mr. Robillier."

The terrain they were travelling was new to Colt. It was mountainous and harsh and when there were no mountains it was a desert that was hot and equally harsh in its own right. A lonely land, not made for man to inhabit. Colt wondered how anything could survive in this territory. He felt small, and at the same time there was an excitement inside him. Starting fresh stirred something inside of him. He couldn't wait for Sacramento.

They had been travelling for two hours working their way through a pass in the mountains when they suddenly heard some yelling and hollering from outside the train. Colt looked out the window and saw a group of Indian riders standing along the ridge above the train. Colt counted seven.

"Indians!" Brick was pointing out the window on his side of the train as well. Colt ran over and looked out, seven more riders on the ridge above them there as well. Colt assumed it was a war party.

"Filthy savages!" yelled Mr. Robillier as he grabbed for a rifle hanging on the wall. He started to aim the rifle out the window, but Jim grabbed the barrel and wrestled it from his hands.

"They're just causing trouble!" Jim said. "They're not going to attack."

"How can you be sure?"

"Each one has a weapon, but no one is firing. None of them are wearing paint, either. They're just trying to scare us. You shoot first, and then there *will* be trouble. They don't want to try their luck with a moving train—it's a much tougher target than they want, especially with only fourteen riders—but they will if necessary. The rest are probably camped up ahead, and if they hear fightin', they'll put together a barricade and knock us off the tracks. That's when they'll pounce."

"They're savages, not strategists! What do you suggest we do? Ride quietly to the slaughter?"

Jim raised his leg, kicked Robillier square in the chest, and knocked him back into his chair. He placed his foot on the man's chest and held him there. "I suggest you sit there and keep your mouth shut before I throw you off this train and give them Indians something to holler about."

Robillier opened his mouth to speak but thought better of it once his eyes met the cold steel glare of Jim's.

"Colt, Brick, back away from the windows a bit and try not

to pay them any mind," Jim said without taking his eyes off Robillier. "They'll leave us alone after a bit."

They had rattled a few more miles down the track when they saw the rest of the tribe. It was as Jim had said, there were forty or fifty more there and Colt could see large logs and rocks they had gathered laying around them. They really had been waiting and if the men on the train had taken the bait, they would have derailed them and attacked them all. Robillier's eyes went wide, but he never said a word. He was quiet the rest of the way to Green River.

Once they arrived, he had food brought for them all. He and Jim were going to head into the town while the boys slept on the train. Colt and Brick found themselves some comfortable chairs to sleep in. They could hear the clamor of the town, voices, music, and the occasional gunshot, and Brick was too excited to sleep. Before Jim left, Colt stopped him and asked. "Jim, how did you know that stuff? How did you know not to shoot?"

"I've spent a lot of time on the trails Colt, and I've tried to make the most of that time. I've listened, I've learned, I've paid attention to what others say has worked for them in those situations. Knowledge is a powerful thing, Colt. Remember what I said about only drawing when you must? A smart man knows when he must."

The two men left. As Colt stared up at the dark ceiling, he heard Brick's voice from the shadows. "Colt, do you think Jim's right? Or do you think Mr. Robillier is right?"

"I'm putting my money on Jim, Brick."

"Why? I thought Indians was bad, and we was s'posed to kill 'em."

"That stuff he said about knowledge and knowing when to draw? It was the same stuff Pa said."

CHAPTER 5

From the windows of the train, the scenery was more of what they had seen yesterday, beautiful, yet scary and dangerous at times. Brick, looking ahead out the window, saw a small shack nestled in amongst the trees and rocks. It didn't look like much, smaller than what they had lived in back in Ash Hollow.

"Someone lives out here?" Brick asked.

"They sure do, Brick. Lots of folks prefer solitude, living off the land with no one out here to tell them what to do. Living with Mother Nature and working together to get along. It's a simple life, but not an easy one. If you don't know what you're doing, what you're looking for, you don't last long."

"Yes, yes, quite right." Mr. Robillier spoke like he was delivering a sermon. "Those poor unfortunate souls live in those ramshackle dwellings while they struggle every day just to try and scratch out a meager existence, and for what? So they can die on a tiny piece of land they can say they own? It would be much easier to move into a town and start a business. Get yourself a decent dwelling and save the money you make. That's the real 'American Dream,' boys: get more money than the rest and have as much power as possible."

Jim stared at Mr. Robillier as though trying to drill a hole in him with his eyes. "Don't listen to him, boys," he said. "There's nothing wrong with working hard, on land you own, to make an honest living. Those people, people like your pa, are the backbone of this country. They're honest, proud, trustworthy folk and some of the toughest people I have ever met. They may not make a lot of money, but they're always willing to share what they have with a fellow in need."

Colt felt pride at the mention of his father, but he was watching Brick as Mr. Robillier spoke and saw his eyes light up. Brick had had enough of the hardscrabble farm life, enough of his school friends having more than him, and what Mr. Robillier was saying was striking a chord. Colt was worried that Brick might be taking the wrong advice to heart, might be choosing the wrong side.

Jim taught more lessons the rest of the afternoon as they rolled along. He pointed out wildlife, where the animals lived, and their favorite things to eat, pointed out what plants had hidden water reservoirs a man could draw on if he was lost and on his own out here, and even gave them more shooting lessons out the windows of the train car.

Jim seemed impressed by both boys' prowess and how easily they picked things up. Even Mr. Robillier seemed impressed at times. It was an invaluable education, and Colt couldn't wait for each new lesson. He wondered how many men out here would give their fortunes for lessons like these.

In between lessons, Colt tried to form a plan for what he and Brick would do once they arrived in Sacramento. He couldn't expect Jim to be there for the rest of their lives. Nor did he want him to be: a man had to learn to stand on his own.

The next few days followed the same routine. There wasn't a lot to do on a moving train. A trip that was supposed to take a week was taking longer because Mr. Robillier stopped the train at every station to conduct railroad business.

Jim expanded the lessons to include some quick-draw practice, and the boys appeared to be naturals. Both were able to pull the gun from the holster, although while Colt could draw it freely, Brick struggled a bit under the weight. They tried to pull with one smooth motion, and their times got faster the more they practiced.

The nightly routine was the same as well, with Colt and Brick left in the car while Jim and Robillier headed into whatever town they were stopped at that day. They could always hear the town from the car, and curiosity and cabin fever were starting to get the better of them. They couldn't wait for the opportunity to finally see one of these bustling frontier towns up close.

"Colt, let's sneak out, go see the town," Brick urged one night.

"No, Brick. Jim wants us to stay here, and I think we should. Besides, Mr. Robillier is looking for any excuse to kick us off, and if that happens, I don't know how we get to Sacramento."

"Please, Colt. Aren't you even a little curious? Don't you want to see the casino or the dance hall? See a real-life gunman?"

Brick was playing on Colt's curiosity, and he finally won the battle. "Okay, Brick. Half an hour. That's it. We'll see what we can see, and then we'll come back. Deal?"

Brick was smiling from ear to ear. "Okay, Colt. Deal."

They crept off the train and stuck to the shadows as they made their way into town. They came across a building from which spilled piano music and the sound of a boisterous crowd. They guessed this must be the casino.

Peering through a window, they saw busy card tables everywhere and a large bar across the room from them. The place was packed with all sorts of men, card sharps, cowboys, miners, and soldiers. Beautifully clad women roamed among the men, stopping to chat one up every now and then. It was a scene unlike anything the boys had seen before. Colt had never seen Brick so wide-eyed and smiling before: he was loving every minute of it. "Let's go see something else," Colt said.

"Okay," Brick replied eagerly.

The next building they came to was the saloon, windows wide open to the cool night air. It was busy, as well, but the crowd was different: mainly cowpunchers, although Colt spotted a couple of professional card players, as well. There were women roaming this room, too, but they weren't as nicely dressed as those in the casino.

Colt spotted Jim sitting at one of the card tables. As he watched, Jim won the hand he was playing. As he reached out to collect his winnings, the man across from him jumped up, kicking his chair out behind him. "You're a goddamn cheat! That's what you are!" he yelled at Jim. Colt could hear every word through the open window.

One of the other men at the table said, "Calm down, Johnny. Do you know who that is? That's Jim Borden." With the mention of the name, some of the bar's patrons stopped what they were doing and turned to stare at the table.

Jim sat quietly in his chair, watching the man opposite him.

"I don't care who he is. He's a goddamn cheat! Ain't nobody that lucky."

Colt, eyes glued to Jim, felt a pit form in his stomach. Jim pushed his chair back from the table, never taking his eyes off the man accusing him. "Friend, I think you've maybe had a little too much to drink tonight. Why don't you just go sleep it off somewhere, and we'll forget this happened?" Jim's voice was cold and level.

"Sleep it off? I ain't drunk. What's the matter? You a coward too?" He turned to the crowd. "Jim Borden is a cheat *and* a coward!" he yelled, then swung back to face Jim again.

"I'm no coward, and I don't have to cheat to beat the likes of you at cards," Jim said. "One more time, how 'bout I buy you a drink, and then you mosey on up the street to some other establishment before this poor barkeep has to clean your blood off his floor?"

"I'm calling you out, Borden. You yella?"

Jim slowly rose from his chair. The other patrons in the bar scrambled to get out of the line of fire. Colt felt the blood drain from his face as he watched, mouth agape, through the window. Brick's eyes were sparkling, and he was so excited he could barely stand still.

Jim spoke again. "If you're gonna jump, then jump, huckleberry. Otherwise, turn around, head to the bar, and I'll buy you that drink."

"I don't sweat you, Borden." With that, the man attempted to draw his weapon.

There was a loud bang, and the room filled with smoke. When the smoke cleared, Colt saw Jim standing, gun drawn. The man across from him clutched his chest, fell to his knees, and then thudded face-first to the floor.

"No! Jim!" Colt yelled from outside the window.

"Colt?" Jim turned to see the boys staring at him. Holstering his gun, he hurried to the door, the crowd giving him a wide berth. Once outside, he strode up to the boys.

"What are you two doing here?" he demanded. "Get back to the train, now!"

"You . . . you killed that man!" Colt stammered.

"You surely did!" Brick said excitedly.

They were interrupted by the voice of the barkeep, who had hurried out in Jim's wake. "You'd better get a move on, Borden. That was Johnny Alsask. He's got a lot of friends in town, and they'll be looking for you."

"I gave him a chance," Jim said. "I asked him to back down three times. It was a fair draw. He left me no choice."

The town sheriff approached, Mr. Robillier beside him. "What happened here?"

The barkeep spoke first. "It was a fair fight, Sheriff. Borden gave him a chance to back down, but Johnny wouldn't do it."

The sheriff stared at Jim and then looked at Colt and Brick. "These your boys, Borden? Not exactly the place for them, don't you think?"

"Not exactly my boys, Sheriff, but I agree." Jim turned and gave the brothers a hard look. "I'm taking them back right now."

Robillier spoke up. "I tried to tell him back in Laramie, Sheriff, that these boys are trouble." He puffed up his chest as though about to launch into another sermon but quickly deflated when he caught Jim's glare aimed at him. "We're just trying to help these unfortunate young souls get to their desired destination."

"Well, see to it that they get to bed for the night, and then I suggest you be movin' on in the morning. I don't want no more trouble around here."

"That's the plan, Sheriff," Jim said. "And for the record, I didn't want any trouble to begin with." Jim shooed the boys toward the train.

It was a quiet walk back to the train. Nobody spoke. Colt couldn't believe what he had just seen and wasn't sure what to say about it. Jim wasn't eager to talk about the event, and Brick didn't know why nobody else was talking about it, so just kept quiet himself, although it required some effort.

Back at the train, as they got ready for the night, Colt finally got the courage to ask, "Jim? What about all that stuff you taught us? Being smart enough to not have to draw on someone?"

"I told you, Colt. Sometimes, you also need to be smart enough to know *when* to draw." Jim's voice had a chill to it.

Colt fell asleep that night with some fear in his heart. Jim scared him a little now.

CHAPTER 6

Over the next couple of days, Jim tried to continue with the lessons, but Colt didn't say much. He was still wrestling with the two sides of Jim he had seen and how they meshed to form one man. He was having a hard time reconciling the man who was helping him and his brother with the dangerous man he had seen in the saloon that night.

The trip was otherwise uneventful until they came to the base of the Sierra Nevada mountains. They had to cross the mountains to get to California, but Brick became anxious at the idea. He pressed himself into the back corner of the train car, hugged his knees to his chest, and kept rocking back and forth, mumbling to himself.

Colt had never seen anything like it. "I don't know what's wrong with him."

"Bad memories, Colt." Jim put his hand on Colt's shoulder. "The last time you crossed a mountain range in a train, you lost your pa, and Brick lost a toe, and that range wasn't near as big as this one. He'll be okay, but it's going to be a rough cross for him. Best you can do is sit with him and try and keep him calm."

Colt sat with Brick and tried to reassure him. He explained that they were in a much better situation this time around. The train was heated, the railmen were prepared for anything, and they had Jim and Mr. Robillier for help. They were going to be okay.

As they started their ascent, Mr. Robillier came out of his sleeping quarters. He noticed Brick in the corner, and a sly smile came across his face. "Well, Mr. Borden," he said to Jim, "I hope you are prepared. As you know, we'll be crossing these mountains through the dreaded Donner Pass and must be ready for any situation." He glanced at the boys.

"Sit down, Robillier, and keep your mouth shut," Jim said coldly.

"Wha . . . what's the Don . . . Donner Pass?" Brick asked between deep breaths.

"Why, my boy, the Donner Pass is the easiest way over these peaks, but it is also fraught with danger," Robillier answered. "It's named after the poor party of settlers who got themselves trapped up here in the winter of 1846. You see—"

Jim interrupted. "Robillier, I'm warning you . . ."

Robillier continued undaunted. "There were eighty-one people in the party. They tried crossing the mountains, headed for California, not unlike you two boys, and their wagons got stuck in the snow. They had to try to winter there with a lack of supplies and no help coming. Only forty-five made it through to California."

Brick was white with fear, and he started rocking faster. Colt looked at his brother and then stood up in front of Robillier, gritting his teeth. "You shut your mouth, mister, or so help me . . ."

"So help you what? This is my train, remember?" He looked directly at Brick. "You know how those forty-five survived, young man? With no food?"

Colt clenched his fists. "Shut up!"

"Some of them ate the others! That's right; they ate their fellow travelers. I wonder, son, how do you taste?" A sick smile came across Robillier's face.

Brick burst into tears, and Colt could see that his brother had wet himself.

"Enough! Leave him alone!" Colt threw a punch into the big man's midsection. Robillier gasped but didn't go down. Instead, he landed a backhand to the side of Colt's face that knocked him to the floor, ears ringing.

"You dare strike me? After what I've done for you? You ungrateful little . . ." Robillier moved closer to Colt.

In one quick move, Jim stepped between Colt and Robillier and landed two quick jabs to the railway man's stomach, followed by an uppercut to his chin as he bent over that caused his large jowls to shake furiously and sent him backward and to the floor.

"I warned you." Jim shook his hand to get some feeling back.

Robillier wiped the blood from the corner of his mouth with the back of his hand and stared at Jim as he slowly stood up. His normally well-kept hair was mussed, sticking up off his head in all directions. He clenched his large fist into a ball and stared at Jim with a hatred that Colt had never seen in a man's eyes before. But after a second, Robillier relaxed his fist. Jim stood at the ready, and Robillier was clearly not prepared to try him.

"Once we get to Sacramento, me and the boys will leave the

train, and you'll never see us again," Jim said. "Until then, you leave them alone, and we'll leave you alone."

"Make sure that's exactly what happens, Mr. Borden," Robillier growled. "If you are on this train one second longer than necessary, I will end this little adventure myself." He spun and went back into his sleeping quarters, slamming the door and leaving the three of them to themselves.

Jim bent down and checked on Colt. "You all right? Let me see your face."

Colt got himself to a seated position. "I'm all right." His head was still ringing. "Brick, you okay?"

"Di . . .did they really eat people?"

"It's all right, Brick," Jim said. "That was a long time ago and in different circumstances. They were using wagons, not trains, and they were ill-prepared." Jim raised Brick's chin and looked him in the eye. "I won't let that happen to you. You have my word. We'll be in Sacramento tomorrow. We'll work things out then."

Colt's face was throbbing as he tried to sleep that night. Jim had said tomorrow they would be in Sacramento. He wondered what California would be like. He hoped that he and Brick could make a life there, that they would be happy.

He allowed himself to dream a little. He wanted a ranch, some cattle, a nice little place in a valley somewhere where water and grass were plenty, where he and Brick could be successful ranchers and businessmen. His pa would be proud of them then.

They didn't see Mr. Robillier the next morning. He stayed in his sleeping quarters, not even coming out for breakfast. They had made it through the Donner Pass without incident overnight and were descending from the mountains now.

"How long until Sacramento?" Colt asked.

"About mid-afternoon, maybe suppertime," Jim answered.

Colt was full of nervous excitement and had a hard time sitting still. He paced nervously around the car and looked out the windows every few seconds at the beautiful country they were passing through.

Tall, strong trees grew in the mountains—Jim said they were Redwoods. As they thinned, Colt could see beautiful green valleys and fields in the distance, stretching all the way to the thin, blue line he guessed was the ocean on the horizon. It was wide-open land, open for opportunity and endless possibilities, the kind of land where a man could make his dreams come true. Colt started to tear up as he looked out over the landscape and thought of his father and the plans he had made for Brick and him.

"You all right, Colt?"

Colt hurriedly wiped his face with his hand. "Yeah, Jim. I'm okay. Just dust or something."

Jim came over and put his hand on Colt's shoulder. "It's okay to cry, Colt. You haven't grieved yet for your pa. Keep your feelings—don't let the world take them from you. No matter what people like Mr. Robillier tell you, being a man isn't about being the toughest guy in the room all the time. Being a man requires some toughness, sure, especially out here, but a good man holds onto things like compassion and empathy. If you can put yourself in the other guy's place, see his point of view, you can avoid a lot more conflict than you can the other way, and avoiding conflict is a good start to living a long, happy life."

"That sounds kinda funny, coming from a gunfighter." Colt was blunt. Jim had been honest with him, and he wanted to return the favor.

"That's fair. It's not always like what you saw the other

night, Colt. I've avoided a good many scrapes in my time, but sometimes you aren't left with any options. The real strength comes from knowing when that's the case and making the decision quickly. Killing a man shouldn't be your first option, Colt. It changes you—changes your soul. Just a little at first, but then gradually more and more, until it gets hard to even recognize your own face in the mirror. You boys stay away from it as long as you can, you understand?"

The boys nodded.

Colt was a little scared of Jim again. Who was this man? Why was he helping them? It didn't seem to fit with the other side of his personality they had seen. What was he getting from it?

Colt was still glad that Jim was on their side, grateful for everything he had tried to teach them, but he was confused and more than a little wary of their traveling companion. As he was mulling the thoughts over in his head, he heard Brick yell, "I think I see it! There it is!"

He was pointing out the window. Colt looked out and saw a large town in the distance, a big one, bigger than even Laramie. He was filled with a mixture of excitement and worry. He hadn't figured out the plan yet and didn't know what he and Brick were going to do.

The first step is to find a place to stay, he thought, but they had no money to pay for one. *First step is to find a job then, earn some money, and then find a place.* But Brick was young and injured. *No, the first step is to get Brick in school, then find a job.* So many first steps he was getting confused. *Where do I start? What should I do?* His head was spinning.

They rode the rest of the way in nervous silence. When they finally arrived in Sacramento, the boys couldn't believe their eyes. This was a city, a full-fledged city, not like the western towns they had seen along the way. There were people everywhere. The train station was full of folks boarding and disembarking from trains, and when they left the station, they discovered the streets were even more crowded. The city was filled with the noise of people living their lives.

Not only that, they appeared to be building Sacramento right under their feet: there was a huge construction project happening everywhere. "What are they doing?" Colt asked.

"They're raising the city, Colt," said Jim.

"What do you mean?"

"Well, Sacramento flooded, boys. Once in 1851 and again in 1862. Folks lost everything, and there ain't no rebuilding after something like that. It don't do no good for one man to build higher if nobody else is, so the city decided they were going to raise the whole place, so it doesn't happen again. They're hauling in dirt and building materials. Whatever was ground level is underground now. It's a big job, and a man can find some honest work doing it if he's willing to work hard."

Mr. Robillier emerged from the train station and came up to them. "Mr. Borden, if we never cross paths again, it will be too soon." he said to Jim. He turned to the boys. "And you boys had better hope we never run into one another under different circumstances." He glanced sideways at Jim as he said it.

Jim ignored the look. "Let's go, boys. See if we can't find ourselves somewhere to stay for the night and maybe get some grub." He turned to the railway man. "Thanks for the ride, Mr. Robillier. Your hospitality is second to none." He chuckled over the last part as he led the boys into the Sacramento streets.

They found what they were looking for in a little boarding house not too far from the train station. Inside, the atmosphere was cozy and homey. They were greeted by a large woman wearing a floor-length dress with an apron around her waist and a huge smile on her face. "Come on in, boys. What can I do for you?"

"We'll be needing a meal and then a room for the night, if possible," Jim explained.

"Well, you've come to the right place! This here is Lillian's Lodgment, and I'm Lillian. We got hot stew on the stove and warm beds for the evening. You gents help yourselves to a table, and I'll get your vittles for ya." Colt liked her; she seemed genuine.

Lillian came back after a few seconds with three bowls heaped with a stew that smelled delicious and a big hunk of bread on the side for each of them. They all dug in and enjoyed the meal. It wasn't as fancy as what they had eaten on the train, but it tasted like home.

Brick had seconds, and then the three of them made their way up to their room. Jim allowed the boys to take the bed while he made himself comfortable in a chair yet again.

After so many nights sleeping in a chair or on the floor of the train, the bed felt wonderful to Colt, even if he was sharing it with Brick. As he lay there relaxed, with a full belly, he had one last question on his mind. "What are we going to do tomorrow, Jim?"

"Tomorrow, Colt, we start our new lives."

A new life! He could hardly wait.

Chapter 7

Colt awoke early the next morning, washed his face, combed his hair, and tried to knock some of the dust off his clothes. It felt good to have the water rushing over his face and to have his hair done; it gave him the feeling that he had value, that he could make something of himself. He wanted to make his pa proud, wanted to prove that he was right when he said coming here would make things better for Brick and him, but he didn't know where to start, and he couldn't wait any longer for Jim and Brick to get up so he could find out.

"Time to get up, boys. Let's get the day started," he said as he nudged Brick and gave Jim's foot a kick with his own.

Brick just moaned and rolled over, and Jim raised the brim of his hat just enough to look at Colt through one squinty eye. "It's early, Colt. What're you doin'?"

"I want to start our new lives. Let's get goin'!"

"Whoa, whoa, hold on there, now. It's been a long trip, and some of us need a little more rest. Look at your brother over there; he's still dead to the world."

"But I want to start now. There's so much to do, so much to figure out, we gotta start earning our keep and . . ."

"All of that can wait until after breakfast, Colt. How about you give us an hour? Go down, take a look around the town. Don't go far, mind you, and steer clear of trouble, but come back in an hour, and we'll start figuring things out, okay?"

Colt wasn't pleased with the idea of waiting, but doing a little exploring didn't sound half bad. He left the two in the room and headed down to see the city of Sacramento. As he exited the boarding house, he had to squint because the sun shone so brightly off all the windows in the buildings across the street. Once his eyes adjusted, he was able to take in the city and all it had to offer.

It was amazing. All the buildings were painted a gleaming white, and there were people bustling everywhere, even in this early hour. Even the air tasted fresher; it didn't have the dusty aftertaste he had grown used to. He walked down the board-walk, looking into each new shop window he passed, his eyes open wide. There was a gun shop, a grocery store, and a hotel, each one larger and fancier than anything he had seen in Ash Hollow or along the way.

At the end of the street, he came to an outfitter. He entered and gazed at the clothes they had for sale. There were fancy dress shirts, church-going clothes, and dresses for ladies that looked like they were made for queens. In the back of the store, Colt found what he was looking for. They had dusters and Stetsons and chaps for riding, everything you needed to dress just like the cowboys he had read about in those dime books. He was standing there, mouth agape, admiring the apparel, when he was interrupted by the shopkeeper. "What're ya looking at, boy?"

"Just admiring your garments, sir."

"Well, unless you got more money than you look like you have, you best be moving on. This ain't no charity, and I don't take kindly to thieves around here."

"I ain't no thief, mister. I was just looking."

"Go on, get outta here! Don't come back unless you got money, you worthless little beggar."

Colt was embarrassed as he left the store. He wasn't worthless, and he was going to prove it. One day, he was going to own clothes like those. He was going to be successful.

He was in his own head as he walked back toward the boarding house. Staring at the ground, he didn't see the man in front of him until he ran into him. The man held a cup of coffee, which spilled onto his shirt in the collision.

"Godammit! Why don't you watch where you're going, you damn runt?" The man was large. Not as big as Patrick Robillier, but more muscular and solid.

"I'm sorry, mister, I didn't see you there."

"Are you blind? Didn't your parents teach you no manners?"

"My folks are dead, mister." Colt was getting angry now. A crowd was gathering.

"Well, that's probably for the best, so they don't have to be embarrassed by your behavior!"

That was enough. Colt balled up his fist and took a swing that landed square on the man's jaw. The man hadn't been expecting it, and it knocked him to the ground. There were some guffaws from the crowd, but it was mostly a collective gasp. The man stood up with rage in his eyes. He grabbed Colt by the collar and threw him off the boardwalk into the street. "Why, you little . . .who do you think you're messing with? I'm gonna teach you some manners myself!"

Colt had sprawled into the dirt when he landed, and he

tried to pick himself up quickly, but the man was on him in no time. He slapped Colt across the face, sending him into the dirt again. His hand was already throbbing from the punch, and now his ears were ringing as well. The man picked him up again and pinned him against the side of a wagon with his left hand as he cocked his right hand for a punch that Colt was sure would knock him out, if not worse.

As the man readied to bring his fist down on the face of Colt the end of a bullwhip wrapped itself around the man's wrist. He looked at his newly collared arm, let Colt drop to the ground, and turned to face this new attacker.

Standing a few feet away, holding the other end of the whip, was a man dressed in black pants, knee-high black leather boots, a white shirt with a bolo tie, and a black vest. On his head, he wore a fine black Stetson.

"Who the hell are you?" said the angry man.

"The boy's had enough. Leave him alone."

"I asked who the hell you are," the large man said through clenched teeth.

"My name is Drake Rockhaven, but that's of no importance to you. Leave the boy alone."

At this point, Jim Borden pushed his way through the crowd with Brick in tow. "What's going on here?"

The angry man spoke. "I was teaching this little bull biscuit some manners when this fancy man made the biggest mistake of his life." He pulled his arm down, and the force on the whip brought Rockhaven in closer. "Do you have any idea who I am?"

Jim spoke first. "I do, Creek." He had already drawn his pistol, and now he cocked it. "You're Creek Masters, and you reckon you're pretty much the toughest man to walk these or any other parts, and you may be right, but beating this boy ain't gonna to prove that to anyone. Leave the boy alone."

Masters had fire in his eyes. He shook the whip loose from his wrist and then assessed the situation. Both Rockhaven and Jim were squared and ready, and Jim had the drop on him. Masters thought better of the situation, wiped his face on his sleeve, and issued a warning. "Fine. This time. But you both better watch your backs 'cause I'll be looking for you. You can believe that."

Masters walked away, and the crowd started to disperse. "Is this your boy?" Rockhaven asked Jim.

"In a manner of speaking. I've taken responsibility for him and his brother." Jim pointed at Brick. "I want to thank you for taking up for him. That Masters can be a real animal sometimes."

"Don't mention it; just doing what's right. Drake Rockhaven." He reached for a handshake.

"Jim Borden." Jim shook back. "This here is Colt Warner and his brother, Brick."

"Well, Colt, you landed a pretty good punch back there. Probably just not the right opponent."

"He was talking about my folks, saying it was good they was dead. He deserved it."

"That's probably true; a man can't have people disparaging his folks, now, can he?" He looked at Jim. "Borden, you say? Didn't I hear about a Jim Borden from out around Wichita?"

"You may have. I've been around there a time or two."

"Well, if the stories I heard are true, then Creek Masters might consider himself somewhat lucky that he chose to walk away. Legend has it that you were quite the hand with that six-shooter of yours."

"Oh, he is," Brick blurted out. "He killed a man in a town on the way here."

Jim kept his eyes on Rockhaven. "Had a little trouble in a town in Wyoming. Misunderstanding over a card game."

"A misunderstanding? I wouldn't expect anything else, Mr. Borden. Have you gents had breakfast yet? I'm feeling a little hungry. Care to join me?"

"Sounds good."

They walked back to the boarding house and indulged in some of Miss Lillian's excellent cooking again.

"What brings you folks to Sacramento?" Rockhaven asked as they ate.

"The boys' father wanted them to come here and start fresh. He unfortunately didn't survive the trip, but the boys wanted to come anyway, so I made sure they got here." The story of the entire trip and ordeal was laid out for Rockhaven as he sat and listened, enthralled by every word.

"Well, that's a hell of a story you boys got there. Incredible, to say the least. Colt, after listening to that, I can see why you popped Masters the way you did," he said with a little chuckle. "What's your next plan, Jim?"

"Gotta get these boys into school. That's the first thing."

"Are you a gunfighter?" Brick asked Rockhaven.

"Well, I can shoot, but I prefer using the whip here." He patted his hip. "I'll leave the gunplay to men like Mr. Borden. I make my living playing cards."

"What if someone pulls a gun on you?"

"I've done pretty well for myself so far. Tried to stay on the straight and narrow as much as possible. I reckon if something gets a little too sticky, I'll have some friends to help me out. Two or three good, loyal friends are more valuable than any other treasure you can find, boys, mark my words.

"To that end . . . I was just in town overnight to get supplies; I've got an old house in a little town just to the east called Monroe. It's nothing pretty, and the food ain't as good as Miss Lillian's here, but it's large and has lots of room for you gents. I was just heading out there now. If you're so inclined as to want to hang your hats there, I'd be more than happy to have you."

Jim stared at the two young men in front of him. "Much obliged. Mr. Rockhaven. Whaddaya say, boys? Might be a good idea to set up in a smaller town, let Creek Masters calm down some."

Colt wasn't sure. Monroe wasn't Sacramento like his pa wanted, but Jim made a good point about Masters, and he figured Monroe was close enough. The boys nodded in agreement.

After breakfast, the quartet made their way to Monroe, where they would start their new lives. It was a lovely town, small but very clean, with all the buildings being well cared for. Drake's place was right on the edge of town. It was a neat little two-story home with a small fence around a dirt yard and a small barn in the back for horses, a porch for sitting on at the front of the house, and a small stone fireplace in the front room. Colt and Brick had to share a room, but it had two cots, so at least they didn't have to share a bed. It felt a little like home. Colt thought it looked like the home of a preacher, not a card player, but it looked like a swell place to start over. They spent the rest of the day getting acquainted with their new surroundings and listening to Drake tell stories about the town and his past.

The following morning, they ate breakfast and Jim made some sandwiches for the boys for later, and they headed out to the school. At the school, Jim introduced himself and the boys to the teacher. She smiled and told the boys they could join the class right then and there.

"Go ahead, boys. Mr. Rockhaven and I will meet you back here when you're done for the day."

The brothers found seats in the classroom. Colt was uneasy as every eye was on them. The teacher called the class's attention back to her, and the rest of the morning was all right as they started learning.

At the lunch break, Colt and Brick were sitting outside by themselves, eating their sandwiches, when they were approached by three boys from class. The lead boy, Troy Benton, was a year younger than Colt and a year older than Brick. He was tall for his age and had a physique that came from working chores at home before and after school. The girls considered him handsome. The kids all called him by the nickname "Pretty Boy Troy."

"Well, looky what we got here. If it ain't our two new classmates, the poor boy and the gimp." Troy laughed with his friends.

"He's not a gimp," Colt said, rising to his feet.

"He's whatever I say he is unless you think you can shut me up." Troy squared up.

"It's our first day. We don't want no trouble. Why don't you just leave us alone?"

"Punch him, Colt! Just like Jim showed us. Beat him good!" Brick shouted.

"Is that right, poor boy? You gonna beat me good?" Troy took a step closer. "There's three of us and one and a half of you." He laughed out loud.

"Enough, Troy, or I'll help even the odds." The voice came from behind Colt. Colt turned and saw a tall boy behind him. He was thin but looked solid. He had messy, brown hair that hung just at eye level and a few freckles scattered across his cheeks and nose. He was wearing overalls with no shirt underneath.

Troy sneered at him. "This ain't your business, Lanky."

"They're new, and they ain't done nothing to you. Leave 'em alone and go act tough somewheres else." The tall boy moved in beside Colt. "There's three of us now. The odds are even-up."

"Damn you, Lanky!" Troy spit on the ground. "Next time, gimpy. You too, poor boy. Let's go, boys." The three turned and left.

"Thanks for the help." Colt shook the hand of the tall boy. "Not sure what got under his saddle."

"That's just Troy—he likes to think he's the toughest guy here. He was just marking his territory. My name's Elijah, Elijah Thomas, but folks call me Lanky."

"I'm Colt. This here's Brick. Thanks again, Lanky."

"Don't mention it. What brings you boys to Monroe?"

Colt told their story to Lanky, who was amazed at the tale. "A gunfighter, eh? That's neat. Man, you guys sure went through a lot just to get here. I'd like to meet Jim; I've never seen a gunfighter up close."

The rest of the afternoon was uneventful, and at the end of class, Jim and Drake were waiting for the brothers. "Hey Colt, Brick, how was the first day?"

Colt explained about the day, and Jim listened intently. "Sounds like you had an interesting day."

"Hey, Colt, see you tomorrow!" It was Lanky.

Colt introduced Lanky to Jim and Drake. Lanky headed on his way, and the four of them started toward Drake's place. Along the way, Jim explained what he had done that day. "I ran into a man named Ed Waters today, boys. Ed runs the livery here. He said they can always use more help, and if you boys are interested, you can head over after school each day and help haul supplies and things. It'll be hard work, nothing fancy, just doing the grunt stuff, but I know you were looking to try and build your life here, Colt. I figured this could be a start."

"It sounds good, Jim. What do you think, Brick?"

"Sounds tough, especially with my foot, but whatever you think, Colt."

Drake spoke up. "Listen, Brick, I understand you walk a little funny, but you can't let that hold you back. If you treat your foot like it's a problem, everyone else will too, but if you don't use it as an excuse, then folks will hardly notice after a while. After school tomorrow, we'll head down and get you introduced to Ed."

Colt was excited; things were looking good for them already. It had been two days, and they had already gone to school, found a place to live, and now had jobs. Maybe their father was right; maybe this was the land of opportunity.

The four of them ate some supper, Colt and Brick read aloud to the two men, and then the boys went to bed for the night.

So far, Monroe was working out. Colt liked it.

CHAPTER 8

———

After the best night's sleep that he had had in recent memory, Colt awakened to the smell of coffee and bacon. He woke Brick, and the two of them headed for the source of the smell. Drake and Jim were both already up and having coffee at the table. "Morning, boys." said Jim, "You best eat fast and get ready to go, or you're going to be late."

"Late for what?" Colt asked.

"School, of course," Drake chimed in.

Colt had almost forgotten about school. It had been so long since they had had a routine or anywhere particular to be that it had slipped his mind. The two of them did as they were told and ate quickly. They got themselves dressed and ready to go, and then Jim escorted them to the school again. Colt was still feeling good about things; it felt like they might be starting their new lives now, the lives their father wanted for them. "Jim, you don't have to walk us to the school. Brick and I can manage."

"It's a nice walk in the morning, Colt; it helps me work off that breakfast. It's a new town, and I want to make sure you guys have a routine and you're comfortable before I stop. Besides, some of the men here aren't the most savory of individuals, and I wouldn't want you getting into any unnecessary trouble."

They arrived at the school, and Jim told them he would meet them at the end of the day to take them over to where Ed Waters was working, so they could start their jobs.

Lanky met them at the front door, and he and Colt went in together. Colt could barely concentrate on his lessons that morning, thinking about the jobs they would work later that day. He was daydreaming about earning money and what he would do with it. He wanted some of those clothes he had seen in that store before he had run into Creek Masters. He was dreaming so much that Brick had to punch him in the arm when it was time for lunch.

The brothers chose the same spot they had sat in the day before and started to eat. Colt excused himself and went to use the latrine. Brick was finishing his sandwich when he was approached by Troy Benton and his gang again. "What's the matter, gimpy? All by yourself today?"

Brick looked around for Colt nervously. He was nowhere to be seen.

"Can't find your big brother?" Pretty Boy sneered. "Not big enough to fight your own battles?"

"What battle? I ain't done nothin' to you." Brick quickly got to his feet.

"You ain't got to have done nothin'. I don't like sharing the same air with gimps." Benton pushed Brick back to the ground.

"I ain't no gimp!" Brick got himself up and charged at Troy. A crowd of kids formed a circle around them as the boys locked up and pushed one another around. Then Troy landed a punch to Brick's mid-section that sent him to the ground again. As Troy moved in closer, Brick grabbed a handful of dirt and threw it in Troy's face. The older boy stumbled backward as he tried to clear his eyes.

Colt stepped out of the latrine and saw the crowd that had gathered. He rushed to the circle just in time to see Brick stand up and land a punch of his own to Troy's belly that doubled him over. Brick then landed a punch to Troy's face that laid him in the dirt.

Brick was possessed now. He jumped on Troy and started flailing with both arms, hitting anywhere he could. Benton was curled in a ball, trying to protect himself and no longer fighting back.

At that point, Jessie Mitchell and Tank Jepson, Troy's gang, jumped on Brick and pulled him off Troy. Tank started to punch at Brick, landing one that bloodied Brick's nose. Colt then joined the fray and started swinging as well. He landed one that knocked Tank backward, and then all three boys stood up and took a step back. Colt looked to his left and saw Lanky standing beside him.

The odds were even now, and after the humiliation he had just suffered, Troy had no interest in an even fight. He spat on the ground and signaled for his boys to leave. He gave the trio one last sideways glance and then backed off himself.

Colt turned to look at Brick. "You all right?"

Brick wiped the blood from his nose on his sleeve. "I'll be okay."

"Where'd you learn to do that?" Colt had some pride in his voice.

"You think you were the only one paying attention to Jim on the train?" Brick smiled as he said it.

Lanky laughed. "Boy, you Warner brothers sure ain't nobody to mess with."

"No, I guess we're not." Colt reached out and mussed Brick's hair a bit. "We'd best be getting back to lessons."

The rest of the afternoon went by smoothly, and the boys met Jim after school as planned. Jim took a look at Brick's nose as the boys approached. "Problem today, boys?"

"No," the boys answered in unison.

"All right." Jim turned and started to lead the boys down the street. "Did you win?"

"Sure did!" Brick said proudly. The three laughed and kept walking.

They met Ed Waters at the livery. There were men working everywhere, hauling, repairing fence, taking care of horses. It was noisy and slightly chaotic, and Colt liked it—it felt like work.

Ed extended his hand as the trio approached. "How you doing, Jim?"

"Doin' all right, Ed." Jim accepted the handshake. "These are the boys I was telling you about. This here is Colt, and this is Brick."

"How ya doin', boys? You can leave 'em here, Jim. I'll put 'em to work—they won't have enough free time to get in any trouble."

"I'm not worried about any trouble; these boys can handle themselves. See you boys later tonight back at Drake's." Jim waved and walked away.

Ed got down to business right away. "All right, boys, I've got ten men working for me right now. They're working full days, and they make two dollars a day. You two are gonna work a couple of hours a day, but because of the deal I made with Jim, you boys get one dollar a day apiece."

"Deal?" asked Colt. "Jim said he just ran into you."

"Sure, he would say that. He ran into me at the poker table. I'd been having a rough afternoon, and then I finally had a hand. I thought my luck had changed, but then, damn, Borden dropped four queens on me. He cleaned me out, but rather than take my money, he made the deal that I could keep my cash as long as you two could have some work and you got a dollar a day."

"Well, we do appreciate it, sir."

"Don't mention it. Here's the deal. You two are hauling muck buckets. You're cleaning out stalls. They need new hay, you're putting it in, they need old hay removed, you're taking it out. You're cleaning up after the horses and any other odd job someone needs you to do. It ain't glamorous, and it's damn hard, but it's honest, and it pays. Every day after school, you're here, and you start at noon on Saturday and Sunday. You miss a day, don't bother comin' for the next one."

"Yes, sir."

"Well, get started. They need youse over there." He pointed to his right.

It was hard work, and the boys were tired. Brick fell behind a bit, and Colt did his share for him where he could, as well as his own. When the day came to an end, the two slowly made their way back to Drake's place for the night. "Colt, I'm sorry I couldn't keep up; sorry you had to carry mine, too," Brick said as they walked.

"You're my brother, Brick. We help each other out."

"I know, but I still feel bad."

"You and me is all we got left in this world. We stick together. Whether it's Pretty Boy in the schoolyard or here at work, we do it together. That's what Pa wanted."

"Colt, are you scared?"

Colt took in a deep breath and let it out slowly before he answered. "I think someone's been lookin' out for us—maybe Ma, maybe Pa, but someone. We're in a good situation, Brick. Jim and Drake seem like good guys to have watching our backs, we're going to school, and we've got jobs. I like Monroe. As long as we stay together, we're gonna be okay. I think I'm more excited than scared."

"Me too, then."

Colt put his arm over Brick's shoulders, and they entered the house. There was the smell of stew in the air, and Drake greeted them as they came in. "How're the working men?"

"Tired. I can barely lift my arms," Colt replied.

"Well, we kept the stew warm for you. Pull up a chair and help yourself. Jim is down at the saloon." He looked at Brick's face. "That nose happen at work or school?"

"School," Brick said between mouthfuls.

"Did you win?"

"Yes." Brick smiled wide, thinking about it again.

The boys finished supper, washed up, and then poured themselves into their beds. Colt could feel every muscle in his body sink into the mattress as he lay there staring at the ceiling. He smiled to himself, feeling satisfied and proud. He and Brick were doing it: they were starting their own life. Sure, Jim had been a godsend, and now Drake, too, but they were on their way. Besides, what had Drake said? Three or four good friends were all a man really needed to make his path. Jim and Drake and Lanky made three. Colt was feeling good.

"Colt?" the voice in the darkness came from across the room.

"Yeah?"

"I know we're excited and everything, but I was scared in that fight today."

"It's okay, Brick. You didn't show it; that's what matters."

"Think Pretty Boy Troy will do it again?"

"Maybe. If he does, you'll just whoop him again."

Brick smiled briefly in the dark. "Colt?"

Colt's eyes were closed. "Yeah?"

"I miss Ma and Pa."

"I know, Brick, me too."

"Colt?"

Colt was trying to sleep and getting agitated now. "Yeah?"

"I'm glad you're my brother."

His agitation melted away. "Me too, Brick. Now, let's get some sleep." The room fell silent as the two finally let the day end and sleep come.

EVERY DAY after that followed the same pattern as the months rolled on: school, work, home, and bed. Both brothers had never been so tired in all their lives. Even working the farm back in Ash Hollow, their father had cut them some slack and given them some off time. Other than Saturday and Sunday mornings, there wasn't any off time, and those mornings were spent catching up on sleep.

It was a hard existence, but Colt tried to look at the positive side. If they didn't have time to spend the money they made, they could save it, and every dollar saved put them one step closer to the independence they sought. He knew he was only twelve, but he figured that if he could save it, by the time he needed it, it would be a small fortune, a big-enough stake to set them up properly.

Brick wasn't quite as visionary, and he wasn't happy with

the way things were. He could hear the other kids at school talk about how they spent their evenings, and he wanted to be part of it. Hauling the muck buckets was hard for him, and he couldn't see why he was doing it if he couldn't reap the rewards. He started to act out some at work, not working as fast, and taking more break time. He even had to be spoken to by Ed Waters on a couple of occasions. Colt tried to pick up the slack for Brick as much as possible, tried to reassure him of the plan and how this was a means to an end, but Brick was stubborn, which made reasoning with him almost impossible sometimes.

One evening, Jim took Brick for a walk around the town. "You know, Brick, I know it's been tough for you these past few months," he said as they strolled. "A boy like you should be out running with your friends, not hauling muck buckets, but there's a reason for it, you know that."

"Yeah, I know. Save, so we can get our own place sometime. But do we have to save everything? I want to spend what I make. None of my school friends have jobs, but they all get to buy candy at the General Store, and Colt won't let me spend anything. It's my money; I work for it."

Jim paused before he answered. "Your brother's trying to do right by you, Brick. He just wants to make sure that you two can have the better life you came out here for, an easier life than you had back home."

"Well, he needs to lay off sometimes. He ain't my pa."

"No, no, he's not, but he's your only kin, and he loves you. He's giving up a lot, too, Brick. He's only a couple of years older than you, but he has a stronger work ethic than a lot of full-grown men I know. That's not fair for him. He's growing up too fast, not having much of a childhood."

"Nobody's forcing him to."

"No, you're right, sort of. Nobody here would blame him if he decided enough was enough and he just wanted to be a kid for a few more years, but I think there's another voice, Brick. I think Colt hears that voice, your pa's voice, every day in his head, and I think that's what drives him. I think he wants to make your pa proud, wants to make sure that you two make it so that your pa didn't die for nothing. I need you to do me a favor, Brick. Give your brother a little more rope; don't ride him so tight. He's doing his best for you and him. Just go a little easier on him."

"Okay, Jim, I'll try." He shook Jim's hand.

"Borden!" the silence was broken by a big man in the middle of the street yelling at them. The man took a few steps closer, and they could see it was Creek Masters.

As Brick stared at the man, he saw others moving in his peripheral vision. Creek had brought his friends, and they were surrounding Jim and him.

Jim reached out with his left hand and pushed Brick behind him. "What do you want, Creek?" Jim said, keeping a cautious watch on the men closing in on them.

"I was looking for you. I heard someone say that you had lit out and were hiding out in this Podunk town. I want payback, Borden. I told you months ago that there would come a time. This looks like a good time."

Jim reached toward his gun.

"Uh, uh, uh, Borden, I wouldn't do that." Creek wagged a finger while he spoke. Three men already had their six-shooters pointed at Jim. He motioned to one of the men. "Take his gun, Tex." The man moved in and removed the gun from Jim's holster.

"I'll be getting that back," Jim said to the man. The man sneered at him and gave a sick little chuckle before striking Jim on the side of the head with the butt of the gun. Jim went down to one knee. He turned his head to look at Brick. "Run."

Brick tried to run but was grabbed by one of Creek's gang. The man held him by one arm and wouldn't let him go.

Brick's heart was racing. He balled his free hand into a fist and swung as hard as he could, landing a blow squarely below the man's belt line. The thug yelled in pain, released his grip, and fell to the ground. Brick ran as fast as he could.

"Let him go. We got who we want," Creek yelled.

Brick rounded the corner of a building and then paused to look back. He saw Creek land a blow to Jim's face that knocked him flat to the ground. Scared, he ran as fast as he could to get Drake and Colt.

Jim tasted blood in his mouth as he lay on the ground. His head still spun from the smack with the gun. He grabbed two handfuls of dirt from the road and threw them into the face of Creek Masters as he moved in for another punch. Creek stumbled backward, temporarily blinded, and Jim lunged, landing a solid punch right to the midsection of the large man.

Masters gasped and bent over, which put his face right in the path of the left fist Jim was throwing as a follow-up. It cracked against Creek's jaw, and blood spewed from his mouth, spattering the ground. Jim was preparing to strike again when he was rushed from both sides by two members of the gang. They grabbed his arms and held him up, helpless to defend himself.

Creek smiled a sick, blood-covered smile as he proceeded to land two quick punches to Jim's midsection. The air rushed from Jim's lungs, and as he gasped, trying to get it back, Creek hit him again, this time a right to his head. Jim saw a flash of light as the punch landed and almost lost consciousness, but a second flash of light from the following left hand stopped him from doing so.

Jim's body hung limply, kept upright only by the two men holding him. Creek took a step back and drew his gun. He smiled that sick smile again as he cocked it and pointed it at Jim. "The great Jim Borden, about to meet his end. I'm going to enjoy this."

A shot rang out, causing everyone to pause where they were. Creek Masters looked around.

"Don't do it, Creek! Let him go." Drake was there, six-gun in hand and whip on his hip. "Back away and leave him alone."

"Why should I? There's only one of you. We still got the numbers. You're next on my list anyway."

"He's not alone, Creek," Ed Waters called. He'd taken cover behind a wagon on the street.

Looking around, Creek saw that Colt had taken a position on the other side of the street and was pointing his father's gun at him. Brick stood wide-eyed beside him.

"Two men and a couple of kids?" Masters laughed out loud, spitting blood everywhere. "We'll take our chances. I'm feeling lucky."

He pointed his gun at Jim again. Another shot rang out, and Creek dropped the gun, yelling in pain.

Drake scanned the street to see what had happened and saw Colt staring, scared, as smoke drifted from the barrel of his gun. Reacting quickly, Drake fired at one of the men holding Jim. He fell to the ground as Tex released Jim's other arm and reached for his own gun. Jim swung his arm wildly, knocking Tex's legs out from under him. Tex hit the ground in a heap, and Jim was on top of him in a hurry, throwing punches as best he could.

Creek had reached for his gun on the ground with his one

good hand, but when he stood, he saw Drake's gun aimed at him. He froze, the gun still pointing at the ground. "Damn you, Rockhaven, why'd you ever have to get involved in this? This was never your fight."

"Can't have you beating up kids and ganging up on men unfairly, Creek. That's not how it's done."

"Damn you!" Creek shouted and raised his gun. There was a volley of shots as Drake unloaded his weapon into Creek's chest. The big man's body lurched a few times, his eyes got wide, and his face got a weird look before he fell to the ground. He lay in the street, not moving.

Jim took his gun back from Tex and fired one shot into the man's chest. "Told you I was going to get this back," he said to the dying man before he, too, fell to the ground.

The two remaining men from the gang threw their guns on the ground and ran. Drake and Jim let them go. Ed Waters came out into the street and started to attend to Jim while Drake surveyed the situation. Three men dead in the street, and not one of his group injured aside from Jim. It was a good night. "Come on out, boys, we're safe now."

Colt and Brick slowly made their way into the street and then ran to Jim's side. His face was bruised and bloody, and he was having a hard time breathing. "We have to get him to the doctor's place, but I think he'll be okay, boys."

Ed and Drake each put one of Jim's arms over their shoulders and helped him start walking. "That was a hell of a shot back there, Colt," Drake said. "Shooting a man in his gun hand is no easy feat."

"I was scared. I closed my eyes. I was aiming for his head."

Ed and Drake both turned to look at Colt with stunned looks on their faces before Drake let out a hearty laugh, and everyone else followed suit. Even Jim managed a little chuckle.

OVER THE NEXT FEW DAYS, Jim recuperated at home while everything else went back to the normal routine. That night was not anything that anybody talked about. It felt awkward to Colt that no one talked about it, and he was embarrassed that, in spite of all the training they had done with Jim on their way here, when push came to shove, and he was needed, he was scared and had closed his eyes before firing.

He was passing by Jim's room when Jim called him in. He sat in a chair next to the bed and stared at Jim lying in bed. It had been a week, and his face was still bruised and had a few cuts on it. His ribs were still bandaged, and he winced every time he adjusted himself in the bed.

"How are you doing, Colt?"

"I'm all right, Jim. You feelin' any better?"

Jim coughed a little. "I'm okay. Been through worse, though not much. That Creek could hit like a sledgehammer."

"I know." Colt said, instinctively rubbing his cheek where Creek had struck him.

"I suppose you do," Jim said. "I want to make sure you're okay, Colt. I mean, really okay. Drake says that you haven't been yourself since the fight. What's bothering you?"

"It's nothing. I'm okay." Colt lied.

Jim reached out and put his hand on Colt's leg. "Remember what I told you about feeling your feelings? Don't bottle them up, Colt."

Colt raised his eyes to meet Jim's. "Everything you've done for Brick and me, all the help, all the training, and the one night you really needed my help, I was too scared. I got lucky, but I couldn't do anything you had taught me."

Jim stared at Colt for a while before he responded. "Colt, shooting a man is very different from shooting at targets or practicing drawing, and it's damn sure different than firing out a train window at a tree trunk. You should have been scared because that meant you were thinking about it, and you understood the importance of the decision you were about to make. I told you once before, taking a man's life, even a man like Creek, changes you. I'm glad you weren't trigger-happy. That means you're becoming a good man, Colt, one who thinks instead of going straight to the gun. Keep that up, and you'll live a good, long life."

Colt felt better after the talk. He focused on school and work and pushed the incident to the back of his mind. Lanky sometimes brought it up, asking for details. His eyes always danced when he asked about it; he was in awe of Colt and his makeshift family. Colt tried to give him some information without reliving the night.

Nobody in the house ever spoke of it again. Colt wondered if it was because they felt the way he did.

CHAPTER 9

"Happy birthday, Colt!" the clan shouted as they approached the table with a cake. Drake, Brick, and Jim were all there. Even Ed Waters and Lanky had shown up. It had been a long three years, long but gratifying. Colt was now fifteen and growing into his body more every day. The hard work had sculpted and toned him so that he was lean but powerful. At thirteen, Brick had followed suit, and both boys now cut handsome figures, turning the heads of the schoolgirls whenever they walked down the street.

They had left the jobs at the livery and the brothers had caught on as ranch hands for a man named Shepherd Broxton. Shep had brought them on much as Ed Waters had: they mucked the stalls and fed the horses and cattle. It paid the same dollar a day as the livery work, the difference being that it was the first jobs they had acquired on their own, no help from Jim. It was another step toward independence. Colt paid attention and watched the cowboys as they worked. It was a lifestyle he admired, but he really wanted to be Shep: to own some land and cattle, a ranch, and be a success that way.

Brick's three years had been a little different. Since the fight in the schoolyard, he and Pretty Boy Troy had become fast friends. Troy brought Jessie Mitchell and Tank Jepson with him, and the four had become a tight-knit group. While Brick still worked the ranch with Colt, his heart and mind weren't in it, and Colt ended up covering for him on more than one occasion.

Brick and his friends had garnered a reputation of being the town mischief-makers, causing some minor property damage on occasion and courting trouble on a few more. Colt wasn't sure what to do. He could feel Brick growing farther and farther apart from him. Becoming friends with Troy and his gang was just the first step. Ditching work and causing trouble was the next.

He had tried talking to Brick, steering him straight, but it had been no use. Brick was incredibly stubborn and seemed to hold a grudge against Colt. Talking to Jim had been the next step, but Brick hadn't listened to him, either. He had decided to let it be and hoped that Brick would come around on his own as he got older.

As Colt rounded the corner into the kitchen, he bumped into Drake. "Oh, hey, Colt, didn't see you there," Drake said with a little chuckle. It had been Drake's favorite joke for the past year as he now wore a patch over his left eye, the result of a poker game gone wrong.

Drake had been in the game with a cowpuncher from somewhere in Texas. The man thought he had the hand to beat and was right furious when Drake threw down his full house. The cowboy stood to fight, while Drake never left his chair. It looked at one point like Drake might have calmed the man down, might have settled the situation, when from nowhere, the cowboy's whore, who had been seated at the table, pulled her hairpin and stuck it in Drake's eye.

It had been chaos at that point. Guns were drawn, and both the cowboy and the whore had ended up dead, while Drake made a trip to the doc's. The doctor had been able to remove the pin but couldn't save the eye. Under that patch was a cloudy mess that looked like Drake's pupil was trapped under a sheet of ice. It didn't affect his card game any, and he could still shoot straight, but he wasn't as good with his beloved whip anymore as his depth perception was quite off now.

When the cake had been eaten, and the guests had left, Colt borrowed Drake's horse and headed out to see Shep. He was excited and could hardly sit still in the saddle. He had been practicing his riding and was getting very good, almost as good as some of the ranch hands. He had made this trip in the wagon numerous times for work, but today, it felt different. The trees seemed greener, the birds sang louder, and the sky seemed bluer. He patted his pocket and felt the wad of bills there as he rounded into the ranch. He rode up to the house and was greeted with a wave by Shep.

"How you doin', Colt? Good to see you. Happy birthday."

"Hey, Shep, is he ready?" Colt said excitedly.

"Waiting for you in the barn."

Colt dismounted and walked the horse toward the barn, his feet barely touching the ground. He opened the door, and his heart jumped a little.

In front of Colt stood the finest horse he had ever seen. He had been a maverick mustang, collected in a valley somewhere north of Sacramento. Shep had him brought to the ranch, and he'd been broken by the ranch hands. The animal stood sixteen hands tall and had a coat so black and shiny that looking at it was like staring into the midnight sky.

Colt approached the animal, who whinnied softly. He reached out his hand and placed it on the horse's neck. "Hey, boy, it's me. You ready to come home with me?" The horse huffed its breath and stamped its feet a little bit. "Goddamn, he is beautiful, isn't he?"

"One of the best I've ever had come through this ranch, Colt. Are you sure you can handle a horse of his size?"

"I can handle him just fine. We've been getting to know one another for the past six months." Colt's gaze never left the horse as he spoke. "He and I are best friends, aren't we, big fella?"

"All right, then." Shep sighed. "I hate to sell such a fine animal, but you two obviously have some sort of connection, and you've been a good worker for me. You got a name for him, or you just gonna keep calling him 'big fella'?"

"Thunder. His name is Thunder." Colt's eyes were wide, and he kept stroking the animal's neck.

"Hell of a name for a hell of a horse. We said two hundred dollars, right?"

Colt reached into his pocket, pulled out the money, peeled off some bills, and gave them to Shep without taking his eyes off Thunder. Shep gave it a quick count and said, "All right, he's all yours, son. You must have been saving for a long while to get this kind of money. Take care of him."

"A big chunk of everything I've ever made, but I've been saving for a day like today, and he's worth it. I'll take care of him like he's never been handled before," Colt said.

Smiling widely, he led Thunder out of the barn. He switched the saddle from Drake's horse to Thunder and swung into it like a real cowboy. "Thank you, Shep. Much appreciated."

"Don't mention it, Colt. I'm glad he's going to someone who appreciates him."

"Let's go, boy," Colt said. He slowly sauntered Thunder out of the yard with Drake's horse in tow.

Colt's chest swelled with pride as he rode atop Thunder. He rode the horse hard, enjoying the feeling of the wind in his hair. He could feel Thunder's every muscle move underneath him as he pushed the horse harder. Drake's horse struggled to keep up and Colt had let him go a few times, circling back to get him after he and Thunder had had their fun. He knew he needed to get back home, but he had a mission today. He rode Thunder into Sacramento. He had worked hard for the last three years and had saved as much as he could, and now here he was, sitting on top of one the finest horses he had ever seen. He wished his folks could see him now.

As he rode through the city, he caught a glimpse of himself in a store window. Thunder looked magnificent, but he looked like little more than a stall boy sitting on him. This was his mission today. He veered Thunder to the left and continued down the street. They stopped in front of the same store that Colt had been kicked out of for not having money when they first arrived in Sacramento. Colt dismounted, tied up Thunder and Drake's horse, and entered the store.

In the shop, Colt looked at new clothes and a hat. He was examining a black Stetson when the store clerk approached him. "Put it down and get out, boy. This ain't no charity."

A customer on the other side of the store let out a whistle as he looked out the window. "Have you seen this horse out here? That is one fine animal."

The clerk took his attention from Colt and went to the window to see for himself. "Now, who do you suppose owns him?" the clerk said.

"I do," Colt said as he ran the felt of the Stetson through his fingers. The clerk turned and stared.

"I'll take this hat here, I want that leather duster right there, I want three pairs of these pants, and I want three of those shirts right there. Better give me some new socks too, couple of pairs." Colt was enjoying himself. "I want this vest, too. I'll change into one of the pairs of pants and a shirt right here, and I'll wear the duster and hat out. Wrap the rest and have it ready to go when I'm done changing." He noticed some new boots on a shelf and said, "I'll take these too."

He changed in a back room and looked at himself in a mirror. He had never looked so well-dressed in all fifteen of his years. He thought to himself that it was a foolish buy, but he loved the idea of sticking it to the store clerk, and he looked the part of a cowboy wearing these clothes. He exited the room and handed a stack of bills to the store clerk.

"Thank you, sir. I'm sorry for the misunderstanding earlier."

"You should be." Colt grabbed his package and made his way out of the store.

Thunder had gathered quite a crowd of onlookers, who turned to look at Colt as he came out. The crowd split and gave him a path to his horse. Colt untied both horses, mounted, and as he rode away, he could hear whispers in the crowd.

This was the best birthday he had ever had. He and Thunder continued the same fun they had had on their way to Sacramento as they headed back to Monroe. God, this horse loved to run.

As he approached the house, he saw Lanky sitting on the front steps waiting for him. "Whoo-eee!" Lanky let out a yell as Colt rode up. "Look at you! Wow. You weren't kidding when you said he was a good horse. Jee-pers!"

They were joined by Jim, Drake, and Brick from inside. "My, my Colt. My horse looks like a nag compared to yours," Drake said.

Colt smiled with pride. "Nah, Jake's a good ride, but Thunder sure is something else, ain't he?"

"Thunder? Well, ain't that a name?"

"Drake, can Lanky and I borrow Jake for another couple of minutes? I want to ride over and see about a new saddle—maybe stop and see about a new six-shooter, too. Pa's is getting old."

Jim stepped down off the porch and came to speak with Colt. "Colt, you look good, and you sure have done a damn fine job saving your earnings. Right now, you're probably one of the richer men in town, and you've earned it. It's yours to do with as you please, but keep one thing in mind for me, having a gun in a drawer upstairs is different than putting one on. If you're gonna put one on, you best be ready to use it."

Colt stared down at Jim from atop Thunder. "I understand, Jim. I'm ready. I've been practicing." Since the night of the incident three years ago, Colt had been shooting every chance he had—shooting bottles off fence posts at Shep's ranch and shooting gophers and other varmints out in the fields surrounding town. He had become a very good shot, and his draw speed had improved from what it had been during the lessons on the train.

"Sure, you can borrow Jake a while longer, Colt. I'm sure he don't mind the exercise none," said Drake from the porch.

"Can you ride him down there bareback, Lanky?" Colt asked.

"Heck, ya, no problem." Lanky jumped up on Jake.

"Can I come too, Colt?" asked Brick.

"Jump on up here." Colt helped Brick up to sit behind him.

"Man, he's tall, ain't he?" asked Brick.

"He sure is." Again, Colt was beaming with pride.

They set out at a saunter and found their way down to the livery, where they asked Ed Waters about saddles. He directed them to the tack shop up the street.

It turned out the tack shop was right next door to a gunsmith. The boys hitched their horses and went into the tack shop first to see what was available. The saddler met them at the door. He was a large, sweaty man with a bald head and a bushy red mustache. "Howdy, boys. Fine-looking horse you got there. How can I help you?"

"I need a saddle for my ride," Colt said. 'A quality one, too."

"Well, of course, if you want a good saddle, it's gonna cost, but it's worth the investment. A good saddle can last a long while with proper care and make riding easier for both you and the horse."

"The money's no worry. Show us what you got."

The saddler took them to the back, where there was a fine black leather saddle with some intricate colored beadwork on the skirt. Colt ran his hand over the smooth leather of the seat. He liked the feel under his fingertips. There was more design work engraved on the fender and pommel.

Lanky let out a whistle again. "Damn, Colt. All that black, you and Thunder are gonna look like the Reaper himself riding across the plains."

Colt again smiled with pride and let out a little chuckle. "How much?"

The saddler rubbed his large hand on the back of his

sweaty neck as he spoke. "Well, that there is some of my finest work. I'd say maybe a hundred dollars."

Colt stared at the man. One hundred dollars was half as much as he'd paid for Thunder. "Seventy dollars," he negotiated.

The man threw him a sideways glance. "Do you understand the work that I put into this thing, boy?"

"I do, and I'd be proud to ride it. For seventy dollars. Mister, I've been saving this money for a good long while. If you don't think I've been pricing in my head that whole time, well, you would be mistaken. A good saddle runs about sixty dollars. I appreciate that your craftsmanship here is better than good; I'm offering seventy dollars."

"Eighty." the man offered back.

"Fine," said Colt. "But throw in that saddle blanket right there, too."

"Deal." the saddler said grudgingly. "You drive a hard bargain, son. What's your name?"

"Colt Warner."

"Well, Colt Warner, you and your animal sure are going to be a sight."

The boys put the new saddle and blanket on Thunder and switched Drake's saddle back to Jake before they headed into the gunsmith's. Colt had had a little over one thousand dollars saved to start the day. He had never spent so much in one day in his life, and he doubted that his father ever had, either. He felt simultaneously great and shameful, but new clothes were needed, a good horse was a man's best friend, and a good gun could save your life out here.

They entered the store and saw the gunsmith behind the counter. He was a small man, not much taller than Colt, with a thin body like Lanky's. He had a long, sharp nose that made him look like a weasel and a pair of small round glasses. He had a full ring of hair around his head but only a few up on top, which he combed to his left.

The trio walked up to the counter and looked at what the man had for sale. The guns under the glass looked amazing. All were shiny and new, not like Pa's old Navy revolver, which was tarnished with age. They all gleamed in the light.

Colt pointed at one and asked to see it. The weasel-like man pulled it out and placed it on the counter. "That's a Smith & Wesson Model 3 .44 caliber pistol. It's a large gun, but if you're looking to shoot to kill, it packs a wallop every time. It's the favored gun of Buffalo Bill Cody."

Colt felt the gun. It was heavier than Pa's, but it felt good in his hands.

"That one's only twenty dollars." said the gunsmith. "Holster and gun belt another seven."

"Wow. What a gun." Brick said, his eyes the size of saucers.

Colt was about to agree when something at the end of the case caught his eye. He moved down and saw a pair of pearl-handled six-shooters. Their silver shone in the store light, and the pearl handles made them look majestic. The final selling point was the black leather gun belt and holsters that came with them. "How much?" Colt asked.

"Son, why don't you look at that Model 3 again? I think these two are a little above your means."

"How much?"

"They're a hundred and twenty, son. They're 1860 Colt Army revolvers. They shoot .44 like that last one, but they're a little lighter and easier to handle. The James Boys swear by them."

Colt put the money on the counter. "I'll take 'em."

The gunsmith stared blankly for a second and then took Colt's money and handed him the guns. Colt fidgeted with the belt as he tried to strap them on in a position that felt comfortable on his hips. Once he found the spot, he drew both guns a couple of times to get the feel.

"Damn, Colt. You're getting faster on that draw every time I see you," said Lanky.

The trio left the store smiling and laughing. It was getting late and they mounted their horses and headed for home. They turned down an alley and were met by three men who stepped out of the shadows. The man in the middle spoke first and appeared to be the leader. "This here the one you were talking 'bout, Stan?"

"Sure is, Ned. He was flashing money around town." the one on the right answered.

"He's just a kid. That true, boy? You been flashing money around town? Where'd you get that money?"

"I earned it." Colt was a little scared but tried to answer as confidently as he could. Stan and the third man had grabbed the reins of Jake and Thunder. Thunder could feel the tension and was getting anxious under Colt.

"Get down off that horse, boy and hand over the money."

Colt stood his ground. "Mister, I ain't leaving this saddle, and neither is my brother."

The man grabbed Colt by the leg and ripped him down. He and Brick fell off Thunder into a heap. The big horse whinnied and raised his front legs in the air. The third man was having a hard time keeping him calm.

Stan threw Lanky off Jake in the same manner Ned had to the boys. "I said get off the horse and hand over the money," Ned growled.

Colt got to his feet in a hurry. Brick and Lanky got in behind him. "Back off, mister. I'm warning you."

Ned laughed out loud and struck Colt with a backhand across his face. "Don't make me kill you, boy."

Colt had matured over the last few years, and while those kinds of blows used to knock him to the ground, now he barely fell off balance. He wiped the blood from the corner of his mouth with his sleeve. "Hate to disappoint you, mister, but I've been hit by Creek Masters, and you ain't no Creek Masters."

Ned's face went red. "So, you're a smart mouth, are ya? Well, them are mighty fine-looking weapons you got hanging off your hips. Let's see if they're just for show."

"I don't want to shoot you, mister. You and your friends leave our horses and back out of here, and we'll all just forget about the whole thing." Colt was standing at the ready, but his insides were quivering with nerves. He swept his duster in behind the guns on either side to make drawing easier. The third man finally spoke.

"Ned, that's the kid that's been living with Jim Borden and Drake Rockhaven. I don't think you want a piece of him."

"Shut up, Harvey! Living with him doesn't mean he is him. He's a damn boy." Ned turned his attention back to Colt. "When I kill you, boy, I'll be taking those guns and that mighty fine horse of yours, too."

Ned drew his gun.

Smoke filled the alley. The horses neighed loudly and stamped their feet wildly. Ned stumbled backward and stared at Colt with a stupefied look as he clutched his chest with both hands. He fell to his knees and then face down in the dirt.

Stan and Harvey, still holding onto the horses, stared at Ned's body and then looked back at Colt. Colt stood with one of his new guns in his right hand, smoke coming from the barrel.

"You killed Ned!" Stan yelled. "You little bastard, I'm gonna…"

He drew his pistol as he screamed. Colt drew his second gun with his left hand and shot Stan dead before he had a chance to fire.

The commotion drew a crowd to the alley as Colt turned his weapons to Harvey. Harvey raised his hands. "Don't shoot, kid, don't shoot. I ain't drawing."

Brick and Lanky stared at Colt with blank amazement on their faces.

The sheriff pushed through the crowd and came to the forefront. Sheriff Lee Van Atten was well-known around California. He was an average-looking man, fair and well-dressed. He looked more like a store owner than a lawmaker but was better than average with a six-shooter. "What the hell happened here?"

Colt couldn't speak. He stood with his guns drawn, his body tense from the showdown.

Lanky was the first to speak up. "These three tried to rob us, sir. Colt tried to tell 'em to back off and leave us alone, but they wouldn't listen. Ned drew first, and Colt killed him. That feller tried to get him next, and Colt shot him, too."

The sheriff looked at Colt, still standing with his weapons drawn. "Harvey, is that what happened?"

Colt turned his head to look at Harvey, and the man wilted under his gaze. "Ye-yes, sir, Sheriff. That's what happened. Ned thought the boy would be an easy mark. I tried to tell him. I tried to tell him that the boy lived with Jim Borden, but Ned wouldn't listen. The kid got him and Stan fair and square, Sheriff."

Colt's feet felt glued to the ground as the sheriff turned to look at him. The sheriff spoke gently. "Why don't you put those guns away now, son?"

Colt stared blankly until the sheriff asked a second time. Then he snapped out of his trance and put the guns back in their holsters.

"You boys get on your horses and get on out of here. I've heard all I need to. Harvey, you'll be coming with me."

The boys mounted and headed out of the alley for home. Lanky and Brick were full of excitement and kept talking about the incident the whole way home. Colt was very quiet, wrapped in his thoughts. Jim had warned him that wearing guns would bring trouble, and he hadn't lasted fifteen minutes before he proved Jim right. He had just killed two men.

They were just coming up to the house when Colt's whole body started shaking. He could barely hold the reins, his hands were trembling so much.

"Colt, what's wrong with you? You're shaking like crazy," Brick asked as he could feel the shudders with his arms around Colt. Colt didn't answer but sat in silence.

Jim came out to greet them as they approached, and Brick yelled, "Jim! Something's wrong with Colt. He's shaking all over."

Jim rushed to the side of the horse and pulled Colt down. "Colt, you all right? What the hell happened?"

Lanky explained the whole story as Brick sat atop Thunder with tears running down his cheeks. Jim looked at Colt and then held him in a hug. He could feel him shaking in his embrace. "It's all right, Colt; that's just your body reacting to what happened. You'll be okay; you just need some time. Brick, Lanky, take the horses 'round the back. Colt and I are just gonna sit here for a while."

The two sat in silence on the porch steps. Colt's hands slowly stopped shaking before he finally spoke. "I tried not to do it, Jim. I gave him a chance. I wasn't giving him my money, and he was gonna have to kill me before I ever gave him Thunder."

"I know."

"It all happened so fast, I can't even tell you what happened. I don't remember."

"That's the shock, Colt. You'll get used to it."

"I don't want to get used to it."

"I know."

The two sat silently for a bit more before Jim spoke again. "Colt, you did good. You did right. I'm proud of you."

Colt managed a small smile.

Jim spoke again. "You sure do make quite the picture, you and Thunder." He chuckled a little.

Colt chuckled, too, and then the two went inside to eat.

Later that evening, lying in the dark of the bedroom, Brick spoke. "Colt? You awake?"

"Yeah."

"You were amazing today."

"Thanks."

"Colt?"

"Yeah, Brick?"

"Thunder is amazing, too. He's the best horse I've ever seen."

"I know." Colt yawned as he said it.

"Colt?"

"Yeah?"

"I want a horse, too. I ain't got as much money as you, though."

"I know, Brick, you spend too much. You gotta stop paying for your friends."

"They ain't got a job like we do, Colt. Besides, I like spending money, and they're my friends."

Colt was too tired to argue. "Let's talk to Shep tomorrow at work and see what he's got left. Maybe I can help you out."

Chapter 10

The next morning, the boys rode Thunder to school. The kids in the schoolyard stopped what they were doing and turned to stare. Some of them backed away as though they were scared of Colt--he guessed those ones must have heard the story of the previous day. As they approached the hitching rail, a girl walked over to them. It was Sadie Walcott, a year younger than Colt and very smart in class. Her father, Sterling Walcott, owned a big cattle ranch just east of town and was very successful.

As she approached, the wind blew her bonnet off her head so that it hung around her shoulders by the knot at her neck. Her blonde hair fluttered in the breeze, and her blue eyes sparkled as she looked at Thunder.

"That's a pretty horse," she said shyly as Colt tied him to the rail.

Colt bristled a bit at the thought of Thunder being called pretty, but he knew what she meant. "Thank you," he said. "He sure is." He patted the horse's neck as he spoke.

"Okay, well, bye." Sadie turned and hustled back to her group of friends, who giggled as she joined them.

Lanky joined the brothers, and he and Brick laughed a little at Colt's expense.

"What?" he asked.

"What do you mean what?" Lanky said. "Don't tell me that you're so in love with this horse that you don't recognize when a girl is sweet on you."

"What? Oh, shut up, she is not."

"Well, if she ain't, then I don't know what sweet means. She ain't never talked to *me* like that."

"You don't have a pretty horse." Colt laughed and threw a punch at Lanky's shoulder. All three of them chuckled and headed into school.

After school had finished for the day, the boys headed to Shep's ranch to start work. They had just finished moving a load of hay into the loft when Shep came by to talk to them. "Hey, boys, how y'all doin'? I heard there was a bit of a scrape in town after the party. You okay, Colt?"

"I'm all right, Shep. Thanks for asking."

"Good to hear. I've got a proposition for you, Colt. What if you came to work for me full-time?"

"You mean doing this stuff all day? I appreciate it, but I've got school and . . ."

"I don't mean mucking stalls and the like; I mean working as a ranch hand. You'd be doing all the stuff you've been watching those cowboys do for years now. It'd pay three bucks a day."

Working as a ranch hand? Colt could hardly believe it, and three dollars a day was better than most ranches paid. "You got a deal."

"Colt, what about school?" Brick asked.

Colt shrugged him off. "When do you want me to start? And Brick still keeps his job after school?"

"You can start tomorrow, bright and early. And, of course, Brick keeps his job. We still need this stuff done, too. In fact, you gotta friend lookin' for work, Brick? Need to replace your brother."

Colt was excited and could barely speak. Brick gave him an elbow to the ribs and then a nod in Shep's direction. "Oh, oh yeah." Colt stammered. "Shep? You got any more horses for sale? Brick was looking for one, and if I'm going to be here all day now, he'll definitely need one."

"I've got a few. Let's go take a look."

They headed out to the corral, where there were some more maverick horses. Colt stared with anticipation as he watched the ranch hands break in the animals. He couldn't believe he would be doing that stuff now.

"This little Appaloosa over here is a pretty good bet. Didn't take long to break him in, and he's been pretty calm ever since. Took a while to catch him, too. Bastard runs like a deer."

The pony wasn't as tall as Thunder, standing only fourteen hands high. He had a gray coat with the obligatory overlaid pattern of spots that was indicative of the breed. His spots were black.

The pony came over to them as they stood on the fence, and Brick reached out to him. The horse instinctively nuzzled Brick's hand.

"Ain't that the damndest thing?" Shep said. "You Warner boys sure do have a way with horses."

"How mruch do you want for him, Shep?"

"Well, he ain't as fine as your animal, but he's a good saddlehorse. I can let you have him for one hundred dollars."

Brick's heart sank. "I've only got forty dollars."

"Forty dollars won't get you much as far as horseflesh goes, I'm afraid, Brick," Shep said.

Colt thought it over. Another hundred dollars would put him at almost half of all his savings spent. He looked at Shep, and then at the Appaloosa, and then finally at Brick, whose eyes were pleading with him to do it. Finally, he spoke. "If I give you the hundred for the horse, do you have a saddle you can sell Brick for his forty dollars?"

"I reckon I can round up a saddle, and it won't be no broken-down claptrap either. I'll find you a good one for the forty, boys," Shep said with a smile.

Brick was ecstatic. "Thank you, Colt! Thank you! Can you pay now? Can I ride him home tonight?"

"Yes, I can pay now." Colt ripped off some bills for Shep. "Give him your forty for the saddle."

Brick handed over his money and then hugged the neck of the horse. "If he's that fast, I'm going to call him Lightning."

"Lightning? I shoulda known—two brothers riding Thunder and Lightning. Makes sense." Shep laughed as he went to go find a saddle.

After the work was done for the day, the brothers rode their horses back home. Drake was sitting on the front porch when they pulled up. "What do we have here? I'm going to need to build a bigger barn back there if you boys start coming home with a different horse every day."

"This is Lightning," Brick said excitedly.

"It's the last one for a good while, I promise," Colt said. He hopped off his horse and gave the reins to Brick. "Put him away for me, please."

"Sure thing, Colt. Thanks again." Brick rode around the back with Thunder in tow as Colt went to talk to Drake.

"Shep offered me a full-time ranch-hand job. Three dollars a day."

"What about school?"

"I'm done with school. I can learn more about real life working the ranch than I can in that schoolhouse."

"Okay, Colt," Drake replied. "You're fifteen. That's old enough to make your own choices, but you have to tell Jim."

"Okay, deal. There is one more thing, Drake. You've been more than kind to Brick and me these last three years. You let us stay in your house, you fed us, and you never asked for anything." He reached into his pocket. "Here's two hundred dollars. It's not what it should be, but it shows my appreciation for what you've done."

Drake balked at taking the money. "Colt, that's not necessary. Having you boys here has been good for me too. I told you when we met that all a man needs is three or four good friends, and I count you boys and Jim as my good friends."

"I know, but if me and Brick are gonna make it on our own, then we need to be responsible and pay the debts we owe. Take it, please. I want you to have it."

Drake reluctantly took the money. "Tell you what. I'll take it and hold on to it for you. Consider us square. This is a stand-up thing you're trying to do here, Colt. It shows the type of man you're becoming, one I'll be proud to say I know."

They shook hands and then went inside to join Brick and Jim for supper. After the meal, Colt asked Jim if he could talk to him. They went outside and sat on the front steps. "Jim, I offered Drake two hundred dollars for all the help he's given Brick and me," Colt said without preamble. "It's not enough, but it's all I could afford to spare."

"Sounds good, Colt. I'm sure he appreciated the gesture."

"He did, but there's nothing I can offer you, Jim. You've

done so much right from the beginning. I'll be in your debt forever. I want you to know how much I respect your opinion and everything that you've done for us." He reached out to shake hands.

Jim took his hand. "Just keep living, Colt. Live the life your father wanted for you. You're off to a good start; just keep working for it. There's nothing shameful about working hard to get what you want. Your brother's gonna be a challenge for you—he's got a wild streak, that one—but do your best to keep him grounded, and you boys will be okay." He drew back his hand. "Are you leaving? This feels like a goodbye."

"No, not leaving just yet. Just wanted you to know that I've been listening to you and appreciate everything you've said." Colt paused. "Jim, Shep offered me a ranch-hand job. It's an opportunity I want, so I'm going to take it. I won't be going to school no more."

Jim thought for a second. "Okay, Colt. A man's gotta make his own path, and if this is what you want for yours, then you go get it. Shep's a good man. He'll look out for you."

The following morning, Colt rode off to his new job while Brick rode Lightning to school. As Colt approached the ranch, he was greeted by Shep and a group of the cowhands that worked there. "Hey there, Colt. These are a few of the guys you'll be working with. This is Ty Wilson, Luke Carson, and Ridge Holloway. We're gonna be moving some cattle from the south pasture to the west one today; you'll help drive them. And this here is Eagle Feather; he's our scout. He keeps us out of trouble with the natives around here."

Colt nodded at each man as he was introduced. Ty and Luke looked like they were maybe ten years older; Ridge maybe only had a few years on him. Eagle Feather was the only man not to nod back at introductions. He sat stoically on his horse and stared at Colt without blinking. It was hard to gauge his age or his feelings at the moment, but Colt felt at ease around him.

Ty gave the signal, and the five rode off towards the south pasture while Shep headed back to the ranch. It was clear that Ty was the ranch boss and that Colt would have to pay close attention to his actions throughout the day.

As they rode out, Ridge pulled up beside Colt. "That's a hell of a horse you got there. Yes, sir, that's a mighty fine animal."

"Thanks," Colt said, "Yours looks to be in pretty good shape too." Ridge was riding a tan-colored bay that stood not quite as tall as Thunder. Muscles rippled beneath the hides of both horses with each stride they took.

"Yeah, Roscoe and I have been in our share of scrapes, and he ain't let me down yet." Ridge gave the horse a pat on the neck as he spoke. "He ain't got no give up in him—he'll just keep going, no matter how hard I push him. I reckon I ain't got a better friend in the world than this old boy right here. How about yours?"

"We ain't been together long enough to have that kind of relationship yet, but I'm hoping we get there." They rode silently until they reached their destination in the south pasture. As they crested a small hill, Colt saw the cattle laid out ahead of him. He had never seen so many cows in one place; he guessed there must have been a hundred to two hundred head in that field.

Ty started handing out assignments. "Colt, you're gonna ride down the left side. I know it's your first time, so nothing fancy—just keep them going straight, and if one gets out of line, you get them back in as fast as you can. If you run into any sort of trouble, you get our attention, and one of us will come to give you a hand. First and only rule: if they start to stampede, you get out of the way. You do *not* want to get caught in the middle of a stampeding herd."

Colt nodded his head in agreement and started to round the cattle into the group to start the drive. It was hot and dusty work. The cattle moved slowly, which gave ample time for the sun to beat down on a man. The dust caked on your skin as it mixed with your sweat, and your upper lip tasted like salt and dirt.

Colt looked around as they rode. Eagle Feather had gone well ahead of the group to scout the territory and keep an eye out for any rogue hostiles that might be wandering on the land. Ty was leading the herd, Ridge was on the right side, and Luke was bringing up the rear. They moved slowly but deliberately. The cattle were used to this and plodded along behind the lead steer as they had done numerous times before.

He knew it was supposed to be work, but Colt was enjoying himself. It felt freeing to be out on the grass, riding Thunder, working for a living. He hadn't known the boys for very long, but he had a good feeling about the group. A couple of times, he had a lone cow try and break away from the herd, but Thunder understood their assignment and was galloping up beside it and pushing it back to the group in no time.

Sometime in the early afternoon, they came to a river. Ty stopped the herd and let the cattle take on water. The horses drank, too, and Colt washed some of the dust off in the cool water. He filled his hat with water and then put it on his head so the water washed down his face and the back of his neck. It felt refreshing in the heat.

They hitched their horses and sat down for a quick lunch while the cattle drank and grazed. "Those are some pretty fancy guns you got there, Colt," Luke said. "You got yourself a rifle?"

"No, I don't."

"You should get yourself one. Out here, those six shooters aren't much help—you need to be close to hit what you're shooting at. By the time you get close enough to fire, the other guy is going to have put three shots into you. A long gun makes more sense out here. I use a '66 Winchester myself. If you can't afford one yet, Shep always has some spares he can lend you 'til you get paid."

Colt nodded in agreement. "I think I can afford one—I'll check it out. Thanks for the advice. Is there much call for that? I mean, we're staying on our own land and everything, right?"

"This time. But even on your own land, there's always the possibility of rustlers, natives, or just some random outlaw making his way through who wants what you got. Things happen."

They mounted again and started the herd back on the trail to the west pasture. The rest of the afternoon was uneventful, and they pulled the herd into their new home in the west pasture right around suppertime. They made sure everything was settled and then hightailed it for the ranch. They rode into the yard and saw Shep out in front of the barn with Sheriff Van Atten.

"What's going on, Shep?" Ty asked.

"Howdy, boys. The sheriff here is just letting us know that the stage was robbed today."

"Whereabouts?"

The sheriff spoke. "Just south of town, late morning. Four men were waiting for it. Nobody was killed, but they beat up the driver and the shotgun rider pretty good."

"What'd they get?"

"That's what don't make no sense. It was mid-week—there wasn't an army payroll or a bank sum on it. They got less than a hundred dollars from the passengers and some of their jewelry and such. Why hit an empty stage?"

"Maybe they didn't know it was empty," Shep offered. "Maybe they had some bad information and were expecting more. You got a description of 'em?"

"Not much of one. They hit pretty fast. Four men, lean builds like cowboys, two of them on the smaller side. They were wearing bandanas on their faces. There were four of them, but the driver only saw two guns."

"You hit a stage, and you're not all armed?" Luke asked, a little shocked. "These guys sound like amateurs. Shouldn't have too much trouble finding them, I wouldn't think, Sheriff."

"Here's hoping. Thanks for your time, Shep; you, too, gentlemen. Keep your ears open for me, if you don't mind. I would appreciate the help."

"Sure thing, Sheriff." Shep tipped his hat. As the sheriff rode away, he turned to the ranch hands. "How was your first day, Colt?"

"Exciting. Real informative. I learned a lot today. Thanks again for the job."

"No problem, Colt. You better get on home now. Get some food in you and get some rest. You're back early in the morning."

"Brick leave already?"

"About an hour ago. Him and his friend Troy. You know, Colt, there's room in the bunkhouse. You can stay here on the ranch and cut out all that ridin' back and forth."

"Thanks, Shep, but I'm gonna stay with Brick and Jim for a little while longer; make sure Brick is getting along okay. Besides, Thunder and I like the early morning ride."

It was dark by the time Colt rode up to the house. Drake

was sitting on the front porch with Jim having coffee. "How was your day, Colt?" Drake asked.

"Long and tiring, but it was good."

"Well, it must have been a tough day. Even a one-eyed old gambler like me can see that you're worn down." Drake laughed a little. "It's good for you. A little hard work is good for a man's soul."

"Is Brick inside?"

"He sure is," Jim answered. "I think he's been waiting for you. He's been wound up since he got home like he's riding with a burr under his saddle."

Colt put Thunder away for the night and, after he finished brushing him down, went in and helped himself to some supper. While he was eating, Brick came in to talk to him. "How was your first day as a hand?"

Colt explained about his day and driving the cattle to their new pasture.

"Sounds neat. You were a real cowboy today, Colt."

"How was your day? You seem pretty excited."

"My day was nothing special. School was a little weird without you there. Working with Troy was all right, though. Maybe one day we'll be ranch hands with you."

"That's it? Nothing else? How come you can't sit still?"

"I dunno. Just a good mood I guess."

"Well, I'm glad you're in a good mood. I'm feeling pretty good too. I like Monroe, Brick. Pa might have been right when he thought this was gonna be the place for us as a family. It's working out pretty well so far."

"I like it, too."

They both went to bed that night with smiles on their faces.

CHAPTER 11

The next few months were busy for Colt. Work filled his days, although he did manage to arrange to be part of a trip back into town for supplies, during which he was able to stop at the gunsmith's and purchase a Winchester rifle as Luke had suggested. Other than that supply run, the only time Colt saw the town was when he came home at dusk each night. His days were filled with moving cattle, trips to round up maverick horses in the hills surrounding the ranch, learning how to rope, and watching Ty and Luke break the ponies they collected. There was always work on the ranch. Colt enjoyed it and worked hard to prove that he belonged there.

Sheriff Van Atten had stopped around a few more times. Those amateur stage robbers had been busy too. There had been three more stage robberies, each one netting around the same as far as collected monies went. Again, none of the fleeced stages had carried bank or army money, the marauders making away with only what they took from the passengers. They were perfecting their craft, though, as their chosen locations were proving more and more conducive to ambushes, and they were getting on the stages and in the faces of the drivers before they even knew what was happening.

The descriptions hadn't improved any either, as their routine got quicker and quicker each time. The best anybody had to offer was still "four men and only two guns." Some of the men in town had been impressed that it took only two guns for the men to paralyze the drivers and their passengers. No one had even so much as attempted a shot at the assailants.

It was a warm, beautiful morning, and Colt and Thunder were headed to the ranch yet again. As they sauntered down the trail, Thunder's ears perked up at the sound of gunshots to their right. Colt paused. "You hear that, boy?"

Just as he said it, a second volley of shots rang out. "Should we go check it out? Sounds like someone has themselves in a pickle. Let's go." He wheeled the powerful house around, and they plunged into the brush, racing toward the sounds. As they approached a ridge, Colt dismounted. Staying low to the ground, he approached the crest. Many a man had been shot after foolishly cresting a ridge without caution and creating a silhouette that made for an easy target.

Colt looked down into the plains below. A single man was hunkered down behind an overturned buckboard. He was firing out into the open, and it took Colt a minute to figure out what he was shooting at. There was a group of Indians in the tall grass, looking to overtake the lone traveler. It was a small party, four that he could count; they must have been scouting when they came across the gentleman. From his vantage point, Colt could see that two had started slinking through the grass in an effort to flank the man on either side.

Colt backed away from the ridge and mounted Thunder again. "Okay, boy, here we go. We've got surprise on our side, but we got to hit 'em fast. Ride straight for that buckboard and shoot at anything that's moving. That's the plan, got it?" He patted the horse's neck as it whinnied as if in confirmation.

Colt dug in the spurs, and they took off over the ridge. It wasn't long before Thunder was in full gallop, and they were closing fast on their target. Colt hadn't had much practice time with the Winchester and definitely hadn't practiced firing from the top of a horse in full flight. His first few shots were wild, nowhere near their intended targets. He held his left elbow up in a crooked position and laid the rifle across it. He did his best to aim amid the jostling, and his next few shots were close enough to the intended targets that they backed off a bit.

They reached the buckboard, and Colt dismounted quickly, laying Thunder down behind the board for shelter as well. "Looks like you've got a situation here. Need a hand?"

The man seemed startled by his sudden appearance. "Absolutely!" he said. "Glad to see you. They just came from out of nowhere."

"They'll do that sometimes. There's only four of 'em. They were trying to flank you, but I think we scared 'em back a bit."

Colt laid his rifle on the buckboard for support. Now that he wasn't moving, his aim was better, and his next shot winged the brave trying to come up on the right side. He yelped with pain, and Colt could see him trying to slide back to the others.

There were a few more shots exchanged, and one more brave was hit before the party thought better of their actions. A single man made for an easy target, but two men evened the odds more than they liked. Whooping and hollering, they rode away over the plains.

The two men stayed crouched behind the buckboard for a few moments longer just to ensure their safety. When they felt it was safe to stand, they emerged from behind their protection, and Colt extended his hand. "Colt Warner. Nice to meet you." He surveyed the smaller man in front of him. Well-dressed as he was, he looked more like a schoolteacher than someone fit to ride across the open prairie in Indian territory.

"Alex Lashburn," said the man as he shook Colt's hand. "Damn glad you came along when you did. Those Apaches were looking to end me."

"Modocs."

"Excuse me?"

"They were Modocs, not Apaches. The Modocs are usually more peaceful, but they've been riled up lately since the government is trying to move 'em all to a reservation in Oregon. If they had been Apache, we'd still be fightin'."

"Well, that's certainly good to know. I wish to thank you again for your timely arrival."

"What you doing out here, mister?"

"I work for the R.B. Higgs Steel Company. It's based out of Ogden, Utah. I was sent out here to check our supply lines and make sure everything is still functioning at full capacity. Steel is a very strong commodity right now and only getting bigger."

Colt mounted. "I'll take your word for it, mister. You best leave your buckboard here. Just get on your horse and head for Sacramento before those braves get their courage up and decide to come back." He started to ride off.

"Wait, how can I repay you?" the man called.

"No need. Just get to town."

"Will I see you there? Can I buy you a drink?"

Colt chuckled. "Mister, I'm only fifteen. I'll be around, though. Maybe I'll see you again."

"Fifteen. Damn. They sure grow up fast out west, don't they?"

"We surely do, mister, we surely do." He hit the spurs, and he and Thunder rode off toward the ranch.

As they pulled into the yard, they were met by Ty. "You're late, Colt. We don't take kindly to that around here."

Colt apologized and explained his morning to Ty.

"Well, shoot, I guess I can cut you some slack on this one, then. Don't let it happen again." Ty was smiling. Colt relaxed and got to work.

His story spread like wildfire around the ranch, and Colt was answering questions about it all day. He felt like he was famous, like Wyatt Earp or someone. He liked the feeling.

When he arrived home that night, it was more of the same. It seemed as though Alex Lashburn had been telling his tale around town all day, and word had gotten back to Drake and Jim.

"You do all right, Colt? You were careful?" asked Jim.

"Remembered everything you taught us, Jim. Made sure I crept up to the ridge and everything."

"It was an honest-to-goodness Indian fight? You're so lucky." Brick was jealous.

"It wasn't a game, Brick," Jim said. "Colt was in real danger."

"It wasn't that bad," Colt said. "I think they were just bored and thought they'd give it a try. They didn't even shoot his horse."

"Still a dangerous situation, Colt, especially with those Indians as angry as they are right now, but it sounds like you handled it well. I'm proud of you."

"Thanks, Jim." Colt turned to Brick as Jim was exiting the room and whispered, "It *was* pretty neat, though."

Brick smiled and laughed a little.

An uneventful two days followed. He worked hard and for

long hours. Then, breakfast on the morning of the third day was interrupted by a knock on the door. It was Alex Lashburn.

"Sorry for interrupting, but I asked around Sacramento, and was told that the guy I was looking for sounded a lot like the kid living over in Monroe. They figured I could either find you here or out at some ranch, so I thought I would check early in the day."

"What can I do for you?"

"I'm eternally grateful for what you did for me the other day, and when you told me that I couldn't even buy you a drink, well, I wanted to do something to show my thanks. To that end, I got in touch with my employer, and he authorized me to gift you with this." He handed Colt a piece of paper.

"What is it?"

"That is ten shares of stock in the R.B. Higgs Steel Company. You are now a part owner."

Colt was confused. "What do I do with it?"

"Well, whatever you want. You can trade it in for cash value, or you can trade it for another stock—it's yours to do with as you please. My personal opinion is that you should hold onto it. As I said the other day, steel stock is getting stronger every day. Once the transcontinental railroad was completed, they started building smaller regional railways, and now every little town wants to be a rail stop. It's big business and only getting bigger."

"This is worth money?" Colt asked.

"Oh yes, currently a hundred dollars, but as I said, it's increasing all the time."

"Well, thank you very much, but it isn't necessary."

"Please take it. What's my life worth, if not at least a hundred dollars? And thank you again."

He left, and Colt sat back at the table, a little confused and a little proud. He put the piece of paper in his pocket and thought that on his next supply run, he would stop at the bank and put it in a deposit box. He had never even seen a stock or share before, and now he was part owner of a steel company. He couldn't wait to tell Lanky about it.

Work that day was particularly rough. It had been hot and dry the last few days, and moving cattle was dusty work. The herd stirred the ground something fierce, and the particles hung in the windless air. The dust was so thick at times that Colt couldn't see the herd in front of him. It coated your mouth and throat, even through the bandana worn across your face. Every breath felt like you were swallowing sand.

It was tiring work, made worse by the heat. By the end of the day, Colt was dead tired. His limbs felt thick and heavy from exhaustion. As he and Thunder made their way back to town for the night, Colt pulled up at a river and watered and washed off Thunder. The horse was caked with dust, his coat grey rather than its usual lustrous black. Thunder whinnied in approval; the water clearly felt good on his hot flesh.

Once Thunder's color had been restored, Colt took a look at himself and realized he was in the same shape as his horse. He removed his duster and shirt and rinsed them in the river, draping them over Thunder to dry. He placed his guns across his saddle before submerging himself in the cool water of the river. A cloud of milky grey extended out from him as the layers of dust were washed off his body and clothing. His skin tingled as the water enveloped him.

He sat for a minute, enjoying the refreshing feeling after a day in the sun. Then he stood and stretched, his muscles tensing and his body glistening in the sun.

There was a rustle in the nearby bushes, and Colt grabbed a gun from its holster. "Who's there? What do you want? I suggest you come out, and you do it nice and slow, before I start shooting at whatever moves next." He had a gravel in his voice that he hadn't heard before. It scared him a little.

"Don't shoot." The voice was female. Colt looked on in puzzlement as Sadie Walcott made her way slowly from the bushes. "I wasn't spying, honest. I was picking berries and just happened to stop where you were."

Colt blushed a little and then grabbed his shirt and put it on. He stared at Sadie for a moment and then asked, "Where's your basket?"

"What?"

"You said you were picking berries. What were you putting them in? I don't see a basket." Colt smiled as he said it.

Now it was Sadie's turn to blush. "Okay, I wasn't picking berries. I don't know why I said that, but I wasn't spying, either. I was riding home and saw you in the river. I only stopped for a second. I . . ."

"It's okay," said Colt. "I ain't angry. It's good to see you again. It's been a while."

"Yes, it has," she agreed.

"Can we ride back to town with you?"

"We?"

"Me and Thunder."

"Oh, of course. I'd like that."

They rode back to town at a saunter while they chatted.

"Why did you leave school?" Sadie asked.

"I was offered a job. I'm a ranch hand for Shepherd Broxton. Need to make some money, so Brick and I can secure our lives out here."

"Well, you're missed there."

"Oh, I doubt that."

"No, really. I mean, poor Lanky is just lost without you

there. And the rest kinda miss you, too. Without you there, Brick and Troy are sorta runnin' wild."

"What about you?"

"Oh, I don't worry about Brick and Troy. I've known Troy since we were little. He gives me any grief, and I'll tell his ma."

"I meant, do you miss me?"

"Oh?" Sadie blushed again. "Yes. I mean, of course. You were fun to have in class."

"That's all. I was fun in class?"

"Colt Warner! Don't you dare make me say it. It wouldn't be lady-like."

Colt reached over and grabbed her reins to stop her horse. He stared at her as they sat in the middle of the trail. "Well, that's just fine. Then, I'll say it. Miss Sadie Walcott, I would like to court you if that suits your fancy."

Sadie's cheeks flushed red as she stared back at Colt. "Well, Mr. Warner, I do believe that would suit me just fine." She smiled.

"Well, that's good news." Colt smiled, too. "Sadie, I have the day to myself tomorrow. Would you like to accompany me on a ride?"

"Yes, I believe I would. You may pick me up at my house after school is out."

Colt smiled again and tipped his hat. They rode back the rest of the way in silence.

As they approached Sadie's place, they saw her father standing out front, waiting for her. "Sadie, your momma's got supper on. You go on and get in and get yourself cleaned up. And who might you be?"

"Daddy, this is Colt Warner."

"Colt Warner, you say?"

Sterling Walcott was a man of average size but not average

wealth. He was the only rancher in the area that had both a house in the city and a house on his ranch. He was dressed very well and had his grey hair combed back and well-kept at all times. He had grey eyes, which were currently burning a hole through Colt as he examined this boy his daughter had brought home. "The same Colt Warner that killed Ned Shiffly and Stan Lamont?"

"It was self-defense, sir. Those men were trying to rob me, my brother, and my friend. I tried to warn them off, but they wouldn't back down."

"I heard it was something like that. Just what would you be doing with my daughter?"

"Daddy, stop," Sadie begged.

"I met your daughter on the road, sir, and escorted her home to make sure she was safe. With your permission, sir, I'd like to court Miss Sadie."

"I don't think that's going to happen, son. If I've heard correctly, you live with that Jim Borden and Drake Rockhaven. Is that correct?"

"Yes, sir."

"Well, Mr. Borden is a gunfighter, and Mr. Rockhaven hasn't been known to shy away from trouble much, either. You're a boy, I'm guessing fourteen, fifteen by the looks of you, and you've killed two men already. You can see why I wouldn't want that kind to come courting my daughter, now, can't you?"

"I can assure you, sir, that that situation was a one-time incident. I . . ."

"Save your breath, Mr. Warner. You can assure me all you want, but those two guns on your hips tell me all I need to know. Inside, Sadie. Good evening, Mr. Warner." He turned and walked into his house.

"Meet me tomorrow where we met today. After school is out," Sadie whispered quickly before she hurried to put her horse away and go inside.

Colt rode the rest of the way home conflicted. He wanted to court Sadie, but he wanted her father to be amenable to it. It wasn't fair for the man to look down on him like that; it had been self-defense, and he didn't go looking for trouble. Just because Sterling Walcott had a ranch and money, that didn't mean he was better than Colt. He had to have started somewhere, too. Those two guns had saved his life once already, and he wasn't about to take them off for anybody.

He arrived home, brushed Thunder quickly before he put him away for the night and stormed into the house. He went straight to bed without eating and lay there staring into the dark. He would prove to Walcott what he was worth. He would prove it to them all.

Chapter 12

The next morning, Colt was starving. He headed straight for the table without changing. Skipping supper the night before had not been a good idea.

He sat at the breakfast table, eating all he could, barely stopping to give one-word answers to questions he was asked. After he had finished, he leaned back in his chair and patted his stomach happily.

Drake laughed. "Shep not feed you out at that ranch?"

"This is my own fault. Shouldn't have skipped supper last night."

"I noticed. Any particular reason?"

"Just a guy. Said some things."

"I see. Anything specific?"

"Just some crack about me not being good enough to court his daughter."

"Ah." Drake chuckled a little. "I should have known. There's always a woman. Only two things can make a cowboy miss a meal: trouble chasing a herd—or a woman. And no mistake about it, you are definitely a cowboy, Colt."

Colt felt some pride again. He hadn't ever thought of himself as a cowboy yet, but hearing Drake say it felt good; made it seem real.

"So, what's her name?"

"Sadie Walcott. I met her at school."

"Daughter of Sterling Walcott? Well, you certainly don't shoot low, do you? I reckon old Sterling certainly *doesn't* think you're good enough for his little girl. I don't reckon he'd think God himself was good enough for her."

"Doesn't like the fact that I've killed two men, even though it was self-defense," Colt said. He left out the part about keeping company with Drake and Jim.

"Thinks you're a bad seed, hey? Only one thing you can do to change his mind."

"What's that?"

"Not be a bad seed," he said.

Colt gave him a confused look. He had been hoping for some actual advice.

Drake continued, "Colt, you're probably the best young man I have ever met. You have goals, you work to reach those goals, and you listen when people offer advice. If it stays that way, you're going to be one of the two or three best men I've ever encountered. Stuff like that changes people's minds."

"What if while I'm waiting to change his mind, someone comes and sweeps away Sadie?"

"You won't have to wait that long. You save money like a miser—you're better off than most of the men walking the streets right now. You spend that wisely, make a place for yourself, and you'll change his mind pretty quick. He wants a future for his daughter, and if you show you can give her one, he'll come around."

"Thanks, Drake." Colt got up from the table. He wanted

to change his shirt before he headed into town; he had some errands today before he met Sadie.

He opened his dresser drawer to find the steel shares Alex had given him, and as he grabbed the certificate, he noticed his Pa's old revolver wasn't there. He tried to remember if the gun had been there last night when he put the shares in the drawer before bed, but he'd been so angry when he did it that he couldn't recall. In fact, the more he thought, he couldn't recall when he had seen it last. He wondered where it had gone. Maybe Jim had taken it to clean it or something?

He would ask him later. He changed and headed to the bank.

He rode by the school on his way and saw Lightning tied up outside. He wondered how Brick was doing. Sadie had said he and Pretty Boy were running wild, and he hadn't asked exactly what that meant. He had been working so much that there hadn't been a lot of time to spend with Brick lately. He decided he would have to make an effort to speak with him more.

It was a pleasant morning. The sun was shining, and it wasn't too hot to start the day. He tied Thunder to the hitching post and walked into the bank. At the wicket, he asked for and received a safety deposit box. Colt put the shares in the box, paid the fee, and walked out into the sun again.

He strolled the boardwalk, just taking everything in. He had been working since he got to Monroe and had never really had the time to just wander the town and look, not since the day that they had arrived.

It was a busy place, with people walking up and down the boardwalks on both sides. The casino had a crowd already, and music was loudly playing. The saloon was also at capacity.

Some of the working girls were already sitting out front of the casino, trying to drum up business.

Colt enjoyed the sight and sound of it all but couldn't imagine living with it every day. He enjoyed the solitude and silence working the ranch provided. When you were out riding fences, it gave you a chance to think, to gather your thoughts and make plans for the future. That was where he wanted to be, on a ranch of his own with no neighbors in the immediate area. Just him and his thoughts, and maybe a family.

He was standing on the walk staring into a store window when a rider came barreling down the street and stopped in front of the sheriff's office. The sheriff came out to meet him. "The stage has been hit again," the man said excitedly. "This time, one of the thieves has been hit. They rode off to the south. We can maybe catch them, Sheriff!"

Sheriff Van Atten and his deputies mounted quickly and followed the rider out of town. Colt rushed back to Thunder and thought about following the posse. He decided that they had a decent head start, so instead, he decided to see if he could head off the gang—get where they were going before they did. He rode Thunder hard out of town. He had a pretty good guess where the gang might be riding to and hoped he was right.

It wasn't long before he realized that he had guessed correctly but had been too slow getting there. He could see dust and four riders ahead of him. They were going at a break-neck pace.

He pulled Thunder to a halt and pulled a spyglass from his saddlebags. From where he sat, he was able to see that the last rider in the group was favoring his right arm and sitting hunched in the saddle. He watched through the glass as the lead rider hung back while the others veered off to the east. Just before the gang rode behind some brush and out of sight, he was able to make out the lead rider's horse: a grey Appaloosa with black spots.

It was Lightning.

Colt was sitting stunned in the saddle when the sheriff and his deputies rode up. "Did you see a group of riders come this way, Mr. Warner?" asked the sheriff.

Colt paused before he spoke. "Yes, sir, four of them. One has a wounded right arm. They headed straight south, and then by that boulder there, they turned and headed west."

"Thanks, Colt. Let's go, boys." The posse rode after the gang.

Colt turned Thunder around and headed back to town, his mind racing. It couldn't be Brick. He was in school. Besides, he had no idea how to rob a stage—he was only thirteen. And he had no reason to do it. He had a place to live, and he had a job where he made money—why would he need to risk getting shot by robbing a stage?

As Colt got back to town, he rode past the school. Lightning wasn't tied out front anymore. If he had thought it wasn't Brick, then why had he lied to the sheriff about which way the gang had turned?

Colt stopped for lunch at the local eatery. Colt sat down, and his thoughts went back to Brick. If it was, in fact, Brick he saw, then it was assuredly Pretty Boy Troy, Jessie Mitchell, and Tank Jepson rounding out the group. This was what they had been doing? Cutting class to rob stage passengers for a few measly dollars? And why? If Brick and Troy were both working for Shep now, then they weren't hurting for money. Was this what Sadie had meant by running wild? Did she know what they were doing?

So many questions, and just when Colt was starting to feel

comfortable with their positions here in Monroe. Things were starting to pick up, and now Brick might be a thief. He was going to have to talk to him later and figure out what the hell he was thinking.

He finished his lunch and stopped by the General Store and picked up some pieces of sweet fudge for when he met Sadie later that afternoon. He had just mounted when Alex Lashburn came out of the casino and spotted him.

"Hey there, Colt!" he yelled as he waved and approached. "How are you doing this fine day?"

"I'm doing fine, Mr. Lashburn. What are you doing here in Monroe? Shouldn't you be in Sacramento? Any more Indian trouble?"

"Oh, no, none at all, thank goodness. And please, call me Alex. I owe you my life; we can at least be on a first-name basis."

"All right. Alex it is. What have you been doing around town?"

"Oh, as I said, I've been checking supply-line paths and speaking with vendors, making sure our products are still getting through. To tell the truth, though, I think I may stay here in Monroe. The town is lovely, and I quite enjoy the weather. Mr. R.B. Higgs may need to find another logistical supply reporter."

"What would you do around here? You don't strike me as the ranching type."

"Oh, goodness, no. I'm sure I can find something. Maybe open a shop of my own or be a Faro dealer for the casino."

"Alex, do you know the law at all?"

"Some. Why do you ask?"

"Well, when you do your checking of supply lines and

things, I imagine you come across situations where you need to buy land and that sort of stuff?"

"On occasion. Why?"

"What're the rules to land ownership? How old you gotta be and stuff?"

"Well, usually you need to be twenty-one, but the government passed the Homesteader Act in 1862, and that says if you're the head of a family and you work the land for five years, it's yours. You looking to buy some land?"

"Maybe. I've been looking but haven't found anything yet."

"Well, with just you and your brother, I imagine you qualify as the head of a family, which entitles you to sixty-five acres under the act, if you find a spot."

"Thanks, Alex. Good to know . . ."

Colt's voice trailed off as he spotted Sadie riding down the street toward him. She smiled and waved as she approached. "Aren't you supposed to be in class?" he asked.

"Well, that's a fine greeting for someone. I thought you'd be happy to see me."

"I am glad to see you—just surprised. What are you doing here? How'd you find me?"

"Well, that's a little better. I was excited about our ride later and bored with class, so I left early so we could get a head start. Just don't tell Daddy. And if you think you can ride that horse of yours through town without causing a stir, you're mistaken. All I had to do was ask one question, and they pointed me right to you." She giggled a little.

Alex cleared his throat.

"Oh, I'm sorry. Sadie, this is Alex Lashburn. Alex, this is Miss Sadie Walcott."

"Nice to meet you, Mr. Lashburn."

"The pleasure is mine, Miss Walcott."

"Well, Alex," Colt said, "as you just heard, I'm wanted for something else right now, so I'd best be going. You take care, and good luck with your plans."

"Absolutely, Colt. Good afternoon to you both."

The two rode off to the north at a slow, easy pace. They talked as they rode, and Colt told her about his parents, life in Nebraska, and his father's plans for them.

"That's incredible," Sadie said. "You have such a story already, and you're only fifteen. I've never been anywhere or done anything. My father says we came here from Arizona, but I was so young I don't remember any of it, and it definitely wasn't a story like yours."

"Yeah, it's a beginning, all right."

"It's more than a beginning, Colt. Some people live their whole lives and don't have a story like that to tell. What do you want to do with your future?"

"I'm going to have myself a ranch one day, Sadie, like Shep's or your father's. A nice little place where a man can work, raise a family, and make something of himself and the land."

"Sounds nice."

"And what about you?" Colt asked. "What's your future?"

"I don't know, I haven't really thought about it. Get married, I guess. Daddy wants to see me with some fancy businessman or doctor."

"What do you want?"

"Your dream sounds nice."

They continued to ride and talk. It was easy talking to Sadie; she was a good listener and genuinely seemed interested in what Colt was saying.

They had ridden northeast and had been talking for so long

that they hadn't realized how far they had traveled or how long they had been gone—until Colt suddenly realized there was no way they could be back in town before dark.

They rode to the top of a small hill and came to an abrupt stop. They were looking down over a piece of pastureland in a valley with mountains at the east end. Colt sat staring out over the land, watching the sun kiss the grassland, and the wind gently sway the blades back and forth. From the hill, the motion almost looked like waves in the ocean.

This was his place. He looked around and could not see any of the tell-tale signs of ownership. There were no fences, no lodgings, nothing to indicate that anybody had claimed it. A small river ran through from north to south, providing water for food and livestock.

"What do you think, boy?" he said to Thunder. Sure is beautiful, ain't it?" Thunder whinnied slightly. Then he turned to Sadie. "This is it. This is my ranch." He glanced over the valley again. "I wonder why no one has claimed it?"

"It's beautiful, Colt. It'll make a fine ranch."

"I'm sorry, Sadie, but we've come too far. We'll have to camp here tonight and then head back tomorrow."

Colt dismounted, took the roll off his saddle, and spread it on the ground before starting a small fire. By the time he had unsaddled and hitched the horses and started some coffee on the fire, the sun had set. He pulled some jerky and the fudge from his saddlebags, sat beside Sadie on the blanket, and offered her some of each. "It ain't much, but it'll have to do. I didn't realize how far we had gone. I apologize."

"For what?" asked Sadie as she took some jerky. "I'm having a wonderful time, and this is a beautiful place." She looked up at the darkening sky. "Look at all the stars. Why would I want to be anywhere else?"

"Your pa ain't gonna like that you aren't back. He's gonna skin me alive when we do get home."

"Daddy's all bark, Colt. Just get me home safe, and everything will be fine."

When they'd eaten their jerky and fudge, they lay down on the blanket side by side. Sadie nestled her head on Colt's shoulder, and the two of them fell asleep under the stars.

THE NEXT MORNING, they awoke a little shivery from sleeping in the night air. They had coffee and jerky again and then prepared to leave. Colt hurried through saddling the horses. "We need to go back. I have to see about claiming this land before someone else does."

They swung up into the saddles, turned the horses to head back to Monroe, and came face-to-face with two Modoc braves about fifty yards away, just riding over the hill. The two parties sat staring at one another for a surprised second. Then one of the braves let out a yell, and the two Indians charged toward Colt and Sadie.

"Sadie! Ride!" Colt slapped her horse hard on the rump, and the animal jumped into a gallop toward the Indians. Colt urged Thunder into his own gallop and raced out in front of her. He turned Thunder right into the path of the brave on the left, bowling over the horse and rider. The brave howled in pain as the animal landed on his leg—Colt heard the snap of the bone breaking.

With Sadie and her horse close behind, he and Thunder charged on up the hill. A rifle cracked behind them, and bark spit into Colt's face as the bullet struck a tree they were passing.

They pushed the horses harder. Thunder was young and strong and seemed to be enjoying the workout, but Sadie's mare was older and hadn't been run like that for a good long while. The horse was breathing heavier and fighting the pace more and more with every step.

They topped the hill. With the following brave out of sight, Colt pulled both animals to a stop. He tried to hide Sadie and the horses among some nearby bushes, but Thunder was still clearly visible. Colt found himself a large fallen log to take cover behind and pulled his guns from their holsters.

It was only a few seconds until the brave appeared. As he could no longer see Colt or Sadie ahead of him, he slowed his horse and looked around. Just as the brave noticed Thunder behind the bushes, Colt fired a warning shot that sent him scrambling off his pony and into a ditch for cover. Colt could see him looking about furiously, trying to figure out where the shot had come from. He sat up to shoot in Thunder's direction, and Colt fired another warning, this time closer to the brave's position.

The Indian ducked as bark flew off a tree not far from him. This time he knew where the shot had come from, and Colt ducked as the brave fired his rifle into the log Colt was hiding behind.

"Colt!" yelled Sadie. "Colt, what do we do?"

"Stay covered, Sadie. Keep the horses covered as best you can." Colt raised up and fired another shot into the ditch as he yelled, then ducked behind the log again. He tried to think of a plan. It had been a great time with Sadie until this point, but this was not how it was supposed to end. He hadn't wanted to put Sadie in harm's way, and he was positive that once Sterling Walcott heard about this, Colt would no longer be welcome anywhere near his daughter, let alone allowed to court her.

He stayed hidden for another minute or two. A couple of more shots from the ditch hit his log, and he made a decision.

In one move, he leaped up from his refuge and ran towards the ditch, cocking and firing both guns over and over as fast as he could. He leaped into the ditch, surprising the cowering brave, dropped the guns, and landed a hard right hand on the Indian's chin. The brave fell backward, and Colt jumped on top of him. The two wrestled in the grass, each landing blows before Colt finally regained the upper hand and landed two quick punches to the Indian's face, knocking him unconscious. He stood up quickly, grabbed the Indian's rifle, and threw it into the bushes. He then slapped the brave's horse, sending it running off alone. He picked up his guns, reloading them as he walked back to Sadie and the horses. Then he holstered them and slung himself back into the saddle.

"Colt, you're bleeding!" Sadie yelped.

"It's nothing. We need to get out of here before he wakes up. Let's go."

They rode back to Monroe in silence until just before they reached the town limits. Then, Sadie broke the silence with a question. "Colt, what were you thinking back there?"

"What do you mean?"

"You stood up and ran right toward someone who was shooting at you, without any cover. You could have been killed."

"I don't know. He wasn't shooting at the time. I was angry and wasn't gonna take it anymore. I needed to get you out of there, and that seemed like the best way. I guess I wasn't thinking, really."

"Well, don't do that again. You scared me."

They arrived in town and headed for the land office. Colt explained where the land he wanted was.

"How old are you, son?"

"I'm eighteen, sir," Colt lied.

"I'm afraid you need to be twenty-one to own land."

"The Homesteader Act says if you're head of a family, age doesn't matter. There's just me and my brother, sir."

The clerk looked him over and then looked at Sadie, who nodded her head in agreement. He thought for a second, then shrugged. "All right, fill out this form with your family name and the rest of the information it asks for. That's sixty-five acres at five dollars an acre for a total of three hundred and twenty-five dollars. Plus, the fourteen-dollar homestead filing fee. That's three hundred and thirty-nine dollars."

Colt didn't have three hundred and forty dollars. "I'm a little short. Can I maybe take less land?"

"Son, the act says you can have the land, but you gotta work it, and you gotta take sixty-five acres. That's the least I can give you."

"Look, mister, I've got about two hundred and fifty. I'm good for the rest. Ask Shep Broxton; he'll vouch for me."

"If he'll vouch for you, why don't you see if you can borrow the rest from him?" asked the clerk.

Colt was dejected. That was *his* place. From the moment he saw it, he could picture everything in his head, the ranch, the family, all of it. He needed to find the money.

"Colt? I have some money. You can have a hundred dollars," Sadie offered.

"I can't take your money, Sadie. Your father . . ."

"My father doesn't matter. It's my money; I can spend it how I choose. And you wouldn't be taking it. We could be partners, own the ranch together."

"Partners?"

"Yes. You asked what my plan for the future was, and I

didn't have one. Investing in a ranch operation sounds like a good place to start."

"It won't happen right away. This will break me. If I need to work the land, I can't work for Shep. It'll be a slow process, but little by little, we can build it and get it ready. It'll take time."

Sadie laughed. "I have time. I'm only fourteen, silly."

Colt turned to the clerk. "Get that claim ready, mister. We'll be right back."

The two went to the bank and withdrew their funds. "Thanks again, Sadie," Colt said as they stepped outside. "I just couldn't imagine not having that land. Did you see it? Did you see how amazing it was?"

"I did. It's really great, Colt. I'm happy for you."

"For us. We're partners now."

They purchased the land, and Colt held the deed in his hand as they left the claims office. "Who would have thought I'd ever be a landowner? Pa would be proud."

He rode with Sadie back to her place and was again met out front by her father, who was in a panic. "Sadie! Where the hell have you been? My God! Your mother and I were scared to death. The sheriff is looking for you right now. And you!" He turned his attention to Colt. "You're a stubborn one, aren't you, Mr. Warner? I thought I made myself clear that you were to stay away from my daughter."

"You did, sir, but I think you've made a mistake."

"Oh, you do?" Sterling Walcott sneered as he said it.

"Yes, sir and no disrespect meant, but I'm gonna keep coming around as long as she'll have me and until you can see the mistake you've made. I like your daughter, sir, and, God willing, she likes me too." He tipped his hat and turned to leave. "Good day, sir. Good day, Miss Sadie."

"Good day, Colt."

As he rode away, he fought the urge to look back. He could only imagine the state Sterling Walcott was in. He laughed to himself, thinking about Walcott standing there, mouth agape, wondering what had just happened.

He rode up to the house and saw Brick sitting with Jim on the front porch. It was at that point that he remembered the goings-on from the day before. He put Thunder away and then yelled for Brick. Both Brick and Jim came around the house.

"What's the matter, Colt?" Jim asked.

"Just need to speak to Brick alone, if you don't mind, Jim."

"Fair enough. I'll be inside if you boys need me."

"What's going on, Colt?" Brick asked.

"Where were you yesterday?"

"I was at school, Colt."

"You're sure you weren't out robbing stagecoaches with Troy and the gang?"

Brick stared at the ground. "How'd you find out?" he said sheepishly.

"I followed you guys after it happened. I was gonna try and stop whoever it was. I saw Lightning, Brick. What the hell were you thinking?"

"I don't know, Colt. Troy thought it would be easy, and it was, Colt, it was so easy. Troy's plan wasn't good—he's got more strength than brains. I went along at first to give him a better plan and make sure no one got hurt. If you catch them by surprise, move fast enough, and yell loud enough, then you can scare them into not moving at all. They just sit there staring at you while you take their stuff."

"Who got shot?"

"It was Jessie. He turned his back on the stage passengers and one dandy who thought he was Wyatt Earp pulled a derringer out of his vest pocket. A derringer, a stupid little lady gun. He had Jessie dead to rights, but he ain't never shot a gun before. The guy was so scared he missed and just grazed Jessie's arm. Troy put a whoopin' on the guy real good for that. I was scared right then, so we just rode to beat hell as fast as we could away from there."

"You're an outlaw, Brick. After all we've accomplished, all we've . . ."

"What have 'we' accomplished, Colt? What have 'we' done? You've done it all. You've got the fancy clothes and the fancy horse, the ranch-hand job, part of a steel company. What do I have? A messed-up foot and a job mucking stalls and feeding horses."

"Everything I've done has been for us. We're brothers. I'm not going anywhere without you, Brick."

"Don't do it for me, show me how to do it!" yelled Brick. "Treat me like an equal, not some little baby you need to coddle. I can be a man, too. At least with Troy and the boys, it feels like we're equals. It feels like a family."

A thought struck Colt. "Was it you that took Pa's gun? Is that what you're using to do this?"

"I don't want your help no more, Colt. I can do things on my own. Yes, I took Pa's gun. You don't need it anymore."

"The sheriff is looking for you guys, Brick. If they find you, you'll hang. You're only thirteen. Tell me you're going to stop this."

"Nobody's been hurt, and there's no big money taken. Ain't gonna hang us for that, some prison fort somewhere more than likely. Are you gonna tell Jim and Drake?"

"That's what you want? A prison fort? Are you gonna stop this? Brick, you have to stop before someone really gets hurt."

"Are you gonna tell, yes or no?" Brick's voice was flat.

"We're brothers. I won't say anything for now. You need to fix this, Brick."

"All right then, thanks." Brick turned and went inside.

Colt followed after a few minutes. The rest of the day was a waste. He didn't even show the deed to Jim or Drake. He hadn't shown up for work, and he knew he was going to have to answer to Shep and Ty for that, but he couldn't stop thinking about everything that had happened over the last day and how he was going to deal with Brick.

He never left his room and finally decided that he would have to get that land ready and move Brick out there as soon as possible. Maybe getting him away from all of this would cause him to see what he was doing, and he would come around and work the ranch with Colt.

He went to bed that night wondering how he could help his brother. He couldn't tell anyone. They'd arrest Brick and the gang for sure. How far would he be willing to go to keep his brother safe?

It was a question he was still trying to find the answer to when sleep finally came.

CHAPTER 13

Colt woke the next morning feeling conflicted. On the one hand, he was ecstatic to have a land deed and to get started on his dream of a ranch. On the other, he had no idea how to help his brother get off the outlaw path he was on without sending him to jail.

He rode out to Shep's that morning and explained that he wouldn't be able to work for the rancher anymore.

"This is pretty sudden, ain't it, Colt?" Shep said.

"Yes, sir, it is, and I'm sorry, but this land just came up yesterday. I couldn't miss the chance."

"I understand. Whereabouts is your land?"

Colt explained the location and how beautiful it was.

"It does sound pretty, Colt, but if it's where I'm thinking it is, you may have some trouble. The Modoc are runnin' through there pretty regular. Not normally an issue, but with the way things are now, it could stir some problems."

"I got no quarrel with any of them. We'll make our peace."

"Good luck to you, Colt. I hate to lose you, but I hope you make it out there." Shep reached out his hand.

Colt shook it. "Thanks, Shep. For everything. Don't be a stranger."

Colt wanted to head out to his place, but he needed a few supplies first, so he went back to town. He figured he needed to tell Jim and Drake what was happening, as well.

He found Jim just outside the hotel and stopped to talk. "I found myself some land, Jim. I'm gonna start my own ranch."

"Where? How'd you do it, Colt?"

Colt explained the location and how Alex had told him about the Homesteader Act. He also told Jim about Sadie giving him the money and being partners.

"You be careful, Colt. Men like Sterling Walcott don't take kindly to new competition, and if he finds out you took money from his daughter to do it, there's no telling what he might do."

"I didn't take her money, Jim. She's a partner. I've got no trouble giving her her share of everything. Besides, I'm gonna marry her someday."

"I understand, Colt. Just watch your back. You need some help getting started out there?"

Colt smiled. "I could surely use some."

Colt started a credit note at the general store and picked up some of the supplies he would be needing. He and Jim then rode out to where his ranch would be. As they came over the last hill, they paused for Colt to show Jim what he had purchased.

"It truly is a beautiful piece of land, Colt," Jim said. "You've done well."

The sun was just starting to set, and the sky had a lovely pink tone to it as the men started out over the grass. They set up a makeshift tent that would be Colt's home for the foreseeable future and then set about starting to build the foundation of what would be a more permanent ranch house. They made a fire, ate, and then slept for the night before starting again the next morning.

They built close to the base of the mountains on the east side for protection from sneak attacks. They built a bridge over the river, so they wouldn't have to try to drag the wagon through the water anymore when carrying supplies. They worked all day, and by the time the sun was setting, they had the start of a solid rock foundation for the house. The mountain base supplied a good number of loose stones that were large enough to build with, and Jim was very knowledgeable when it came to stone houses.

Colt caught himself staring at Jim on more than one occasion. The man fascinated him. He had all the knowledge of the mountains, plains, and deserts that he had shared with the boys on the train, he was very skilled at both cards and guns, and now it turned out he could build houses as well. Who was Jim, and what kind of life had he led? Every time Colt thought he had him figured out, there was another layer to discover. He was glad Jim was his friend.

"Have you told Brick about this place yet?" Jim asked as they sat around a fire.

"Not yet. I'm not sure what's going on with him, Jim. He's fighting everything I'm doing, pulling away. I don't know how he can't see that I'm doing all of this for us."

"A man's gotta make his own way in this world, Colt, and Brick's just trying to figure out what kind of man he's going to be. Just keep working; he'll come around."

"I don't think so, Jim. He's pretty angry with me." Colt didn't offer up Brick's secret.

"He's young. He will be for a while. Eventually, things will clear up for him, and he'll see what's right."

"How can you be sure?"

"He's from the same family as you, Colt. He was raised the same way. He'll come back."

"I hope he does."

A few weeks later, the stone house was complete, and the two had moved on to cutting trees from the west end of the land to build a corral and start some fencing. Jim went back to town for a few days to check in with Drake and Brick and pick up some more supplies. Colt took those days to explore the mountain face behind his home.

He found a small cave almost directly above his house that went back into the mountain for about fifteen feet. From the mouth of the cave, he could look out over his entire homestead. A natural wall that had formed five feet from the mouth made it hard to see the cave from the valley floor. Colt built the wall a little higher, and by the time he was done, the cave was invisible from lower down the slope. A slight ledge above it meant it wasn't visible from higher up, either.

He hauled a few supplies up to the cave and stocked it with firewood, as well. If something should happen and he needed to retreat from the house, this would be a good hideaway.

He had heard about men mining the mountains for silver, and he needed money. His credit note at the store was getting larger, and he currently was not making anything from the ranch or the little farm he had started to satisfy the requirements of the Homesteaders Act. Each day, he would head up the mountainside and try digging into the rock, looking for some trace of the silver or gold men had been finding. He chipped away at the surface, breaking off pieces of the dark, glass-like stone.

As he paused for a break, he spotted a lone rider approaching his ranch. Colt worked his way back down the mountain and started walking toward his home. He adjusted the gun belt on his hips and made sure everything felt right if he needed to draw.

As he came up to the back of the house, the rider was finally close enough for Colt to identify him. It was Alex Lashburn.

"Howdy, Alex. What brings you out here?"

"Hello, Colt. I ran into Jim Borden in town, and he told me that you had been working out here, trying to get yourself established to start ranching. He went on about how beautiful your land was, and I thought I'd take a ride out and see for myself. He wasn't lying."

"No, I don't suppose he was. It might be the best place I've seen in my life."

"Looks like you've done a great job on the house, too. Colt, you might truly be the most remarkable young man I've ever met. There are full-grown, tough men back in Sacramento that don't have half of what you've got or the will or desire to get it. It's incredible."

"Well, thanks, Alex, but the house was mainly Jim. I just helped out. There's an incredible man for you! There's no limit to what he knows."

"What have you been up to out here all by your lonesome? I don't think I could handle that much alone time."

"I been climbing that mountain every day trying to see if I can't maybe find some of that gold or silver you hear stories about. My funds are mighty low, and I don't think the general store is gonna take kindly to me racking up too much more credit." Colt wiped his brow as he said the last part.

"Really? You've been mining? Can I see where you're digging?" Alex's voice carried some excitement.

"Sure. But it ain't much, really, more like chipping than digging."

They climbed up to where Colt had been chipping at the mountain's surface. "Like I said, there's not much to it," he said.

Alex stared at the crevice Colt had made. It wasn't very deep, and it sure didn't look like there were riches to be had. He bent down and picked up a piece of loose rock. He studied it, turning it over and over in his hand. "You might be right, Colt. There may not be any gold or silver in your mountain, but I don't think you need it."

"What do you mean?"

Alex turned the stone over in his hand again. He looked up and down the mountain as he spoke.

"There might not be obvious riches here, but I think you've got enough to keep you living. You see this piece of rock you chipped off? If I'm not mistaken, this rock is obsidian."

"Obsi-what?"

"Obsidian. It's not worth what gold and silver are, but there's a real healthy market for it right now. It's got some qualities that make it useful in the making of tools or jewelry. Even some surgical tools can be made with it. It's a handy little stone and quite popular right now, as I said." He looked around as he continued speaking, "And by the looks of it, you've got quite a large amount of it here. You could collect and trade it and make enough money to keep yourself afloat until you got your ranch going."

Colt picked up a piece himself and stared at it. "Who knew?" he said with a grin. He stopped and stared at Alex for a minute. "You're quite a useful guy, aren't you? You know a lot of stuff about a lot of stuff. You find a job in town yet?"

"Not currently. They don't need any more Faro dealers right now."

"How do you feel about working out here? With me?"

"You're offering me a job? I thought you just said your funds were low, and it doesn't look like there's too much ranching going on right now."

"That's where you come in. I can use a smart guy like you to help run the business side. I can run cows, but someone with your brains can help really make a go of it for me and Sadie. If you can trade this obsidi-stuff like you say you can, then I reckon there's enough rock here to meet my needs and pay you until the ranch takes off. What do you say?"

"It sure does sound good, Colt. I believe I can do that for you. Thank you." He grinned. "For you and Sadie, you say?"

Colt felt his face turn red, and he smiled a wry smile. "Shut up, Alex."

"Yes, sir, Mr. Warner, sir." Alex gave a little salute as he said it, and then they both started laughing.

The two worked hard at chipping away as much rock from the mountainside as they could, then hauled it down and loaded it into the wagon. Alex had to head back into town to grab his things, so he hitched his horse to the wagon and said he would try and trade the obsidian while he was there. Colt warned him about riding in the dark, but Alex wanted to be able to trade the rock as soon as business opened.

Colt watched him drive away, then headed back into the house. His mind was going over the day. Who would have guessed that the rock under his feet might be worth something? He wondered how many men had lost everything searching for hidden riches when all along, they were standing on what they needed to keep going.

He couldn't believe his good fortune in having met

someone like Alex. He thought about what Drake said about a man needing two or three good friends to get by in the world. He counted Lanky as one of his friends and was starting to feel that Alex could be one, as well.

He was feeling pretty lucky, but then his thoughts went to Brick. Until a few weeks ago, he'd had Brick as one of those friends, but then Brick had started pulling away, and after what Colt had found out, he wasn't sure Brick could be counted as a friend anymore, though he'd always be his brother.

He hoped Jim was right and Brick would come back, but he wasn't sure. He wasn't sure if he had done the right thing by not telling Jim what Brick had been doing. Jim might be able to do something to make Brick stop. On the other hand, knowing that Colt had told on him might make Brick go even further to the other side, and then there would be no chance of the two of them ever being side by side again.

What would Pa want him to do? He would want his boys to stick together, but he was a strict follower of law and order. Pa had fought in the war because he'd felt the other side wasn't right in what they did. He would want Brick to learn a lesson, but Colt didn't think that lesson included prison at thirteen. Colt spent a restless night tossing the possibilities around in his head.

A beam of sunshine crept through the window and found Colt's eyes, causing him to squeeze them more tightly closed as he slowly came out of unconsciousness. He rolled over and then sat up in his bed, feeling like he had just fallen asleep. His body felt heavy as he hauled himself to his feet. He slowly made himself some coffee and breakfast and dropped into his chair to eat it. He was still thinking about Brick and was so lost in his thoughts that he didn't hear the wagon approach the house until the driver yelled from the yard, "Hello? Hello? Are you home?"

In a panic, Colt was up and at the window with a gun in his hand in an instant. He peered out cautiously and saw that the driver of the wagon was Sterling Walcott. "I'm home," Colt called. "Just give me a minute." He hastily put on a shirt and then opened the door, gun still in hand. "What can I do for you, Mr. Walcott?"

The older man looked him over as he stood there in his underwear and a shirt. He smirked slightly. "Mr. Warner, I understand this is your land?"

"Yes, sir."

"And I also understand that my foolish daughter took it upon herself to loan you some money in order for you to acquire this land?"

"No, sir."

"She didn't loan you money?"

"No, sir. She bought half this place for herself. We're partners."

Sterling Walcott laughed out loud. "Boy, didn't I tell you to stay away from my daughter? How is taking her money . . . correction, *my* money . . . staying away from her?"

"She's an equal partner, sir, and with all due respect, she's a woman with a mind of her own. She wants to see me, and I want to see her. I don't think you're going to stop us."

Walcott's face darkened, and his expression became hard with anger. "You listen to me, boy. You *will* stay away from her, and you will pay me back every last dime of that money, or so help me God, son, I will . . ."

Colt raised his gun and cocked the hammer with a single motion. "You will what, sir?"

Walcott's eyes widened, and he froze.

Colt spoke again. "Now, I don't want no trouble with you, Mr. Walcott, but I do love your daughter, and I *will* see her again. If you want your money back, that's fine. You just go on home and convince Sadie that she ain't my partner in this anymore, and I will get it back to you. But if you can't convince her, and I don't reckon you can, then you won't see anything from me, cuz the way I see it, it's her money, and she did what she wants with it. If I owe anybody, it's her."

"Why, you smart-mouthed little . . ."

At that point, another rider came into the yard at a furious pace. It was Jim. "Are we having a problem here, Colt?"

"No problem at all. I was just explaining to Mr. Walcott the nature of the business agreement between Sadie and myself." Colt's voice was flat, and his eyes never left Walcott.

"Borden, you would be well-advised to tell this little gutter snipe exactly who he is talking to." Walcott spit the words through clenched teeth, never taking his eyes off Colt.

Jim chuckled a little. "Mr. Walcott, I don't think it's Colt that isn't aware who he is speaking to. If you're done saying your piece, I would suggest you turn that wagon around real slow and head yourself back into town before things get any more serious out here."

Walcott turned the wagon and slowly headed back towards town, turning in his seat only once to look back at the two men in the yard. Once he was out of sight, Colt lowered his gun.

"You doing all right, Colt?" asked Jim.

Colt blinked a little and then shook his head. "I'm fine, Jim. Nothing I can't handle."

"I can see that. Maybe next time you'll be prepared to handle it with your britches on."

Colt looked down and laughed. "Coffee's on, Jim. Come on in and sit for a minute." Colt went inside, and after tethering his horse, Jim followed, throwing two saddlebags full of supplies on the table.

"What's new in town?" Colt asked.

"Not much, Colt. Little bit of lawlessness. The usual. Walcott been bothering you a lot?"

"First time I've seen him. Sadie must have just told him about the money. How's Brick?"

"He's a little angry, Colt. He wants to know why he hasn't seen this place yet, why you just up and left. If you head in and talk to him, he'll settle down. Anything else exciting happen while I was gone?"

Colt explained about hiring Alex and the plan to trade the rock from the mountainside.

"Well, I'll be. Who would think that some rock would be worth anything to anybody? And Alex thinks he can trade it?"

"Took a wagonload with him when he went back to town. He should be back in a day or two, and I guess we'll see."

"He sounds like a good man to have around."

"Can't really shoot worth a plugged nickel and has about as much cowboy in him as somebody's grandma, but he's smart and knows some business stuff better than I do. I trust him." Colt started putting away the supplies Jim had brought.

"That's good, Colt. Trustworthy men are hard to find out here."

"I found you. And Drake. And Lanky, and now, Alex. I don't think they're that hard to find if you're really looking."

"You've done well for yourself, that's for sure. What's your next big plan?"

"I guess next is to get some more fencing up and get this land staked out so people know I'm here. Then hope that Alex comes through, and maybe we can get some cattle out here. And then build a better ranch house."

"What's wrong with this house?"

"Nothing, for you and me or me and Brick, but if Sadie's moving out here, she deserves a nicer house. One made from wood and glass, not a rock hut in a field." Colt was ashamed just thinking about it.

"Moving out here? Didn't Walcott just warn you to stay away from her?"

"Jim, I wasn't kidding when I said she was a partner. Half of this is hers until she tells me it ain't. She's gonna be my wife one day, and Sterling Walcott can just learn to live with that."

"Ok, Colt. I just hope you know what you're getting into. Sterling has enough money and influence that he can make some real trouble for you if he chooses. He's not a man you want to make an enemy out of."

"I didn't want to make him my enemy, Jim. He's done that on his own."

"All right, Colt. Well, you got some big plans, so we best be getting started. Let's get that fencing going today, and then I think tomorrow I'll keep working on it while you head into town and talk with Brick. I don't know what happened between you two, but it don't do no one any good hiding out here away from him. You guys need to talk."

"I'm not hiding, Jim. He's got a room right there—we built the place for him and me. Hell, I couldn't have even gotten the land if it wasn't for him being my family. I just wanted it done before he came out, that's all."

"That's not how he sees it, Colt. That's why you need to talk."

"Yes, sir."

The rest of the day was spent cutting trees and hauling the logs into place for the fence. It was a hot day and hard work, but Colt liked it. The hard work loosened up his sore muscles and made his body feel better, plus it gave him an opportunity to focus on something other than the problems happening in his life. He hated feeling sorry for himself, especially since everyone kept pointing out just how charmed his life had been to this point.

After supper that evening, Colt took Jim up the mountain and showed him the cave he had stocked with supplies. "This is a good job, Colt," Jim said. "A place like this might come in handy one day."

"Yeah, I figured you never know who might come calling unwanted, and the situation might arise where it's best if I just adios away from the house and get a better perspective. Live to fight another day."

"It's thinking like that that has gotten you where you are so far, Colt. Always a step or two ahead, looking into the future; that's why you've had success so far. It's not luck, and don't ever think it is. Most men don't have half the forethought you do."

Colt hit the bed that night with a different feeling than he had had for a while. His body was tired and felt worn out, but he felt pride—pride in what he had accomplished so far. If Jim and Alex were willing to heap praise on him, why shouldn't he allow himself to feel some of it? He needed to stop thinking like a scared boy trying to prove his worth to everybody and start thinking like a man that had earned everything he had.

He was smiling to himself as he drifted into sleep.

CHAPTER 14

The next morning, Colt was up early. He left Jim sleeping as he saddled Thunder and headed into town. His first thought was to speak to Brick and try and clear the air some more. Colt didn't like what he was doing but was willing to try to overlook it, to let Brick learn his own lessons, instead of trying to be his pa and not his brother.

When he arrived in town and rode up to the house, Drake was sitting on the porch with his coffee cup in his hand. "Well, hey there, Colt. Long time no see. How's that place of yours looking out there?"

"Evening, Drake. It's looking all right. It's coming along. Jim's been a big help."

"Glad to hear it. It's good for a man to strike out on his own, find what he wants, and chase after it."

"Is Brick here?"

"Sleeping. Put Thunder in the back and come on in for some supper. He'll be moving once he smells the bacon. He always does."

Colt came inside and sat at the table. Drake poured him a

cup of coffee and then went back to frying bacon. "Missed you around here, Colt. Little bit of excitement in town."

"Really? Jim said it was pretty normal."

Drake chuckled. "You know Jim. His life could be on the line, and he could have only one bullet left, and it would barely raise his heartbeat. Two more stages were robbed. Gang got away clean both times."

Colt felt a pang in his chest as Darke said the words. At that moment, Brick came down the hall into the kitchen. "Smells good again, Drake. You sure can cook bacon." Brick's eyes narrowed as he saw Colt at the table. "What are you doing here? I thought you had your own place now and were too good to come back here."

"It's our place, Brick. You've got a room in the house. I was just trying to get it ready before you came out. I wasn't leaving you behind."

"Didn't feel that way." Brick grabbed two more pieces of bacon and headed out the door. "Thanks again, Drake."

Colt went after Brick and caught up to him on the back porch. "Brick, come on. I don't know what I did, but whatever it was, I'm sorry. We've got a spot now, our own place. We can start a ranch and make some money. Alex is gonna help us. We can be businessmen, Brick. Just like Pa wanted."

"I don't need your help no more, Colt. Troy and the boys are my family now. I'll make my own way; I don't need no handouts from you. That time has passed. I ain't no baby anymore."

"Brick, you're thirteen."

"That's a man by West standards. You were working and saving by thirteen, Colt, why can't I?"

"You can! Just come work with me on our land, making

our own way. You can't keep robbing stages. You're gonna get caught."

"We ain't getting caught. We're good, Colt. I know you don't think we can cuz we're young, but I'm thirteen, Troy is fourteen. Think back to you at thirteen and the things you were doing. Age don't mean nothing. Anything you can do, I can do. You earned your money your way; I'm getting mine my way."

"Your way gets you in prison or in the ground. Come to the ranch and work with me. We're family. We can build a real thing here, Brick. We can make a good life."

Brick readied Lightning and climbed in the saddle. "Your way gets you tired and broke, Colt, just like Pa. I'm gonna have a good life, and I'm not gonna have to bust my hump like you will to do it. Pa's dead, Colt. You can stop trying to impress him. You ain't impressing me." With that, Brick rode away.

Colt was left standing in the yard, staring after his brother. He shook his head and made his way back into the house. After a little more small talk with Drake, Colt said goodbye, mounted Thunder, and rode down to the main street. With no real destination in mind, he tethered the horse, dismounted, and started down the sidewalk, running the conversation with Brick over and over in his head. With every step, he felt angrier. How could Brick say those things? Did he really believe all of it?

In his own head again, Colt wasn't paying attention to where he was going. He bumped into a man coming out of the casino, knocking him to the ground. The man got back to his feet in a hurry and muscled up to Colt, yelling, "Watch where you're going, you little pissant! You . . ." The man stopped when he saw the guns on Colt's hips. He'd clearly thought he'd bumped into a shopkeeper or the like, not someone who was armed.

Colt stared at the man. "I'm sorry. My fault."

In response to the apology, the man steeled himself. "You should be sorry. You're lucky I don't squish you right here."

Colt wasn't in the mood. "Go ahead. Squish me."

The man's eyes widened for a second, and then he balled his fist and swung at Colt's head. Colt sidestepped the punch, and the man fell forward with momentum. As he fell, Colt swung a left that landed behind the man's right ear, accelerating his plunge to the ground. The man crashed to the sidewalk and lay there motionless.

Colt was feeling real anger now. Everything swelled inside him as he looked at the helpless man on the sidewalk, and he kicked him twice in the midsection. "When you gonna squish me? Get up." Colt kicked him again. "Is this what you meant? Is this what you wanted?" Colt was seeing red as all his feelings boiled to the surface. He was punching the man wildly now, landing blow after blow. He heard the man grunt and moan with every punch, but he wasn't moving. Colt kept swinging. His arms were getting tired.

"Colt! Colt, you have to stop!" Alex Lashburn had joined the crowd and was now trying to pull Colt off the fallen man. Colt struggled as Alex pulled him back.

Sheriff Van Atten pushed through the crowd. "What's happening here?" he demanded.

"Simple disagreement, Sheriff," Alex offered.

"Doesn't look so simple. Mind telling me what's going on here, Colt?"

Colt just stared at Van Atten, staying silent.

"That's right, Sheriff. Just a disagreement." An old-timer on the porch added to the conversation. "The big guy there wasn't happy with the young'un for being in his way. The young'un apologized, but the big guy wanted to teach him a lesson. Turns out the young'un can fight." The old-timer whistled. "Can he ever. Don't think the big guy expected it."

The sheriff looked over the scene once more. He pointed to a couple of bystanders. "You men get this guy over to the doc's. Colt, you best get out of here before I change my mind and take you in."

"We're leaving right now, Sheriff," Alex said. He pulled Colt off the sidewalk into the street. After a few steps, he looked at Colt and asked, "What was that?"

Colt had calmed down. "I don't know, Alex. I just saw red and couldn't stop swinging. This feeling just built up in me, and it all came out when that guy tried to push me around."

"You could have killed him, Colt."

"I know. Thanks for pulling me off him."

"Don't mention it."

"What were you doing there?"

"I had just finished having supper and was on my way down to the trade market. I ran into the broker at dinner, and he told me he has our money from the obsidian."

Colt was hardly listening. "I was just so mad, I wanted to keep punching. It felt so good to get it out."

"Stop thinking about it. Think about something else."

"Like what?"

"Like your new money." Alex smiled and gave Colt a little smack on the chest. "Let's go get it."

Colt smiled back. "Okay."

Colt returned to Thunder and grabbed his saddlebags, then the pair entered the trade market and headed towards the broker. The man looked up from his desk and smiled. "Ah, Mr. Lashburn. Good to see you. Glad you could make it—I opened this evening just for you. Don't like having this much money here just lying around. How are you feeling after a meal like that?"

"I'm doing well. This is my employer, Colt Warner."

"Good evening, Mr. Warner." The spun his chair and bent down to a large safe behind his desk, spinning the dial left, then right, then left again. "You know, when your man here showed up with a wagon full of rock saying he wanted a trade, well, I just about laughed out loud at him. I hadn't ever heard such a thing." The safe's lock clicked, and he swung open the door.

"I felt the same way when he first told it to me." Colt agreed.

"But one wire was all it took. I sent one message to see what could be done, and I had a taker right away. Took the whole wagon. I couldn't believe it." He put two large boxes on his desk. "There you go, sir. Five hundred dollars, can you imagine?"

Colt smiled a little as he opened one of the boxes. He pulled out thirty dollars from the bills stacked inside and handed it to Alex. "Here you go; job well done."

"That's too much, Colt," Alex objected.

"Take it for now; we'll work out a salary later. Consider it wages and a finder's fee for getting this started. If it wasn't for you, I never would have known this was even a possibility."

Colt shoved the rest of his money into the saddlebags, and the two exited the building, discussing what the next step should be. They parted for the evening, and Colt rode back to Drake's to sleep.

The next morning, he met up again with Alex, and they had breakfast at the eatery. After breakfast, they headed to the general store, where Colt paid his credit note in full. He thanked the shopkeeper for his generosity, and the two headed back out into the morning light. "What's next, Boss?" Alex asked.

"Why don't you go grab your stuff? You can stay at the ranch tonight; a room has opened up. Then meet me at the stockyard. And don't call me boss, Alex. It feels weird. Colt will do."

"Whatever you say, Boss." Alex laughed as he said it and walked away.

Colt shook his head a little and turned Thunder toward the stockyard. He hadn't gone far when he heard his name yelled from the sidewalk. He looked over and saw Lanky waving at him. Colt smiled. "Hey, Lanky! How you doing this morning?"

"Hey, Colt. Long time no see. I hear you and Sadie are partners in some land now." He chuckled. "How did you swing that?"

"I didn't have enough to do it on my own. She wanted to help and wanted something she could call her own, not her pa's."

"Leave it to 'Lucky' Colt Warner to end up with the prettiest partner in these parts. You sure were born under a lucky star."

"It's not luck, Lanky. I'm gonna marry that girl one day."

"Does her pa know that?" Lanky chuckled again.

"He does. And he ain't so happy about it." Both boys laughed now.

"Where you headin'?" Lanky asked.

"Down to the stockyards. Gonna see if I can purchase a few head of cattle. I've got a ranch, but it ain't much good with nothing to keep on it."

"Want some company?"

"Sure. You know anything about cattle?"

"Not enough. Didn't you learn nothing when you were ranch handing for Shep?"

"Some. It's my first cattle buy, though, and I don't want to get suckered into buying some old bag of bones."

At the stockyards, things were busy. There were men pushing cattle in and out of corrals, ranch owners overseeing all the movement, and cow hands lounging and checking out the animals. The boys stared wide-eyed at all the bustling and hustling, then found a spot up against a rail and eyed the stock. They were discussing what they were seeing when Colt heard a voice from behind them.

"Hey, Colt. Whatcha up to?"

Colt turned around. It was Ridge Holloway. "Hey, Ridge. Just looking to buy some cattle. You here shopping for Shep?"

"Just here hanging around. Not working for Shep right now. He's lost some of his stock and don't need all the help anymore."

"Lost his stock? What do you mean?"

"There's been some rustling going on. He's lost quite a few head. He's had some die on him too. It hasn't been a good month or so. Anyway, that leaves me looking for work."

Colt was putting a plan together in his mind. "How'd you like to work for me?"

"Work for you? Doing what?"

"Well, you can start by helping us pick out a few good head here, and then I was thinking ranch foreman."

"Ranch foreman? Well, I'm much obliged for the job offer, Colt, but who exactly am I looking after? My understanding is you currently only have land, no stock or cowhands to speak of."

Colt looked at Lanky with a smile on his face. "You got your first cowhand right here."

Lanky was confused. "Me?"

"If you want it."

"Colt, I ain't never worked a ranch before."

"Ridge can teach you what you need to know. I ain't got enough yet to need an experienced staff, Lanky, but I sure do need some trusted friends helping me out."

"Well, then, I guess I'm in."

The three men shook hands, and Colt continued. "You guys are gonna need some tents to start with; Jim and I ain't built the bunkhouse yet." He reached into the saddlebags and handed each man some money. "This here is your starting wages. Now, let's get some cattle."

"What are we looking for, Colt?" asked Ridge.

"I've only got about two hundred dollars right now."

"Well, you're going to need at least half that for a good bull. You can probably get three cows and a couple of calves for the rest if we get lucky."

"Well, it ain't much, but it's a start. Let's see what we can find."

Things fell their way, and in the end, they had the six head of cattle they wanted. Alex rode up with the wagon and joined the group as they were looking over their stock.

"Alex, this is Ridge Holloway," Colt told him. "He's our ranch foreman. And this here is Lanky. He's gonna be our first ranch hand. Fellas, this is Alex Lashburn."

"And what does Alex do?" asked Ridge.

"Alex is a useful man. That's his position. He knows a lot about a lot."

"You've been busy, Colt. Got some cows *and* a staff," Alex said.

"Cattle." Ridge corrected him. "There's cows and a bull here. Together they are cattle."

"Right," said Alex. "Cattle."

"What's next, Boss?" asked Lanky with a smile on his face.

"You three take the cattle to the Whistlestop. I need to pay a visit to Sadie."

"Take the cattle to the where exactly?" asked Alex.

"I think that's what I'm calling the place. Whistlestop Ranch. I've been mulling it over, and it seems appropriate. The train played a big part in bringing me out here; seems fitting to make sure I remember that."

"I like it," said Lanky. "Sounds real professional and homey at the same time. 'Who you working for? Well, I work for Colt Warner over at the Whistlestop Ranch.' Sounds good."

"I like it, too," said Alex.

"Well, lead the way, Mr. Useful," Ridge said with a chuckle. "Let's get these cattle moving."

"Jim should be there when you get to the ranch, Alex. Fill him in on everything, if you can, please."

"Will do."

The three moved off, with Alex leading the cattle with the wagon and Ridge and Lanky riding in the rear. Colt rode off toward the house of Sterling Walcott. What should he say when he got there? he wondered. How should he handle Walcott after the altercation at the ranch?

He rode Thunder up to the gate at a casual pace and was greeted by Sadie, who was in the front yard. "Hey, Colt. How are you doing?"

"I'm doing real well, Sadie. I wanted to come see you."

"I wanted to see you, too, but you better get out of here. Daddy's real mad about the last time you guys talked. He isn't going to want to see you around here."

As she spoke, the front door of the house opened, and Sterling Walcott appeared on the porch, rifle in hand. "You get the hell away from here, or I'll shoot you where you stand, you little pissant!"

Colt gave him a cold stare. "I came to talk to your daughter, sir. Wanted to let her know about the progress of her ranch." He looked at Sadie now. "We have a house to live in, the fencing is up, we have corrals, and as of a half-hour ago, we have some cattle and a staff to work them. It's a real ranch now, Sadie."

Sadie smiled.

"What do you mean, you have cattle?" Walcott bellowed from the porch. "How can you afford cattle?"

"Only six head right now, but it's a start."

"Six head?" Walcott laughed. "That's not a ranch. That's a petting farm."

"With all due respect, sir, even you had to start somewhere. I'm sure there was a time that you had only six head, and look where you are now." He looked to Sadie once more. "I've named it Whistlestop Ranch, Sadie. I hope you like it."

"It sounds lovely, Colt."

Colt turned his attention back to Sterling Walcott. "I'm a rancher, sir. I plan to be successful at it. I also plan to marry your daughter. I don't want to be your enemy; I've never been dishonest with you. I hope that's something you can respect. Good afternoon, Miss Sadie." Colt tipped his hat and then turned and rode off, heading for the ranch.

Walcott was left steaming on his front porch. Colt never looked back, so he never saw the hatred stirring in Sterling Walcott's eyes.

CHAPTER 15

Months passed, another birthday came, and Colt, now sixteen, stood at his front door and looked out over the Whistlestop. They had worked hard and now had something to show for it. Alex was living in the stone house he and Jim had first built, Lanky and Ridge were in the newly built bunkhouse with two new ranch hands, and he and Jim were living in the ranch house they had just constructed. It was a fine building, one that Colt was proud of and felt was fitting for someone like Sadie.

Thanks to Alex and his obsidian trading, there was enough money to build everything, pay the wages, and increase the size of his herd, which now numbered seventy-five head. He had continued to spend time with Sadie Walcott, and their relationship was stronger than ever.

Things were just about perfect. The only thing missing was Brick. Brick was still angry with Colt and had turned his back on him. The brothers hadn't seen one another since that last blow-up they had had in town. Brick was still robbing stages with Pretty Boy and their gang, only now they were hitting stages with larger bounties, even one carrying a military payroll. In one final insult to Colt, the gang was now calling themselves "The Brotherhood." There was a reward being offered for any information on The Brotherhood, proclaimed on posters all over town.

Colt drank his coffee as he surveyed the ranch. A voice came from inside the house. "Morning, Colt. Whatcha doin'?" Jim asked.

"Nothing. Just staring. This is some beautiful land, and every now and then, it catches me off guard, and I just need to look at it for a while."

Jim joined him on the porch. "You've done well, Colt. You should be proud."

"I am. Couldn't have done it without you. Thank you again."

"No need for thanks. I'm glad things are working out for you."

"Have you heard anything about Brick? Do we know where he is?" Colt asked.

"Last I heard, he and that Troy Benton were living somewhere. He hasn't been back to Drake's place in a while. He'll come around, Colt. Give him time."

"You said that months ago, and it hasn't happened yet; it's just gotten worse."

"He's young and stubborn. It'll happen."

Alex emerged from his house and rearranged the gun he now wore on his hips. He gave a wave to Colt. Colt had been teaching Alex how to shoot, and he was getting better. Alex had never wanted to use a weapon, but Colt had softened him up on the subject, reminding him that the first time they had met was in a shootout and explaining that for protection from predators of any kind, a man should know how to use a gun.

The bunkhouse door opened, and the ranch hands made their way out to the yard as well. Charlie and Lane Trotter, the two newest hands, were brothers, drifters looking for a stable place to hang their hats. Ridge had hired them, and they were hard workers who enjoyed the ranch life. They reminded Colt of himself and Brick, even though both were older than he was, and their relationship with one another made Colt wish he could get that back with Brick.

"Hello, Boss. Beautiful morning, isn't it?" Lane asked as he strode across the yard.

Charlie was the older of the two, but Lane was the talker. While Charlie was a steady, hard worker who preferred to focus on getting a job done, Lane would work hard but work his vocal muscles at the same time. It never took away from the quality of his work; it just made your ears feel tired by the end of the day.

"Morning, Lane. It sure is," Colt replied.

The rest of the men joined Colt and Lane. "What's the plan for today, Ridge?" Colt asked.

"We need more land, Colt. Seventy-five head is too big for sixty-five acres. It's all right at the moment, nobody owns the land adjacent, so we can graze 'em there, but I'd sure feel better if we owned it and nobody could take it from us."

"How much you figure we need?"

"If you want to keep expanding at the rate you are, you need at least two hundred acres more. That's a big buy, Colt. You'd be almost as big as Shep's ranch and roughly two-thirds the size of Sterling Walcott's if you did that."

"What can we manage, Alex?"

Alex cleared his throat. "Currently, we have enough for seventy-five more acres. If you let your credit run a little longer at the store, we can get eighty. We can trade some more obsidian, but our stockpile of loose stuff is gone. We're going to have to break some more off the mountain, and that's going to take time. We'll need two more wagonloads to get all two hundred acres and still have funds for other ranch needs."

"Will eighty do for now, Ridge?"

"It's a good start, but you're likely to have another problem if you buy your land piecemeal like this."

"What problem is that?"

"Sterling Walcott. He don't want you expanding none, and he definitely don't want you being as big as him. If you only buy a bit at a time, he's gonna catch word and might be inclined to purchase before you, so you can't take any more."

Colt nodded slowly. "All right, then. Charlie and Lane, you guys head up and start chipping obsidian off that mountain. Alex, you head in and secure the eighty for now. Do it as quietly and discreetly as possible. Ridge and Lanky, you two look after the herd. Graze 'em on the adjacent land for now. Alex is gonna secure that for us as soon as possible. I'm gonna go see Sadie, let her know what's happening, and try and avoid Sterling as much as possible. Jim, wanna keep me company, or you wanna hold down the fort here?"

"I reckon I could use a little trip, and it sure is a lovely morning for a ride. I'll come with you."

The men each finished their coffee and started their tasks for the day while Alex, Colt, and Jim got ready for their ride into town. Just as they were leaving the yard, two riders appeared on the ridge up ahead. From their silhouettes, it was apparent they were Modoc. The three men stopped their horses and stared up at the riders. Alex pulled his gun from his holster.

"Calm down, Alex," said Jim. "They aren't fussin' about

up there. I think they're just passing through. Re-holster that, and we'll just wait a few minutes."

Alex put his gun away. The men sat and watched as the riders on the ridge slowly walked their horses, continuing along their path. Once they had cleared the area and were no longer visible on the ridge, the three men continued their ride.

"That's the second group in as many days, Colt. Things are getting a little more interesting around here." Jim said.

"If they don't bother us, I got no problem with them passing through. I'm just trying to raise cattle, not become an Indian fighter."

Alex was a little more nervous. "What if they decide they don't want to just pass through? I've been in one shootout with them already. I'm not fancying another, even if I am better with a gun now."

"If they want a fight, they'll get one. I've worked hard for this land, and I'm not giving it up easily. Not to a band of Indians and not to Sterling Walcott."

Once the three reached the town, Alex split from the group and went to visit the land office while Colt went looking for Sadie. Jim decided to head to the casino and see if he could find Drake, maybe get in some cards and conversation.

As he started out, Colt mulled over an idea. Once he had made up his mind, he turned Thunder around and made a stop downtown before going to find Sadie.

Colt found Sadie's horse hitched out back of the church, and stopped and knocked on the rear door. A lady answered, and Colt removed his hat as he took a step inside, where Sadie and several other women sat around a table in a small room. "I'm sorry to interrupt, ma'am," he said humbly. "May I speak with Sadie Walcott for one minute?"

"Something important, Mister Warner?"

"Yes, ma'am, it is. It has to do with her ranch, ma'am."

"Very well. Sadie, please meet with your guest outside. Our Bible study will continue in your absence. I do hope everything is all right with your family."

"Thank you, ma'am," Sadie said as she rose from her seat and went to meet Colt. Once they got outside, Sadie asked, "Colt, what's going on? Is everything all right with Daddy?"

Colt turned with a smile on his face. "Not that ranch Sadie, *your* ranch. The Whistlestop."

Sadie blushed a little. "Sorry, Colt. I sometimes forget we're partners. I live here, and you're way out there—I forget it's mine, too. What's going on?"

"Just wanted to let you know that we're looking to expand. Ridge says we need more land for the number of cattle we have. Alex is buying some as we speak."

"Do you have the money to buy more?" Sadie asked. "I thought you had put it all back in to expand the herd?"

"We have enough to buy some. Not everything we need, but a start. We're working on some plans to get the rest. I just wanted you to know because we're going to move as fast as possible, but if your father catches wind before we get it done, there may be some more tension between us."

"Okay, Colt. But why?"

"When we're done, we'll be a sizable ranch. Your pa ain't gonna take kindly to another big operation setting up out here. Right now, he leaves us alone, except for him hating me, cuz we ain't so big that he needs to worry, but this land buy will change that."

"Is there anything I can do to help, Colt? Maybe if my money bought the land, then Daddy wouldn't be angry? He's loud and hot-tempered, but if it's me, then maybe . . ." She paused. Colt had gone down to one knee in front of her. "Colt? What are you . . .?"

"Miss Sadie Walcott, I know we're young, and I know people won't like it, but everything I have right now I have because of you, and I would like nothing more than to spend every one of my remaining days enjoying every bit of it with you. Would you consent to be my wife?" He showed her the ring he had just purchased from the jeweler in town.

"Colt, I'm only fifteen! I . . . I . . . I don't know what to say."

"Say yes."

"Daddy would lose his mind! He'd come after you. You think he hates you now? Just wait."

"Do you love me?"

She stared down at him. Of course, she loved him. He was so different from the other boys she knew. He was sixteen and already had his own horse and his own ranch, and he ran a crew of men that worked for him. Other boys were still *playing* at being a cowboy. Colt was living it. She admired him for his passion and his willingness to work for what he wanted. "Of course, I love you."

"Well, then, that's all that matters. Say yes, and we will make a life together. You said it was hard to picture owning it because you didn't live there. Say yes, and you can live at the Whistlestop. You can see what it is you own every day."

Sadie had tears in her eyes. "Oh, Colt. Yes! Yes, I will marry you."

Colt stood up, and they embraced. "I promise you, Sadie, I will love you and protect you with everything I have."

"I know you will, Colt." She put her head on his chest while they hugged. It felt safe. "I guess I should go and tell Daddy. Come with me, please?"

"Of course." Colt helped her up on her horse, and they rode out towards the Walcott ranch.

Colt's heart held excitement as they rode. "I can't wait for you to see the Whistlestop, Sadie. There's a ranch house for us, a bunkhouse for the guys, and Alex has his own place. It's a real ranch. You'll love Charlie and Lane; they're stand-up guys. Ridge is our foreman, he knows a lot about cattle, and he's a good guy to know in a scuffle too. You already know Lanky."

"Elijah's out there? I hadn't realized that. That's nice. I miss seeing him around."

The two continued to chat about the ranch and the future as they rode along. The sun was setting as they approached the ranch, where they were met at the gate by Sterling Walcott. Behind him, three men were busy in the corral nearest the house, mending fence, it looked like. Their saddled horses were tethered nearby.

"Young lady, why aren't you at your Bible study?" Wolcott demanded.

"Sir, if you don't mind, I'd like to speak to you . . ." Colt began.

"I wasn't talking to you, Warner. You sit there and keep your mouth shut."

"Daddy, stop. I'm going to marry him," Sadie said as she dismounted.

"The hell you are." Walcott's face was red with anger.

"That's why I'm not at study, Daddy. Colt just asked me, and I said yes."

Walcott raised his hand as though to strike his daughter but thought better of it when he heard the sound of Colt's hammer cocking.

"I hope you don't do that, sir. I'd have to shoot you, and the wedding wouldn't be nearly as festive if I had to explain how I shot my soon-to-be father-in-law dead cuz of his bad temper." Colt had his gun aimed at the middle of Walcott's chest.

"Get in the house, Sadie," Walcott said through clenched teeth. "And you get the hell out of here, Warner."

Sadie ran into the house. Colt holstered his gun and met Walcott's gaze squarely. "I have been honest with you from the start, sir. I told you my intentions toward your daughter. I never lied to you. I was hoping we could maybe behave like men, but you always wanna try and lord over me. You see me as a child instead of seeing me for what I've done."

"You are a child. A child who thinks he's a man because he can fire a gun."

"No, sir, I'm not. I don't want to use these, but they are an unfortunate necessity in the times we live in. I was told while I was being taught that I should always look for a way to avoid shooting and only let the bullets fly if there's no other way. I can provide for your daughter, sir. I want to. I've got a ranch, and it's doing well. I love her and want to share that with her."

"Like hell. My daughter can do better than some uneducated cowhand that got lucky and found some money somewhere. I'm still not sure how you and that odd little man managed to turn rock into cash, but my daughter can do better. Now, you've got ten seconds to get out of here, or I'll rip you off that horse and give you a beating, gun or no gun."

Colt nodded coldly. He turned Thunder. As he rode away, he heard a whistle behind him. He looked over his shoulder to see Sadie running out of the back of the house, out of sight of her father, with a suitcase in hand. She waved at him, and he galloped Thunder in her direction.

"What are you doing, Sadie?" he said as he reached her.

"I'm leaving with my future husband. I don't care what my father says. Now help me up."

He helped her up onto Thunder just as Walcott rounded the house at a run. "Get back here, Sadie. Now!" he roared.

"Let's get going unless you want him to catch me," Sadie said with a giggle.

"Yes, ma'am." Colt hit the spurs, and Thunder took off, leaving Walcott yelling in the dust. Colt heard another whistle and looked back to see Walcott and the men who had been working in the corral saddling up and coming after them.

He pushed Thunder harder, and they covered ground toward town rapidly with the mob in pursuit. By the time they reached the town, it was almost full night. Drake's place came into sight, and Colt saw Jim and Alex out front, talking with Drake. "We gotta go!" Colt yelled as they galloped up. He reined Thunder to a halt and pointed behind him.

Alex and Jim looked at one another, looked at the group of men galloping in hot pursuit, led by Walcott, and hurriedly mounted. Colt spurred Thunder again, and all three galloped away, Walcott and his men now much closer.

Thunder's hide glistened from sweat under the light of the full moon as Colt kept pushing him to gallop faster. Gunshots rang out behind them, but the pursuers were too far away for that to pose much threat. They kept the pace for a good long while until Alex's horse looked like it couldn't keep up anymore. Finally, Colt slowed Thunder to a trot as they topped a ridge and rode down the other side. Jim stayed at the top of the ridge to keep an eye out for their pursuers. After a few minutes, he rode back to the group.

"Looks like they gave up. Probably ran their horses ragged tryin' to catch us and didn't want to go any farther in the dark.

Good evening, Sadie. Colt, wanna tell me why we were riding like our tails were on fire?"

"I'm afraid it's my fault, Jim," Sadie said. "Daddy wasn't happy that I left with Colt."

"We're getting married, Jim," Colt said. "I just asked her, and she said yes. Sterling didn't take too kindly to that."

"But they . . . they were going to kill us. Because you want to marry her? That's crazy." Alex was trying to catch his breath.

"Congratulations, you two, but the next time you want to try and run the legs off the horses, can we have a little warning? We don't all ride animals like Thunder." Jim smiled. "Poor Pete here is gonna need a week in the pasture after this."

Colt chuckled. "Sorry, it just sort of happened. It wasn't my intention to leave town so quickly, but it seemed to be the prudent thing to do."

The rest of the travel back to the ranch was uneventful. As they came over the ridge and stared down at the Whistlestop, Sadie gasped at what she could see in the moonlight. "Oh, Colt, it looks beautiful. You've done so much work. It's a real ranch."

"It's been a group effort, Sadie, but it is a beautiful place. All that's been missing is the person it was built for, and now you're here."

Sadie could feel her cheeks blushing.

They corralled the horses, and Colt showed Sadie the house and where she could put her things. Re-emerging from the house, Colt joined Jim, Alex, and the ranch hands, who had gathered by the corral.

"How we lookin' on that land there, Boss?" asked Ridge.

In their haste to exit town, Colt had completely forgotten to ask Alex about the land buy. He turned to him now. "How did it go, Alex?"

"We got the eighty that we could afford today, but we'll need to act fast for the rest. I did some chatting at the land office, and between other settlers and a proposed railroad coming through, the remaining hundred and twenty we want could get bought up pretty quickly."

"Charlie, Lane, how'd the obsidian haul go today?"

"One full wagon loaded. We can get the rest by tomorrow or the next day if the weather holds and everything goes to plan."

"Okay. Alex, you'll take the first wagon into town again tomorrow and get our rock traded. Lanky, you can help Charlie and Lane with the mining tomorrow—maybe we can get it all done. Ridge, Jim and I will work the cattle with you tomorrow. Let's get as much done by the end of the day as we can cuz the day after that, we celebrate."

"Celebrate what?" asked Lanky.

"The day after tomorrow, Sadie and I are getting married."

As Colt said it, Sadie emerged from the house. The men all stared in her direction.

Lanky's mouth had fallen open. "Married?" he said weakly.

"That's right." Colt put his arm around Sadie as she joined them. "We'll do it right here at the Whistlestop day after tomorrow. Alex, when you come back from Monroe, can you bring the preacher with you, please?"

"Will do, Colt. Congratulations."

"Fellas, this here is Sadie Walcott. She's half-owner of this place, and day after tomorrow, she'll be my wife. Sadie, this is Ridge Holloway, the foreman. These are Charlie and Lane Trotter, and you've already met Alex and Lanky."

"Hello, gentlemen," Sadie said.

As the group started talking all at once, offering their congratulations, Ridge slid off to the side next to Jim. "Walcott? As in Sterling Walcott?" he asked Jim in a whisper. "Does he hunt trouble on purpose?"

"Colt can take care of himself," Jim answered. "Besides, with her here now, there's no way he'll let the Whistlestop fail. He'll do whatever he needs to keep it going."

Ridge nodded slowly. "I hope he knows what he's doing. I wouldn't bet against him, but it seems like courting trouble that don't need to be courted."

After a day of hard work, the morning of the wedding day began with a glorious sunrise and a light layer of dew on the grass. As the morning progressed, it stretched into a beautiful day. Mid-morning, Alex came over the ridge with the wagon, a mounted man alongside and someone sitting in the seat with him. As Alex got closer, Colt recognized the mounted man as Reverend Sullivan, the town preacher, and the passenger as Drake.

"Morning, Colt," Drake called as Alex pulled into the yard.

"Morning, Drake. What are you doing here?"

"I ran into Alex here in town, and he told me what was happening today. Once I heard, I hitched a ride. You didn't think I'd miss this, did you?"

"Glad you're here, Drake."

Colt introduced himself to Reverend Sullivan, Sadie was familiar with him since she attended church, and a place was chosen for the ceremony.

Colt's mind was racing as the Reverend conducted the ceremony. Here he was, standing in the grass beside a bridge he'd built over a river on land he owned, marrying the girl of his dreams, getting everything he wanted. He wished his mother and father were there to see him. And Brick. He wanted Brick there. He wished he knew where Brick was.

After the ceremony, there was a picnic set out, and the guys all sat around enjoying the meal and talking about their lives.

Alex approached Colt and let him know how things had gone in town. "You got it, Colt. We sold the obsidian and got another eighty acres. That leaves you about forty acres shy of your goal. Once we get the rest of that rock sold, you'll get those, too. You're a bona fide rancher now."

It was a good day, and Colt's heart was bursting with pride. He couldn't wait to see what the future had in store.

It was the start of a good life; he could feel it.

CHAPTER 16

Three years went by, and they were not a good three years for Colt. One of the cattle contracted splenic fever, and it devastated the herd. What had at one point become a fine, sturdy, plentiful herd of two hundred and fifty head dwindled, thanks to the fever and rustlers, to a mere sixty. As well, the market for obsidian dropped, and they could no longer make the money they had made from selling it. Things were starting to get desperate. For the first time in the last seven years, things were not working out for Colt.

He stood on the porch and stared out over the land that was his. He was muttering to himself, trying to figure out how he was going to get things turned around, when he was joined by Sadie. In her arms, she carried their son. When they found out that Sadie was pregnant, Colt wanted to name the boy after his two father figures. James William Warner had been born one year ago.

Colt put his arm around Sadie's shoulder and kissed both of them on their foreheads. "I don't know how yet, but I promise both of you that I will get this turned around. We'll be okay."

"I know you will, Colt. I'm not worried. You're always good to us."

While it hadn't been a good three years for Colt, the opposite was true for Brick. The Brotherhood had continued to intimidate and menace Monroe and the surrounding territory. They had expanded from robbing stages to robbing trains and banks all over. They had been very successful and had grown in ranks as well. They now numbered eight men in all, and all had become wealthy from their exploits.

In spite of all the offenses they had committed, no one had been able to identify the members of The Brotherhood. They remained anonymous figures, gaining popularity with each new crime. They were starting to rival the James Gang in that the general public saw them almost as folk heroes. Colt had kept his promise and had not told anyone that Brick was leading The Brotherhood, even though the two had not spoken since that last fight they had had in town three years ago.

There were rumors that The Brotherhood had a hideout somewhere in the mountains to the south of the Whistlestop, but no one working on the ranch had ever seen any sign of them. Colt continued to try and work his ranch even as disease ravaged the herd and took away everything he had worked for. He would occasionally hear stories of another robbery by the gang but paid little attention to it other than to make sure Brick was still alive and still doing okay.

One Saturday morning, Colt was sitting at a table in the eatery, having breakfast with Jim and Alex, when Sterling Walcott walked in. Colt hadn't spoken to Walcott since the day his men chased them from his ranch. Sadie had had contact with her family and told Colt that her father had softened his opinion of him, but he had not witnessed it himself.

Walcott walked up to the table. "Warner, I hear you're having some trouble out at that ranch of yours."

"Nothing I can't handle, Mr. Walcott."

"Is that so? That splenic fever is nothing to sneeze at, and I hear that whatever ain't sick, you're losing to rustlers."

"You wouldn't happen to know anything about those rustlers now, would you?" Jim asked.

"Just what the hell are you insinuating, Borden? You think I'd steal from my own daughter?"

Jim met his gaze with eyes as hard as steel. "I think you'd take advantage of any opportunity presented to you and step on anyone you needed to."

Walcott's face turned red. "Listen, Borden, I'm here to talk to Warner, not you. Warner, I'm offering you a chance to get out and save your family. Sell me your ranch."

"The Whistlestop is not for sale, Mr. Walcott."

"Be serious, son. You've got nothing. Your cattle are dead or dying. You've got no way to replenish them and no other prospects. Let me help you save my daughter and your son. They don't need to suffer for your pridefulness."

Colt's face was red now. He stood up from the table. "My family will be just fine, and I'm the one that will make sure they are, not you. Now get away from this table before I lose my control and show you just how prepared I am to fight for what I love."

Walcott chuckled and then backed away. "That's fine, Warner; I'm leaving. Don't say I didn't give you a chance. At least let my daughter know that she and the child can come home whenever she's ready."

Walcott walked away, laughing, and Colt sat back down,

fuming. "That bastard is loving every minute of this. I'm proving every doubt he ever had about me to be true."

"Don't let him get to you, Colt," Alex said. "Everybody hits hard times. You didn't make the cattle sick. Look at how much you've done so far. It's incredible."

The three continued their breakfast. A few minutes later, some businessmen entered and sat at a nearby table, loudly talking. "That damn Brotherhood hit the bank in Elk Grove yesterday," one of the men said.

"I heard that, too. Only I heard that this time it was a larger bank, so the leader had to get off his horse and come inside like the rest of 'em."

"Really? He didn't sit outside and keep watch like usual?"

"No, sir. It was too big, and there were too many people. He had to come in to keep everyone under control."

"What's the big deal?" the third man asked. "So he came inside, so what?"

"Well, he ain't never done that before, that's what. And when he did it, they noticed something."

"Yeah, what'd they notice?"

"They noticed that he don't walk right. He's got a bum foot or something."

Colt froze. He felt the blood drain from his face and Jim's eyes upon him.

"How long have you known, Colt?" Jim said softly.

"Known what?" Colt reached for more bacon.

"Don't play games with me, Colt. You're not good at it. It's not your way. How long have you known that Brick was running the Brotherhood?"

"What?" Alex asked in shock. "Your little brother is an outlaw?"

"How long, Colt?" Jim was more forceful now.

Colt's shoulders slumped, and he stared down at his plate. "Not from the beginning, but pretty close to it. That time I chased them from town after they robbed a stage, I saw that one of them was riding Lightning. I asked Brick about it later."

"And you didn't tell me? What were you thinking? He's gonna get himself killed. It's not just stages now, Colt. They're hitting banks and trains. The marshals, the Pinkertons, they're all after them. If they catch them, they're gonna hang."

"I know, Jim. I tried to tell him that, but he wouldn't listen to me. I couldn't tell you; I promised I wouldn't. He's my brother, Jim. I had to protect him."

"Well, how're you gonna protect him now?" Jim was angry. "He's pretty recognizable with that hitch in his step, and people are furious. He and his friends have caused a lot of trouble for a lot of people. Everyone will be looking for him."

Alex had been sitting slack-jawed. He couldn't believe that Brick was the leader of the gang that had been getting rich off the backs of all the people of the county. "I'll say one thing for you Warners," he finally managed to say. "When you put your mind to doing something, you don't go halfway."

They finished their breakfast in silence and then walked out into the sunlit street. Colt squinted hard as his eyes adjusted. "I'm sorry, Jim. I should have told you, but I gave him my word. He was already so mad at me, I figured it was the least that I could do."

"No sense worrying about it now, Colt; the past is the past. Right now, we have to find Brick and talk some sense into him."

"How are we gonna do that? I haven't spoken to him in three years. He doesn't even know he's an uncle. Nobody knows where the Brotherhood hides out. All we have is rumors."

"Let me talk to some people. We need to find him, Colt. He needs to come home."

"Yes, sir."

"You and Alex go ahead. I'll catch up later and let you know what I find out."

Jim walked away down the sidewalk, and Colt and Alex headed to the general store for the supplies they had come to town for.

"I can't believe your brother is running The Brotherhood. That's amazing. How old is he now?"

"He'd be seventeen," Colt said. "I'd rather not talk about it."

"Seventeen? And he's been doing it for years now? Incredible. Is he as good a shot as you? Do you know if he's killed anybody? How much do you think he's stolen?"

Colt wheeled around and looked Alex directly in his eyes. "Alex, I said I didn't want to talk about it."

Alex paused for a minute as he stared into Colt's steel gaze. He gently approached the topic again. "No, no, of course not. Nobody would want to talk about that. But, Colt, this could be the help you've been looking for. If Brick has enough, maybe he could lend you some until the ranch gets . . ."

"Don't say it, Alex. I'm not using stolen money for the Whistlestop. Besides, I doubt Brick is willing to hand any of it over to me."

"Well, of course, you don't want to use stolen money, nobody does, but you didn't steal it, and money is money. Sometimes you have to do something you don't want to in order to do the things you do want to do."

"That's not me."

"Colt, you remember why you hired me? You said it was because I knew some things about some things. Well, one of the things I know is that there isn't a businessman or successful rancher out there that didn't at some point do something they didn't like to get where they are. That's the difference between success and failure, the willingness to bend your morals, even just for a second, if it's the only way to take that next step."

"I don't believe that's true, Alex."

"Look around you, Colt. Every one of these businesses is here because someone made a sacrifice somewhere. You can bet Walcott has done some questionable things. Hell, even Jim has a checkered past, and you admire him. I've got a few years on you, and I find myself looking up to you anyway, Colt. The things you have done in your short time put me in awe. I admire that you've always done it the right way, for the most part, but even you bend the rules from time to time."

"What are you talking about?"

"You wouldn't have the Whistlestop if you hadn't lied to the land office about how old you were."

"Oh, come on, Alex. One little lie isn't shooting or stealing."

"No, it's not. And like I said, I admire you, but you saw a way to the next step, and you took it. I'm with you whatever you want to do. I was just saying that there might be an option out there for you, you know, short-term."

"I don't think that option is for me, and like I said, I don't think Brick would be too anxious to lend it to me anyway."

They finished picking up the supplies and started the ride back to the ranch. Colt couldn't help but wonder how Jim was going to find out anything. The Brotherhood's hide-out was a tightly guarded secret. And could Jim convince Brick to come home? Would Brick want to?

Colt's mind was jumping as they rode. He was so deep in his own thoughts that he didn't notice the plume of smoke on the horizon until the grey of it stood out against the fast-darkening sky. It was in the direction of the Whistlestop. "You got your gun, Alex?"

"Yes."

"Then get ready to use it." Colt spurred Thunder, and they took off at a gallop. Thunder was the faster horse, and Alex was a good twenty yards behind him when Colt came over the last ridge. He hadn't even stopped to protect himself. All he could think about was Sadie and James.

In the gathering darkness, he could just see a group of Indians in the yard, exchanging gunfire with Ridge and Lanky, who had taken cover behind a wagon. There was no sign of Charlie or Lane. He could hear the shots and see the spurts of flame from the barrels. The barn was on fire.

He urged Thunder to go faster and was already approaching the bridge by the time Alex came over the ridge. Colt crossed the bridge shooting, and his first two shots hit home. Two braves dropped their weapons and fell to the ground, not moving.

The unexpected arrival of two more riders with guns caught the attacking Indians by surprise. Once they saw their two comrades fall, the remaining fighters thought better of their plans and galloped away across the ranch. The yard was suddenly very quiet.

Colt rode in and jumped off Thunder. "Sadie! Sadie! Where are you?"

"She's okay," Ridge yelled as he ran towards the burning barn. "Lane took her and your son up to your mountain hideout. Let's get this fire out!"

Lanky, Alex, and Colt joined Ridge at the barn and attempted to get the animals out while throwing water on the blaze.

"Where's Charlie?" Colt asked while dousing the flames.

"He didn't make it," said Lanky. "They came into the yard all stoic and quiet-like. We thought they were looking for trade or fresh water. They surprised us, and Charlie took one right in the chest before we even knew what was happening. It's a good thing you showed up when you did."

By the time the blaze was out, the barn was half of what it once was. The four men sat quietly on the ground, tired from the battle. "Where's Charlie's body?" asked Colt.

"I managed to drag him in behind Alex's place over there." Ridge pointed.

"We'll have to get him buried. Pick a nice corner some-where, and let's get that done. Does Lane know?"

"Pretty sure he has a good idea. He saw Charlie take the bullet before he got Sadie out of here," answered Lanky.

"Okay. I'll let him know for sure when I get up there. I know you're tired, but let's get Charlie's place dug, then I'll go see to Sadie and James."

"Go get your wife, Colt. She'll be scared to death," Ridge said as he stood up. "We can see to Charlie."

"No. Charlie was one of us, one of my guys. I'll help bury him. Alex, see if you can signal Lane that everything is clear, and they can come back."

Colt looked around and saw the bodies of the two braves still lying in the grass. "Might as well bury them, too; they deserve our respect. Let's choose that corner at the end of the yard by those redwoods. That way, if their tribe wants to pay their respects, they'll have access."

While he was talking, Colt had heard Alex fire three quick shots in the air. Now he heard Lane and Alex yelling at each other. Lanky, Ridge, and Colt gathered the bodies and put them in the wagon to take to the spot Colt had chosen. By the time they had everything loaded, Lane, Sadie, and James had joined them in the yard.

Sadie saw Colt and ran into his arms with James. "Oh, Colt. It was so awful. They shot Charlie before he even had a chance."

"It's okay, Sadie, it's over now." He hugged his family tightly. "Lane, I'm sorry about Charlie. Thank you for protecting my family. I owe you one. Do we know what they were doing here? What made them angry? They've passed through here without an issue for three years."

"They weren't really talking, Boss," said Ridge. "They showed up and just started shooting."

"Well, something got them riled up, and I'd sure like to know what that was. Let's get some rest. Clean-up can wait 'til morning."

It was a sleepless night for Colt. He paced around the house with thoughts running through his head at breakneck speed. Was Walcott right? Should he sell the Whistlestop?

He paused to stare at Sadie and James, asleep in the bed. He loved them more than anything in the world, but they deserved better than what he had been giving them the last few years. They deserved more than a dying ranch and scraping by just to live, and if the Indians were becoming violent now, then that was a whole other element of danger. Maybe they would be safer living in town with Sterling.

The thought put a lump in his stomach. They were his family, and he would be damned if anything was going to happen to them. It was his job to protect them, and he was going to do whatever was necessary to do that.

His father had sacrificed everything when he moved Brick and him out here. He owed his family at least that much.

CHAPTER 17

The sun was just creeping up on the horizon and the fog starting to lift from the ground when Colt took his coffee out to the front porch. As he paced there, drinking and thinking, he spotted a Modoc chief standing over the graves of the fallen men from the night before. Colt slowly lowered his hand toward the handle of the six-shooter on his hip, maintaining eye contact with the stranger the whole time.

The chief stared back at Colt. His eyes were full of sadness and weariness. The moment seemed to last forever; then the chief turned his attention back to the graves, performing a ceremony that Colt didn't completely understand. When he was finished, the chief looked back in Colt's direction. He gave a slight nod of his head, raised his right hand, and then mounted his horse and rode off into the fog. Not a word had been spoken between the two men.

As Colt took another contemplative sip of coffee, the bunkhouse door opened, and Ridge appeared. He stretched and shook his limbs, trying to get some feeling into them in the chilly morning air, then joined Colt on the porch. "How ya doin', Boss?"

"I'm doing all right, Ridge. Didn't sleep much last night. You?"

"I was plumb tuckered, so I slept like a rock. Feeling last night a little bit this morning, though, let me tell you." He rubbed his shoulder while moving his arm in a circle.

"I can imagine. I still don't know what we're dealing with. We've had a visitor already this morning."

Ridge looked around, stunned. "What? Here?"

Colt nodded. "Modoc chief. Just performed a ceremony over the graves and left. Never said a word."

"And he saw you standing there?"

"Looked right at me. Eagle Feather still workin' for Shep?"

"Far as I know, he is. You don't let go a scout like that—too valuable to your survival."

"You feel like riding over to Shep's and see if you can talk with him? Maybe he knows what's got them so riled up."

"Can do. Ain't seen Ty or Luke in a spell; might be good to catch up with them boys. You sure you don't need me here?"

"I think we'll be okay. I don't have any plans to go anywhere, and Alex is here now, too. See what you can find out."

"Yes, sir, I'll get mounted right away."

Colt went back inside. James was just starting to fuss in Sadie's arms, so he picked him up while she continued to sleep. "Come to Daddy, my big boy. Let's let Mommy sleep. Did you sleep all right? Lots of excitement last night, hey?" He made a quick breakfast for the baby, and then he and James went back outside. Ridge was just getting ready to ride and was talking with Lanky and Lane. Alex hadn't yet emerged from his house.

"Morning, Mr. Colt, sir." Lanky chuckled as he said it. He still enjoyed giving Colt a hard time every now and then about being his boss. "And how are you this morning, Master James?"

"Everybody's doing just fine, Lanky. And how are you boys feeling?"

"Little stiff, but don't you worry, the old trigger finger is still nice and limber."

"Hopefully we won't need it. And you, Lane?"

"Spent the night writing a letter to my mother, telling her about Charlie. Ridge is gonna deliver it when he passes through town. I'm wore out, but I'm here if you need me."

"I think we're gonna try and work closer to the ranch house for the next day or two. Let's have you two move what's left of the herd in closer for the next few days so we can keep a better eye on them, and then we'll start collecting wood and get that barn rebuilt."

"Sounds good." The boys went to saddle their horses and collect the herd.

Alex finally exited his house and walked over to join Colt and James on the porch. "Sorry I'm late, Colt. I was pretty tired after last night. I've never been involved in anything like that before."

"Me neither. It was a little harrowing. I think Sadie is still a little shook. She's still sleeping." Colt took a deep breath and let out a sigh. "Do you think maybe Sterling Walcott was right?"

"Right about what?"

"That maybe I should just sell the Whistlestop? That Sadie and James should go live with him? That they'd be safer there?"

"I don't think that those two could be anymore safe anywhere else in the whole wide world, Colt. You'd give your life to protect them. Why would you even consider it?"

"I wasn't here when the fight started, Alex. I wasn't here, and they were attacked."

"Colt, that could have happened at any time. You can't always be here--you're running a business. Running a business to provide for them."

"The business is in the outhouse, Alex. The ranch is dying."

"It's down times, Colt. They come and go. You'll bring it back. If I had to bet all I had on one thing in this life, I'd bet on you turning it around. And as far as protecting your family, that's why you hire hands, so they can be here when you can't, and you've got a good team here. Every one of them cares for your family like it's their own. You're doing a good job."

"Thanks, Alex. I'm just not sure."

"Well, I am." The voice came from the doorway. The men turned to see Sadie standing there. She wrapped her arms around Colt's waist and put her head on his shoulder. "I'm sure that you will keep us safe, you'll run this ranch, and you will be good at it. I don't care what my father says, we're not leaving. This is our home."

"Well, Alex. I guess that settles it, then," Colt said, putting his arm around Sadie and giving her a squeeze. "We best be getting started on bringing in some wood so we can get that barn fixed. If we're gonna have a ranch, we're gonna need a barn."

Colt kissed Sadie, and then the two men stepped off the porch. As they did so, a rider appeared on the ridge and rode down the hill. It was Jim. He gave a little wave as he rode up to the two men in the yard. "Howdy. Ran into Ridge on my way over. He said you had a bit of trouble, said Charlie didn't make it." Jim looked at the burned-out barn. "Everyone else all right?"

"We're good, Jim," said Colt. "Did you find what you were looking for? Do you know where Brick is hiding out?"

"Not exactly, Colt. Any coffee left? Let me get myself a cup and then we'll talk about it."

All three of them went back into the house, where Sadie joined them at the table. Jim took a long drink from his cup and gently set it back on the table. "So, Brick does not have a hideout somewhere in the mountains."

"Really? Where is he? How do you know?" Colt asked rapid-fire.

"Calm down, Colt." Jim chuckled. "We'll get to it. I did some looking into The Brotherhood. I asked some questions and did some checking with an old cowpuncher I used to know, Webb Logan. Webb's done some things in the past, ran with some rough men—he still has some connections. Anyway, Webb says that the 'hideout in the mountains' story is a smoke screen, just a ruse to keep the sheriff and the marshals and the Pinkertons off the trail. He says their real spot is somewhere to the southeast, out near Brela and LaTrobe."

"That's a lot of area to cover. He couldn't narrow it down any?"

"He wasn't sure. Said he heard something about a place called Flat Creek but doesn't know where it is. I checked a few maps and I didn't see it, so it must just be the name they gave the place. I'll need to take a little trip, do some exploring. We got to find him, Colt. We got to bring him home before he or his friends get caught or killed."

"I can't go with you, Jim. I just sent Ridge away for a few days, and with Charlie gone, we're a man down already. I can't leave my family short-handed if the Modocs decide to come back."

"I can understand that, Colt. Honestly, though, I think I would have better luck convincing him if you were there."

"You should go, Colt." Sadie put her hand on top of his. "We'll be okay. There's still Lanky and Lane if trouble comes around, and Alex will be here. He's your brother, Colt. If you can reach him, then you have to try. Go bring him home."

Colt paused for a minute, staring at the table. He raised his head and looked directly at Alex. "You keep my family safe. I'm counting on you."

"Absolutely. You have my word."

"All right, Jim. Let's get packed and go find Brick."

They gathered up the supplies they would need and loaded their horses. As they were getting ready to leave, Lane and Lanky came back into the yard.

"Hey, Colt, you going somewhere?" Lanky asked.

"Jim thinks he has a lead on where we can find Brick. We're gonna go check it out and try and bring him home."

"Oooh. Colt, your brother is stubborn. Good luck with that. Making all that money, I don't know if I'd want to come back."

Colt swung into the saddle. "I'm hoping that getting shot at has gotten old and that ranching sounds like a better way to live at this point. I need you two to keep it locked tight here. Ridge is looking into what got the Modocs riled up, but until he figures it out, we need to stay aware. Keep your eyes open. Keep my family safe." He looked up at the porch and tipped his hat to Sadie. "I'll be back soon. Stay safe. I love you."

Jim and Colt rode out of the yard and headed for Brela. They rode in silence for a few hours before Colt finally asked the question. "What's the plan, Jim? How are we gonna find him?"

"Webb says he's got a girl. She works at the saloon in Brela."

"You mean she's a whore?"

"I don't think he sees her like that, Colt. She's his Sadie. You best make sure you give her that respect. Disrespecting his lady won't help our cause any."

"I wasn't trying to disrespect her, I was just asking. Do we know her name?"

"Webb says it's Ruby."

"How does this Webb Logan know all this? I mean, if the sheriff don't know and everybody thinks the hideout is in the mountains, why is Webb so in the know?"

"I told you, Webb is an old-timer who goes way back. He knows a lot of folks, and most of them owe him a favor or two."

"Do you?"

"I think Webb and I are pretty well even."

They were silent until it was time to make camp for the night. As they were eating, Colt started to talk. "I don't know how things got like this, Jim. How I lost Brick."

"You haven't lost him, Colt. He's just walking his own path."

"But how did this become his path? Nothing we did would have given him the idea. I tried to make sure I steered him right all the time. I look at Charlie and Lane and how they were always together, did everything together. That's how I wanted it with Brick and me. The Whistlestop was s'posed to be for both of us."

"Maybe that was part of the problem, Colt. You were doing the steering."

"He was a kid, I was looking out for him, like Pa would have wanted."

"I understand that, Colt, but maybe he didn't see it. You grew up real fast after your Pa died, and you took to it like a fish to water. The life of working hard, being responsible, getting something of your own, it just fit you like a glove, and you've done real well at it. Brick was a little younger, maybe not quite ready for that yet. He sees the shadow of his pa, everything he had done, and then he sees his big brother do even more, cast an even bigger shadow. He watches you make decisions for both of you. Things like where to work, when to work. Heck, you even made the decision to keep coming out here after your pa died."

"I was trying to look after him, trying to make sure he was okay, that he—that *we* were going to be okay."

"I know that, Colt, and I understand it, even admire it. I think most people do. No one is faulting you for what you've done, but I think Brick was looking for a brother. I don't think he understood your stepping into the role of Pa the way you did. If he wasn't ready for that, that's a lot of pressure. He's feeling that pressure. and then this 'Pretty Boy' comes along and offers him what he was looking for. They pal around, spend more time having fun instead of working, and he brings some other guys with him. Troy offered him the brother that he thought he didn't have with you anymore."

Colt stared up at the starlit sky. "Do you think we can get him back?" he said softly.

"I don't know, Colt. That's a tough relationship to crack. As far as Brick's concerned, those boys are his family, and as hard as you're fighting to get him back, he's gonna fight for them. But we are sure gonna try. Let's get some sleep and we'll talk it out some more tomorrow." Jim leaned his head back on his saddle and put his hat over his eyes.

Colt stared at the stars for a few minutes longer. He was

wondering how his pa would have handled this. He had to convince Brick to come back with himself and Jim. He didn't want to see his brother shot or hung—he had lost too much family already. He was determined that no matter what happened tomorrow, Brick was coming home.

It was the last thought in his head before he finally fell asleep.

<h1 style="text-align:center">CHAPTER 18</h1>

Colt squeezed his eyes shut tighter as the sun crept above the horizon and slowly made its way into the sky. His nostrils flared at the smell of coffee and bacon, and he turned his head to see Jim already up and cooking breakfast over the fire. "Morning, Jim."

"Well, about time you woke up. We got things to do today. We need to get moving."

"Did you come up with a plan?" Colt asked as he stretched and rubbed his eyes.

"We're gonna go see this Ruby, tell her we're lookin' for Brick, and when she tells us where he is, we're gonna go get him."

Colt took some bacon. "Doesn't sound like much of a plan," he said with his mouth full. "What if she won't tell us? Or he doesn't wanna come?"

"She won't have to tell us. If she doesn't say it out loud, she'll get a message to him somehow, and we'll follow the messenger. As for Brick, we'll do what we can. It may take some hard convincing. He has his boys around him, and he ain't gonna wanna look weak in front of them. We may need to get him alone."

"I don't know what else to say. I tried to stop him before it got this far. I don't know what's left."

"Talk to him like a brother, Colt. I suspect the first time, you probably sounded more like a father. Talk to him like he's your equal, that you're the same. He was looking for something when he took up with these boys. Maybe you can convince him he can find that with you. You two are cut from the same cloth. I believe he wants you back in his life. It may just take one big appeal to get him there."

"I hope so. I do want him with me. I want him at the Whistlestop. That's *our* place."

The two finished packing and started along the trail again. After a few hours, they spotted the outline of Brela on the horizon. As they approached the town, they entered an arroyo that skirted the town limits. It looked like it had been a healthy river at one point but had been dry for a while, and it offered them a little cover as they approached, allowing them to check out the workings of the town before they entered the streets.

Colt could feel the eyes of the townspeople on them as they slowly moved down the main street. Western towns were known for the large number of men passing through regularly, and because of it, the townspeople always looked at strangers with caution and suspicion.

They came to a stop in front of the saloon and hitched their horses to the rail. As they dismounted, two cowhands leaning against the wall approached them. "That's a fine-looking animal that you're ridin'," one of them said to Colt. "Any chance you're open to selling?"

"No chance!" Colt said sharply and started past the men.

The cowhand reached out and grabbed Colt's arm. "Where you goin'? I was trying to have a conversation with you."

Colt turned to face him. "The conversation was done. I'm not selling him. Now, kindly take your hand off me."

"You think you're better than me? You're bein' disrespectful. I just wanna talk, and you're acting like you're too good to talk to me."

"I don't think I'm better than you, but I don't wish to talk to you either. I have nothing else to say to you."

"Is that so?" The man squared off and adjusted the gun belt on his hips. His partner moved himself to a position that provided a better shooting angle. Jim returned the favor and did the same. The tension increased, and the four were locked in a stare-down when a voice came out of the crowd.

"Borden? Is that you?"

The cowhand's eyes widened at the mention of Jim's name, and he softened his stance a bit. "Borden? Jim Borden?"

Jim nodded his head without taking his eyes off the two cowhands. "That's me."

The cowhands backed away slowly. "Maybe this was my mistake," said the first one. "Maybe you weren't being rude; you just got things to do. I do apologize. You boys have a good day now. That is a mighty fine animal you have. I was just admiring him."

Colt was impressed. Every time he saw the power Jim's name carried, it was humbling.

The two men left, and Jim led Colt over to the man who had called his name, who gave them a little wave as they approached. "That's Webb Logan," Jim said to Colt.

Colt gave Webb the once-over. He was an older gentleman with grey hair poking out from under the beat-up Stetson he wore on his head. He stood bowlegged and had narrow eyes—narrow but steely and aware—and a face full of grey stubble. His appearance made Colt smile, but Colt could see he was a dangerous man and not someone to be taken lightly.

"Jim Borden!" he said as they reached him. "In town two minutes and already making friends. I see nothing's changed all these years."

"Not me this time, Webb. I was just the backup." Jim shook his hand, then indicated Colt. "This here is Colt Warner. He's the brother of the man we're looking for."

Webb reached out and shook Colt's hand. "Colt Warner? Well, the way I hear it, those two are lucky they backed off when they did. You don't need Jim for backup." He smiled and looked at Jim. "That's a lot of respect you're showing, Jim. We both know you ain't looking for a man. That's just a boy running The Brotherhood."

"What are you doing here, Webb? I thought you were still in Sacramento."

"You think I'd miss a chance to see you in action again? Besides, if you're taking on The Brotherhood, you're gonna need some help. Even with 'Two-Gun Ace' here backing you up."

Colt winced when he heard the nickname. He hated being thought of as a gunfighter; that just brought more trouble. He was about to say something, but Jim spoke first. "I'm hoping we don't have to take on anybody, Webb. We just want to talk to him. Hopefully, he'll come on his own."

Webb laughed out loud. "Well, good luck with that, but you and I both know that things don't work out that easy. Especially with young men feeling their oats."

Colt interrupted. "You said Ruby works here? Is she inside?"

"All business, hey? Yeah, she's inside. You two can't just go in and start asking her questions, though."

"What do you mean?" Colt asked.

"Look around, son. This here is a tough town, full of men with secrets—secrets that they don't want shared. If you give that poor girl the reputation of being a spiller of secrets, she's as good as dead."

"What do you suggest, Webb?" asked Jim.

"You're gonna have to do things private-like. Pay for her time and take her to a room where you can talk in peace."

"I can't pay for a whore, especially my brother's," Colt protested. "I'm a married man."

"Well, good for you, son. You don't have to lay with her. Paying for her time gets you some time to talk and keeps her from being labeled a talker."

"It makes sense, Colt," said Jim.

"Can't you do it, Jim?"

"She's young, Colt. I think it's better if you do it."

Reluctantly, Colt agreed, and the three entered the saloon. They found a table and looked around the room. It was loud as the saloon was full even this early in the morning. There were card players at three different tables, ladies looking for company all around the room, and a line of men at the bar.

It was a rough-looking crowd. Even at the card tables, the men all looked hard and mean. Not one of them dressed like Drake would be if he were playing. *Drake would love it here,* Colt thought. He loved an active saloon, and this was definitely that. "Which one is she?" Colt asked.

"She's the little one over in the corner by the staircase," Webb answered.

Colt looked at her. She was a little shorter than Sadie, with dark-brown hair tied up in a messy bun with some strands falling out and framing her face. She was just a wisp of a girl, very thin, but had a cute-enough face. "What do I do now?" asked Colt.

"I suggest you go talk to her, son. Before some other man does and takes her upstairs," Webb answered.

Colt rose and walked toward the girl in the corner. As he got closer, he saw she had freckles and a scar down her left cheek from her earlobe to her chin. He also noticed she had shining green eyes that danced, even in the poor light of the saloon. He had to clear his throat and swallow before he could speak. "Excuse me?"

"Hey there, cowboy." She spoke softly, almost shyly. "Are you looking for a poke? It's two dollars for a poke."

Colt tried not to cringe. He felt guilty, even though he knew he wasn't stepping out on Sadie. "Uh . . . yeah. Can we go upstairs?" He fidgeted with his hat.

"Sure. Right this way." She grabbed his hand and led him up the stairs to a room at the end of the hall. "This is my room here," she said as she opened the door. Colt hesitated once more before entering. She closed the door behind them and started to untie the corset she was wearing. "Go ahead and take your clothes off. We can start right away."

Colt walked up behind her and grabbed her arms so she would stop what she was doing. "If you don't mind, I just want to talk."

Now it was her turn to hesitate. "You don't wanna poke? It's two dollars either way."

"I'd rather not. I just have some questions for you."

"Suit yourself, mister." She sat down on the bed.

Colt stood in the corner of the room and placed his hat on the dresser beside him. "What's your name?"

"They call me Ruby."

"That's what they call you, but what's your real name?"

"It's Ruby. I guess I was just born to work here." She laughed a little.

"Do you have a last name?"

"It's Munchin. What's this about, mister?"

"Do you have someone, Ruby? A boyfriend? Named Brick, maybe?"

She rose from the bed quickly and headed for the door. Colt stepped in front of her and blocked her path.

"Mister, I don't know what you want, but you better get out of my way. If you know who he is, then you know who his friends are, and I swear, if you hurt me, they'll hunt you down and do worse to you."

Colt grabbed her by the shoulders and gently pushed her back to sit on the bed. "I'm not going to hurt you. I don't want to hurt you. I'm his brother, Ruby."

She stared at him with wide eyes. "You're Colt?"

He was shocked that she knew about him. "He's told you about me?"

"Well, I would say so. He loves me. He tells me everything. What are you doing here?"

"I want to find him, Ruby. I want to talk to him, try and convince him to come home with me."

She laughed. "He said years ago you didn't like him doing what he does. Haven't changed any, I see. He's not coming home with you. He doesn't want to be controlled by you. Besides, he's good at it. He's getting rich."

"What about you? Don't you want something else?"

"He's gonna take me away from here. Just needs some more money first."

"I, *we*, have a ranch, Ruby. A place to stay and call our own."

She paused for a second and looked him in the eye. "Honestly? A real-life ranch with cows and stuff?"

"Well, not many of them right now, it's been some bad years, but yes. You and Brick can come live there with me and Sadie. No more slobbering drunks, no more robberies. Just ranching and living. It's a beautiful ranch, Ruby. Peaceful. I'm sure Sadie and my son would love to have you there."

"Why are you telling me all this?" Ruby was agitated now.

"I'm hoping maybe you can help me convince Brick to come back. Maybe he'll listen to you."

Ruby stood up from the bed. "He don't listen to me. He don't listen to nobody 'cept maybe Pretty Boy. Those two are thick as thieves." She laughed at her own little joke. "Besides, I'm not gonna talk to him. You want to talk to him, you find him on your own, you and your friends down there. I assume that one of them is Jim Borden?"

"He really does tell you everything, hey? If you change your mind, let him know that I want to talk to him, okay?" With that, Colt left the room and went back downstairs to Jim and Webb.

"Did you get what you wanted from the young lady?" asked Webb.

Colt took a seat at the table. "I don't think so. She's a pretty tough girl. I did my best to plant some seeds, but she seems pretty loyal to him. I think we're on our own."

"I think you did more than you think, Colt." Jim nodded toward the staircase.

Colt turned in his chair to see that Ruby had come down the stairs. She was talking to a large cowboy with a dark, scraggly beard in a corner of the saloon. She walked away, and the large man rose from his seat and made his way to the doorway.

"I believe it's time for us to go, boys," Jim said as he rose from his seat. "That man's gonna take us where we want to go."

The three left the saloon and watched as the man rode off out of town. "Shouldn't we follow?" asked Colt.

"Give him some time. He'll be looking to see if anyone's on his backtrail. He won't get too far. Webb's a pretty good tracker. We'll catch up to him when it's time."

CHAPTER 19

Once Jim had decided that enough time had passed, the three mounted and headed out of town in the same direction as the cowboy. They rode at an easy pace across the prairie, keeping their eyes on the horizon, looking for signs that the cowboy knew they were following him, as well as any indication that trouble might lie ahead.

Webb was following the cowboy's trail with Jim and Colt behind. Up ahead was a small butte. When they got close, Jim dismounted and walked up the slope, crouched down with Pete in tow. Once he got to the flat, Jim took a look around, then called for Webb and Colt to follow.

From the top of the butte, they could see the surrounding plains for miles around, broken only by some foothills off to the east, the mountains rising blue in the distance behind them. "Must be headed that way," Jim said. "It's the only cover anywhere around here."

"Looks that way." Webb knelt and checked for tracks, then stood again, brushing dirt from his knees, and peered in the direction of the hills. "Don't see anything that says different."

The three headed in the general direction of the foothills. Though they weren't as large and foreboding as the mountains that rose beyond them, what they lacked in size, they more than made up for in cracks and crevices. There were any number of niches in between the hills that a man could get himself lost in. You could spend days wandering in circles and never find your way back out or, worse yet, get caught up in a chase, lose your bearings, and trap yourself in a box canyon with no way out but to shoot your way clear or die where you stand.

As they approached, Webb kept studying the ground. He looked ahead, then pointed to a narrow pass between two hills. "Looks like he headed in here."

The three rode on in silence. The only sound for some time had been their hoofbeats on the ground when Webb suddenly spoke again. "Jim."

"I see 'em," Jim answered as his eyes narrowed. He slowly removed his rifle from its sheath and laid it across the saddle in front of him.

Colt scanned the hills around them. He caught a flicker of movement, and then he saw them. Two men, up on the hills, one on either side of the pass, hunkered down behind what little cover they could find, rifles aimed in their direction.

"What do we do now, Jim?" Colt asked.

"Just keep moving forward, Colt. Nice and easy. This wasn't unexpected. It means we're getting close. They're just there to make sure Brick doesn't get any unwelcome visitors."

"You think he knows we're here?"

"He will. As soon as they get the message to him."

A whistle rang out and echoed in the hills. In the distance, a cloud of dust rose.

"And there goes the messenger. Brick'll know in a matter of minutes. How many depends on how far out we are from their hideout." Webb smiled a little. "Things are gonna get a little more interesting now." He, too, had laid his rifle across his saddle. They continued forward, weaving through the hills with Webb still following signs.

Suddenly, up ahead, three men appeared in their path. As they got closer, Colt recognized the one in the middle. He was face to face with Tank Jepson for the first time in nearly four years. "Howdy, Tank," he said as he, Jim, and Webb reined their horses to a stop. "Long time. How you been?"

"Colt." Tank lowered the brim of his hat in acknowledgment. "What're you doing here?" He tipped his hat again. "Mr. Borden. I know you." He turned his eyes to Webb. "You, I don't know."

"This is Webb Logan. He's with us," Jim said.

Colt spoke up again. "Tank, I just need to speak with Brick, okay? We ain't looking for no trouble."

"Well, you may not be looking for trouble, but coming here is damn sure a good way to find it," Tank snarled. "Especially bringing a stranger with you." The tension between the groups went up a notch; Colt's arms and neck tingled as the hairs rose.

Tank spoke again, the snarl replaced with a smirk. "The good news for you is Brick heard you were coming, and he wants to see you. Follow us in."

The three gang members turned their horses around and walked them single file down the pass. It was narrow, and the surrounding walls were sheer and steep. Colt looked up and saw men on the ridges above them every fifty yards or so, all armed with rifles.

The pass opened up onto a hidden valley. From the outside, you would never guess that this little gem of land existed. It had lush green grass, a ranch house, two bunkhouses, and a corral filled with horses. Out in front of the ranch house, a well had been dug. It was almost as pretty as the Whistlestop had been in the beginning—much too pretty to be a hideout for thugs and thieves.

"Head to the ranch house. He's expecting you." Tank motioned for the group to move on.

There were cowboys lounging all over the yard. It was obvious that the reported numbers of The Brotherhood had been underestimated, and plenty of able men had joined the group. Some were at the corral, others playing horseshoes by the bunkhouse, and some just relaxing in the warmth of the sun, but every pair of eyes was on the trio as they made their way toward the house. Colt could feel the tension, and Thunder felt it too, whinnying and sidestepping a little under Colt.

"Easy, boy," Colt said softly, patting Thunder's neck. "It's just Brick, boy. We're just here to see Brick."

The door of the house opened, and Brick and Pretty Boy Troy made their way out onto the porch. "Colt! Jim! It's been too long, boys, way too long." Brick sounded almost giddy as he spread his arms wide to welcome the group. "How are things back in Monroe?"

It wasn't the welcome Colt was expecting, but he was going to take it while it lasted. He dismounted and walked toward his little brother. Brick came down the few steps and met him halfway. The two brothers embraced.

It felt good to Colt, good to have his brother back in his arms. And Brick looked good, too, strong and healthy. His hair was longer, gently brushing his shoulders beneath his hat. He still walked with a hitch in his gait but otherwise seemed to be doing just fine. "Things are okay, Brick. How have you been?"

Brick let out a laugh and stretched his arms out again while he did a little spin. "Look around, Colt. Things couldn't be better. Jim, I see you still got those steely eyes. How's Drake, that ol' dry-gulcher?"

Jim got down from Pete and shook Brick's hand. "Everything is all right, Brick. Drake is just fine."

Brick turned his attention to Webb. "Sorry, stranger, don't believe I know you. Brick Warner." He held out his hand for Webb to shake.

"Webb Logan, old ridin' partner of Jim's. Nice to meet you, son."

Brick paused for a moment. "Webb Logan? Well, if you're the Webb Logan I've heard about, then you're a little more than an old riding partner." He turned to Pretty Boy. "Troy, this here is Webb Logan. He's one of the original bad guy desperados from the 'Wild West.' He's robbed more trains and shot more men than the bunch of us together. They say he is one bad man."

Troy smirked, and Brick turned and looked back at Webb, his tone more serious now. "Is that true? Are you a dangerous man? And if so, what's a bad man like you doin' comin' round these parts?"

There was silence as the two men stared at one another. Suddenly, Brick made a move as though he was going to punch Webb. Webb's hand dropped quickly to his pistol, but he didn't pull it.

Brick's hand stopped short, and his mood lightened again. "Whoa, there, pardner, I'm just funning you. Any friend of Jim and Colt is a friend of The Brotherhood. What say we all go in and get somethin' to eat?"

Once inside, they sat around the supper table, eating and reminiscing. The train ride to Sacramento was brought up, minus the death of their father. Brick laughed out loud as they talked about Patrick Robillier and the issues they had with him on the journey. "When Jim had his foot on that fat man's chest, just daring him to make a move, why, I swear that old boy was near gonna soil himself." He laughed again. "I hadn't ever seen a grown man look so much like a little girl before."

Pretty Boy wanted to add his two cents. "I hear you was so scared you pissed your pants." He laughed as he looked around the table, but Brick looked up from his plate and stopped his laughter dead.

"I'm just saying that's what I heard, that's all." Troy looked at his plate and went back to eating.

The stories and the laughter continued until the food was gone. Colt got up from the table and walked outside to stand on the porch. Brick followed him out.

"It's a nice place you got here, Brick," Colt said.

"It surely is. The boys and I like it well enough, anyway. What are you doing here, Colt? You're not here to tell old stories and check up on me."

"Did you know I'm married now?" Colt offered the question, not yet ready to answer Brick's. "Yes, sir, Sadie and I got married. We have a son, too; his name is James William Warner. You're an uncle, Brick. Can you imagine?"

"I always knew you and Sadie were gonna get hitched; that much was obvious. What do you want, Colt?"

"I want you to come back with us, Brick. Quit the Brotherhood and come live on the Whistlestop."

"Same old story, hey? Never a changing tune with you. Why would I quit this?" He waved his left arm out into the night. "Look around, Colt. I'm doing pretty well for myself.

Got me some land, got me a girl, got me some brothers who'll stand by me no matter what. Why would I give that up? For what?"

"You're gonna get caught, Brick. The Pinkertons are looking for you now, plus the U.S. marshals, not to mention every two-bit cowpuncher with a gun who thinks he can score himself an easy reward. It's not gonna last, Brick. Come home before I have to take your body home."

"That ain't my home. This is my home." Brick was more forceful now. "You think I don't ask around, Colt? You think I wasn't checking up? From my understanding, I'm doing a damn site better out here than your run-down ranch is doing. All the talk is about Colt, the kid rancher who's runnin' his place right into the ground. They're laughing at you, Colt. They're saying you might not last another winter before you have to sell. Why would I come back to that? I told you that you were gonna be just like Pa. That ranch will kill you. But you know what they're saying about me? About The Brotherhood? We're famous, just like the James Boys."

"They'll find you, Brick, just like we did, and then what? The Whistlestop is having a rough go right now, but at least it's honest. And you're wrong. It *is* your home; you're just too damn stubborn to accept it. Jim and I built that place for us, so we would have a place of our own.

"These thugs ain't your family, Brick. Jim, Drake, and me, we're your family. Any one of these guys would take you down, given the chance. You heard Troy in there. They're laughing at you, too. They're not your friends. They're looking for that first sign that says you're not up to the challenge of running the gang, and then they're gonna take their shot. Can you live knowing that any one of them would just as soon shoot you in the back as look at you?"

"They're welcome to try, Colt. A few have. I'm not your scared little brother anymore. I lead these men. Me! You think I could lead these boys if I wasn't just as bad and nasty as they are? What I say is what gets done, and ain't nobody challenging that 'less they think they're faster'n me and they wanna try pullin' steel. I'm asking one last time, why are you here? I walked away from you. It's been years. Why now?"

"We want you home, Brick. I guess it's like cattle."

"What the hell are you talking about now?"

"When you get new stock, the first thing you do is slap a brand on them so that people know they're yours. Family is that brand, Brick. Now, some cowboy is gonna come along and steal your cows, and he's gonna try and alter that brand so that you think the cows are his and not yours. Did you know that if you kill one of them cows, skin the animal, and look at the underside of the hide, you can identify the original brand? It's pretty incredible.

"It all boils down to what's inside, just like family. You and me are Warners, and we're the last of what we've got. You're always family, Brick, whether you're at the Whistlestop, running with The Brotherhood, or moving to Utah and becoming one of those Mormon types we heard about. Come home and meet your nephew."

Brick chuckled a little. "I ain't gonna be no damn Mormon. How'd you get so smart?"

"Jim's a good teacher."

"Yeah, that he is."

From the darkness came the sound of a wagon approaching. As the brothers looked toward the sound, Tank rode up first on his horse. "It's Ruby, Brick. She's coming in." The shadowy shape of the wagon emerged from the black, and the driver pulled to a stop. Ruby, who'd been sitting beside him, jumped down and ran to Brick.

He put his arm around her. "How you doin', honey? What are you doin' out here?" He gave Colt a little smile. "I understand you two have met already?"

"Ruby." Colt tipped his hat as he spoke.

"Colt," Ruby said curtly, then turned her attention to Brick. "Baby, let's go inside. I'm cold, and we need to talk."

Brick looked at Colt. "You boys can spend the night in the bunkhouse over there, and then I suspect that come morning, you'll be able to find your way back home. Now, if you'll excuse me, I've got some company to keep." With that, he took Ruby inside. The door closed behind them, and Colt was left on the porch alone.

The door opened again, and he was joined by Jim and Webb. "Any luck?" asked Jim.

"Nothing. He's just so damn stubborn. How does he not see that he's riding right toward his own damn death?"

"He's his own man, Colt; he's making his own decisions. All you can do is try."

"He says we can bunk in the house over there, and then he wants us to leave in the morning."

"Well, sleeping in a bed sounds good to me." Webb started toward the bunkhouse. "You think he'll at least feed us in the morning before we go?"

Jim followed him and gave him a playful shove. "Always thinking with your stomach, you old codger."

"I was just thinking that they appear to be a far sight better at cooking than you. If I have to settle for one more of your hard biscuits or overcooked bacon, I might just turn myself in to the authorities. Even they have better food than what you serve . . ."

Colt took one more look at the closed door into the house, then followed them.

Later, he lay on his bed, staring up into the darkness, wondering if his trip here had made any difference at all. His final thought before his eyes closed was of Sadie and James and how he wished he was at home with them.

CHAPTER 20

Colt squinted against the sunlight coming in through the window of the bunkhouse. He stood and stretched. The bed had felt good after sleeping on the ground the previous night, but his back was still stiff.

Leaving Jim and Webb still asleep in their beds, Colt exited the bunkhouse and looked around the yard. It was a hub of activity already. Clearly, something was going on today. Men were moving everywhere, packing horses, cleaning guns, and just generally looking busy. Across the yard, the door to the house opened, and Brick came out with two cups of coffee in his hand. He joined Colt in the middle of the yard and handed him one of the cups. "Morning, Colt."

"Morning. What's going on here today?"

"Just getting ready for a little excursion, nothing for you to worry about. You've caused me enough trouble already."

"How do you mean?"

"What did you think you were doing, putting that nonsense about your ranch in my girl's head? Telling her we could go live out there. You know, she came all the way out here last night, and there weren't no mister and missus time; all she wanted to do was talk about us leaving here and going to live with you. I've got half a mind to put a bullet in you right here just for that."

"Well, I'm sorry for that, but it wasn't nonsense, Brick. There's room for both of you, and there always will be."

"I said my piece last night, Colt. I'm good where I am. There's breakfast for you boys inside, and then I would appreciate it if you'd get moving on after that."

"All right, Brick." Colt started to the bunkhouse to get Jim and Webb.

"Colt?"

"Yeah?" Colt turned to look at him.

"It was good seeing you again, brother. You take care."

"You too, Brick. You too."

After breakfast, the trio did as they were asked and left the cozy valley, heading for home. "A lot of hustle and bustle going on there this morning," said Webb.

"They've got another job planned," Colt offered.

"Where?" asked Jim.

"He wouldn't tell me—just told me they were heading out, and I shouldn't worry about it."

Webb said nothing.

The three rode back into Brela, where Webb was going to part company with them. The town seemed busier than usual; there were people moving everywhere and a general air of anticipation. Jim stopped a gentleman walking by. "What's happening here, fella?"

"The Pinkertons are here. They say they've got a bead on that Brotherhood gang. They're looking for posse members over at the marshal's office."

Colt, Jim, and Webb made their way to the marshal's office,

where a large crowd had gathered. They pushed their way to the front of the crowd and listened as a man in a grey suit and bowler hat, with a tidy mustache and wire-rimmed glasses, began to speak.

"My name is Douglas Brookdale, and I am employed by the Pinkerton National Detective Agency. I have been deployed by Mr. Allan Pinkerton himself on behalf of his clients to track down and bring to justice the scourge on your good society, the vermin who steal from you and sully your way of life, those scoundrels known simply as 'The Brotherhood.'"

Colt and Jim looked at one another and then back to Brookdale, who continued to speak.

"These men are thieves, thugs, a blight on society, and a symptom of the disease of crime that is sweeping across this great nation. Great men forge ahead every day, risking their wealth and their well-being, to make this country what it is. You folks work hard to scrape out whatever success you can find for yourselves, and then this riffraff, these undesirables, they waltz in and just take whatever they want. Does that seem right to you? Does that seem fair?"

It was hard for Colt to hear his brother described that way. He was starting to feel anger welling up inside himself when a voice rang out from the crowd.

"They don't steal from us. It's the banks and the trains, all you fancy suits, that they're hurting. I got no problem with them."

Colt couldn't see where the voice had come from, but before he could try and get a better look, Brookdale was speaking again.

"That's not true, sir. While it is a fact that they mostly hit banks and train payrolls, isn't it also true that they've robbed stagecoaches? Haven't they stolen from ordinary citizens such as yourselves?"

Another voice came above the crowd noise. "Only the greenhorns and the dandies that ain't got no business bein' out here to begin with." The crowd let out a collective laugh.

Brookdale replied, "I ask you, sir, was that not all of you at one time or another? Didn't you all make your way west from the larger cities? These 'greenhorns' all have the same dreams you did. Shouldn't they be allowed to try and make theirs come true? This gang threatens everybody's way of life, and I'm here to track them down. I'm looking for eight to ten good men who want to track them down with me, eight men who will stand up and put justice first instead of protecting these men any longer. We will pay two hundred dollars to each man once The Brotherhood is captured and in this jail. Do I have any takers?"

Two hundred dollars was a large sum; it would take a lot of hard work for a man to make that much at any one time. Colt could feel the tension in the air as the crowd contemplated the offer.

"Come now; surely there are eight men out there that could use two hundred dollars?" Brookdale asked again.

Colt looked around at the crowd. There was a moment of silence, and then suddenly, there were shouts of acceptance from the mob as men raised their hands and walked to the front of the group. In no time at all, Brookdale had his posse.

Colt studied them. Brookdale had gotten twelve volunteers, more than he had asked for. There were some tough-looking men in the group who looked like they could shoot. Colt felt a lump growing in his stomach as he thought about Brick and these men trying to chase him down.

The speech continued. "Thank you, you twelve men, the

brave soldiers of justice who will put an end to this disease plaguing our society. We have word of where The Brotherhood plans to strike next. You men gather your horses and weapons and meet back here. The sheriff will swear you in as deputies, and then I'll fill you in, and we will be on our way. If we ride fast enough, we may get there ahead of them, and we can set our trap. Hurry now."

The crowd dispersed, and Jim, Colt, and Webb were left looking at one another. "What do we do now, Jim?" asked Colt. "We don't know where Brick was headed today."

Webb cleared his throat. "Happens I do. They plan to hit the bank in Bullard."

Colt stared at him. "Why didn't you say something?"

Webb shrugged. "Ain't in the habit of warning banks someone's 'bout to rob them. 'Sides, if you had gone racing over there and told 'em the Brotherhood was coming, Brick would be in the same predicament he is now, with armed men waiting for him."

Colt couldn't argue the point. He turned to Jim. "So, what do we do now?"

Jim's jaw clenched before he spoke. "I guess we ride hard for Bullard and hope that we get to Brick before they do. Any chance you wanna come along, Webb?"

The old cowboy slowly raised his head and pushed his hat back so Colt could clearly see his eyes. His pupils were small, but Colt would have sworn they were dancing as a smile crept across Webb's face. "Jim, you know I ain't ever been one to miss a good fight. What're we waiting for?"

The three mounted their horses and headed for Bullard as fast as they could.

Thunder liked the run. It wasn't often that Colt let him go like this. His muscles moved easily as he galloped faster and faster across the plains. He set a fast pace, and it wasn't long before he was well ahead of the other two horses. Colt reined him a little and allowed the others to catch up.

"My goodness, that is one heck of a horse you're ridin' there, boy." It was Webb's first time seeing Thunder run as fast as he could. "I thought you were leaving us behind for sure. Heck, he don't even look like he's sweating."

Colt smiled. "He ain't. I don't usually have occasion for him to run like this, and he loves every minute of it." Colt gave the animal a pat on the neck. "He'd go all day if I let him."

"He's gonna have to if we want to get there ahead of that posse." Jim gave his horse a little kick, and they sped up again.

"What's the plan when we get there?" asked Colt.

"Don't know yet. Play it by ear and see what happens."

The trio left a cloud of dust in their wake as they rode over the dry plains. They'd been riding hard for an extended period when the group finally slowed their horses. Thunder was sweating now, and Jim and Webb's horses were looking worn. "We're gonna have to find them some water pretty soon, or we won't be going much farther," Webb pointed out.

"There's a small spring just over the next hill, and Bullard ain't much farther now," Jim said. "I think we've got a good enough lead that we can probably slow some now."

They watered their horses at the spring and then carried on into Bullard. It wasn't much of a town, not even as sophisticated as its already unsophisticated neighbors. The streets were full of tough guys, men who lived on the trails. To his left, Colt saw rows of sheets hung to dry and guessed that this was the Chinese section of the town. The Chinese had come over as railroad workers and, once the track had been completed, had taken to the towns and set up businesses such as launderers or shop owners. They had their own little community in every town Colt had visited, always segregated off to the side. They were hard workers and always kept to themselves. Colt admired them for their work ethic.

They made their way to the middle of town, where all the action would be taking place. They kept the horses at a slow walk as they studied the people in the street.

Colt saw a man he recognized leaning against a pillar outside the casino: he had been at The Brotherhood's ranch house last night. He spotted three more cowboys from the hideout before they dismounted and hitched their horses.

Colt moved closer to Jim. "I've seen four of Brick's guys already. They're definitely here."

"Yeah, Colt. I've seen 'em too. Keep moving, spread out, and make your way to the bank. That posse is gonna be here soon enough, and then the bacon will really be in the fire."

The three each found a place to sit and relax where they could plainly see the bank as well as the roads, keeping an eye out for the posse. Colt had hardly taken a seat on a bench outside the barbershop when he saw members of The Brotherhood approaching the bank. Six of them rode up the street and hitched their horses right in front of it. Brick was there. Colt saw him dismount Lightning and gather his guys for one last talk before they all pulled bandanas over their mouths and entered the bank. A shot was fired, and there were some screams from inside.

Colt stepped off the boardwalk to cross to the bank, then had to jump back to avoid being run over by the galloping horses of the posse as they rode down the main street. He saw Brookdale beckoned to by a man in the street as he climbed off of his horse. The man said something to the Pinkerton man, who looked startled. He called his men over to him. "Take cover where you can see the front door!" he said so quietly Colt had to strain to hear it. "They're in there, already trying to take the bank! Get your pistols ready, but nobody fires until I give the word." The men scattered, Brookdale directing them to their positions like a general commanding his troops, even unhitching a couple of unattended wagons, letting the horses run free, and tipping the wagons over to make more cover.

Jim ran over to Colt. "Get ready. It's about to break loose."

"What are we gonna do, help them escape after they rob it? I can't be labeled a thief, Jim; I've got a family."

"We're not helping anybody rob anything. We're just here to make sure Brick doesn't get himself shot."

Suddenly, the door to the bank opened. One of Brick's men took one look outside and slammed the door again. "Boss, Boss! We've got trouble!" His voice carried into the street. "There's a whole group of 'em out here surrounding the place." It was an exaggeration, they weren't surrounded, but Colt could see why he might think so.

"Who's out there?" Colt recognized Brick's voice calling from inside the building.

"I'm Douglas Brookdale of the Pinkerton National Detective Agency," Brookdale shouted. "I'm here with a group of men who are my sworn deputies. Come out from the bank, throw your weapons to the ground, and put your hands in the air."

"A Pinkerton? A goddamn Pinkerton? My, my! We made the big time now, boys." Glass shattered as one of the bank's windows was smashed outward. Colt caught a glimpse of Brick in the dim interior. "If it's all the same to you, Mr. Pinkerton, I think we're just gonna hold on to these here pistols for a little while longer. How many men you got out there? Who's with you?"

"I can assure you that we have more than enough men to keep you corralled. Throw out your weapons."

Another window shattered on the opposite side of the building, and the voice of Troy Benton came through it. "More than enough? I don't think so!" A shot rang out, and one of the posse members let out a yell, stood up from behind his cover, clutched his right hand to his left shoulder, and fell into the dirt. Troy laughed. "Sounds like one less man already!"

Brookdale dove for cover as the posse fired a volley of shots toward the bank. More glass shattered, and bullets thudded against wood. People in the street ducked for cover and dove into stores as the posse kept firing at the building. Brookdale got his wits about him and tried to yell above the noise. "Cease fire! Cease fire! We want them alive, for God's sake! We can't put dead men in jail!"

The shooting stopped, and the street fell eerily quiet. Gunsmoke hung heavy in the air. The silence was finally broken when Brick yelled again. "You want us alive? We ain't going to jail. You come get us if you're man enough."

Brookdale was crouched behind one of the wagons he'd had overturned earlier. He raised up just enough to see the bank. "You're trapped. You can't go anywhere!" he shouted. "Surrender, and I'll see to it that you're treated with respect all the way until trial."

"Respect this!" A shot knocked the bowler hat right off the head of Douglas Brookdale. He reached down and grabbed the hat out of the dust, then put his finger through the bullet hole in the crown.

Brookdale's face drained of color. "This is unacceptable!" he yelled. "Deputies, fire at will."

But before his men could fire, they were forced to duck for cover as bullets rained down from the rooftops across the street. The bank's front door flew open, and the gang rushed out with their pistols blazing. Once outside, the men scrambled in all directions, forcing the deputies to do the same. The streets of Bullard were now engulfed in a full-fledged shootout.

Colt, staring, was startled by a hand grabbing his shoulder and turned to see Jim's eyes blazing at him. "We need to find Brick and get the hell out of here before we're all full of holes." He jumped off the sidewalk and disappeared between some buildings.

Colt drew both his guns, leaped off the boardwalk in Jim's wake, and ran into an alley across the street, weaving to throw off the aim of anyone who might take a shot at him. He couldn't see Jim and had no idea where Webb was.

He carefully poked his head around the corner of a building, and a bullet crashed into the wall above him in a shower of splinters and sawdust. He whipped his head back into cover and blinked, trying to clear his eyes.

Another shot smashed into the wall above his head. Instinctively, he fired both guns at the rooftop across from him. There was a pained scream, and a man crashed down onto some crates across from Colt. As his vision cleared, he recognized the man as one he had seen at Brick's hideout.

After a few more hard blinks, Colt was on the move again, looking for Brick. So many guns were firing it was hard to tell the actual shots from the echoes. Men were running everywhere, and Colt couldn't find anyone he was looking for.

He fired his gun sparingly, but every bullet hit its mark. He shot three more men before he found himself in the Chinese part of town. It was hard to see anything with all the hanging sheets obscuring his vision. He walked deliberately, slowly pushing aside each sheet he came to.

There was a rustle behind him, and he spun around

quickly with his guns leveled. A Chinese woman cowered in a corner, her hands up over her face, speaking a million words a minute in a panic. Colt exhaled and moved his hands in a gesture for her to calm down. Once she had done so, Colt motioned for her to keep quiet and then continued moving forward, looking for Brick or Jim or anyone that didn't look like they wanted to put a bullet in him.

WHILE COLT WAS STRUGGLING to find his way through the hanging laundry, Jim was having issues of his own. He had shot two men already and had had several close calls since his leap off the sidewalk, with no luck locating Brick.

He was crouched at the back corner of a general store when he heard a man moving some crates. Jim stood up, stepped out, and raised his gun. "Don't move, mister," he said it with the most authority he could muster. The man slowly turned, and Jim was suddenly face to face with Brick. Both had their guns at the ready. As they stared at one another, Jim hesitated for a moment; then, he started to lower his gun.

A shot cut through the silence. Brick stared as Jim's eyes grew wider, and his mouth fell open. There was a red stain at the center of Jim's shirt that was growing larger by the second. Jim dropped to his knees, never breaking eye contact with Brick until he fell face-first to the dusty street.

"No!" Brick shouted. With Jim down, Brick could see Jessie Mitchell standing in the alley behind him. Smoke drifted from the barrel of Jessie's gun as he stared at the body of the man he had just shot. Brick ran to Jim's body. "Why did you do that?" he yelled at Jessie.

"He—he was gonna shoot you, Brick. He had his gun drawn. You're fast, but that was Jim Borden. You weren't gonna beat him."

"You damn fool, Jessie. Jim wasn't gonna shoot me. He was like a father to me."

Colt had heard Brick yell and rounded a corner just in time to see Brick kneeling over Jim's body. He stopped in shock and stared at Brick. "It wasn't me, Colt," Brick said, looking up at him. "I swear I would have never done this. Jessie shot him."

Colt instantly raised his gun and fired in the direction of Jessie Mitchell, who ducked around the corner the instant he saw Colt start to turn. Splinters flew as the bullet took a chunk out the building.

Colt turned back to Brick and Jim, staring down at Jim's body. This man had saved their lives, brought them to Sacramento, practically raised them, and now he lay in the dirt of a town that mattered nothing to any of them because of Brick and his damn gang. "He came here to bring you home, to get you out of here before any of this happened. Dammit, Brick! He loved you like a son."

"You don't think I know that? You don't think this tears me up inside? I didn't want this to happen. Why didn't you just go home like I said?"

The brothers had almost forgotten there was still a gunfight happening until a bullet pierced the air between them and crashed into a crate next to the building.

Both boys spun and fired. The man across the way never stood a chance. The brothers' bullets both found their mark, and he was dead before his body hit the dirt.

"You need to get out of here, Colt," Brick said.

"I'm not leaving without Jim. You gotta help me get him to the horses."

Reluctantly, Brick agreed. Each grabbing an arm, they started dragging Jim toward the main street, his body draped between them, drawn guns in their free hands. No one challenged them; the fighting had mostly moved off into the side streets, and anyone who saw them took one look and found urgent business in a different direction.

As they reached the horses, they were met by Webb Logan, who stared in disbelief. "Damn. Thought that man would live forever. How'd it happen?"

"Shot in the back by a lousy coward who thought he was a tough guy." Colt spit the words with anger while staring at Brick.

They laid Jim's body across his saddle. Pete moved nervously as something about his rider didn't feel right. "It's okay, Pete." Colt rubbed the horse's neck. "We're gonna take him home." Emotions were getting caught in Colt's throat. He looked at Brick. "You coming with us or not?"

"I can't, Colt. This is where I belong. Get going and take care. I don't want to bury you both."

Colt and Webb mounted. "Damn you, Brick." Colt's eyes bore a hole into his brother. He gave a quick kick to Thunder and rode out of town with Pete in tow behind him, Jim's body swaying with the gait of his horse.

Colt rode in silence, fighting back tears. He looked at Webb, who appeared unshaken. How could someone who claimed to be his friend not feel anything for this fallen man? Colt wondered bitterly. Jim had been a great man, a tough guy with a heart of gold. How could Webb just sit there?

"This is where I break off," Webb finally said. "I'm heading back into Brela. I'm damn sorry that this happened, Colt. Good luck to you the rest of the way."

"You don't look damn sorry." Colt finally said what he wanted to say.

"What's that?"

"You don't look sorry, and you ain't said a damn thing since we left. I don't think you care at all." Colt's emotions were starting to come out now.

Webb drew a long breath before speaking. "Son. That man right there pulled my bacon out of the fire more times than I can count. I done the same thing for him. He's the closest thing I ever had to a brother, and I am damn sure gonna miss him."

"Then why don't you show it?"

"It's the life, Colt. Jim always knew that he was probably gonna meet his end staring down the barrel of a gun. There's no such thing as an old gunfighter. Mine's waiting for me out there somewhere, too. You just keep hoping you can ride far enough to stay ahead of it a mite longer. It's a shame it happened like this, but I s'pose it was the only way it could. Ain't nobody could beat him in a fair fight; he was about the slickest I ever seen with a pistol. I've got my sadness, but I've got my memories, too, and I'm gonna get into town, sidle up to the bar, and drink until the memories are all I remember. Make sure you bury him right, Colt. That man deserves it."

Webb headed toward Brela, and Colt was left alone with Jim. He started the long ride back to the Whistlestop and took solace in his solitude. He let his feelings go, and tears streamed down his cheeks. He was glad no one was there to see it.

He made camp for the night and spoke to Jim's body the whole time he was doing it. "I'm sorry, Jim. I'm sorry that we were so much trouble for you. You done what you could to teach us everything we needed to know, and all it did was get you killed. Maybe you should have left us back there in

Wyoming; then you'd still be alive. Why did you help us? What did you get from it? We were just two kids with a dead pa and nothing else. You could have walked away and left us to Patrick Robillier. Why didn't you walk away?"

Colt fell asleep that night with that thought in his head, and sadness in his heart.

Chapter 21

Brick and The Brotherhood had managed to escape the shootout in Bullard, but it had not been without losses. What had been a group of fourteen when they'd entered the town that morning was now a group of five, meeting in a grassy field halfway between Bullard and their hideout, where a lone cottonwood tree and a few small bushes provided a little bit of cover.

Brick was the last to join the group. On his way to the rendezvous point, he had thought about Jim, the words Colt had said, and what had just happened at the bank. His mind was heavy as he rode up to the survivors. Still mounted, they were talking excitedly and laughing.

"What's so funny?" Brick demanded.

"We were just listening to Jessie tell his story, that's all," said Tank.

"What story?" Brick's eyes swung to Jessie.

Jessie stammered a little "No—nothing. Just talking about how crazy that whole fight was."

"Oh, come on, Jessie," Troy urged. "Tell Brick. Tell him why you can barely sit still in that saddle."

"Yeah, Jessie," Brick said. "Tell me why you're so excited."

Jessie swallowed hard. "I was just saying that I'm gonna be famous, that's all."

"How you figure?"

"Well, I mean, I'm the man who killed Jim Borden. That's gonna carry some weight."

"No, you're not."

"Whaddaya mean, Brick? You were there; you saw me. I . . ."

There was a loud crack, and Jessie fell from his horse. The members of the gang scrambled to grab their guns and only then noticed that Brick had already drawn his. There was a thin trail of smoke lifting from the barrel.

"You're the dead man that killed Jim Borden," Brick said flatly to Jessie's corpse.

"Brick, you shot Jessie!" Troy was confused. "Why? Why'd you do that? He was one of us."

"He shot Jim, and he shot him in the back."

"He was our brother. You can't just kill a brother; we have a code. We're family."

"We're not family, Troy. Jim was my family. And Colt is my family, and he almost got killed today, too, because of us. I'm done."

"What do you mean, you're done?"

"It's over. I'm finished. There's no more Brotherhood." Brick kept his gun in his hand, resting on his saddle horn.

"You don't get to make that decision by yourself. We've all got a stake in this!"

"Troy, we lost nine men today. And for what? A couple of hundred dollars? Money won't bring them back. You say we're family, do any of you even know if those men had families? Do you know where they were from?"

There was silence from the group.

"They're coming for us, Troy. The tycoons and the capitalists aren't gonna take it anymore. That Pinkerton was just the beginning. They'll keep raising the reward until someone gets us."

Troy glared at him. "You ain't never been a coward, Brick," he said between grit teeth. "Not from that first day in the schoolyard. Never figured you'd turn one now."

"I'm not a coward, Troy. Just trying to live as long as I can."

"That ain't long for you!" a rider shouted, pulling his gun. Brick shot the weapon from his hand, and the cowboy yelled in pain before the other members even knew what had happened.

"Anyone else wanna take their shot?"

The only sound from the group was that of the wounded cowboy cursing and moaning.

"I thought we could maybe end this peacefully and just go our own ways, but it looks like that might not be a possibility, so I'm gonna need each of you boys to throw your guns in the dirt over there and step down from your horses."

Nobody moved. "You can't take us all, no matter how fast you are," Tank snarled.

"Maybe not, but I noticed you just threw the words out there and didn't bother trying to skin your pistol, Tank. Worried that I might get you?"

"You dirty son of a bitch." Troy threw his gun in the dirt and dismounted. The others followed suit. "You won't get far. We're coming for you."

"I would expect nothing less. Hey, you with the busted hand. Pick up those guns and bring them over here, and then gather those horses, too."

"You bastard! You can't leave us here with no weapons or horses." Troy was seething.

Brick smiled. "Now, you see, Troy? You should have paid better attention in school because I *can* leave you here. What you meant to say was I *won't* leave you here emptyhanded, and you're right." He took a coiled length of rope from his saddlebag, tied it around one of the guns, and threw the gun over one of the limbs of the cottonwood tree. It dangled eight feet in the air above the heads of the men. He leaned over and tied it off on a broken branch lower down and then turned his attention to the wounded man again. "Okay, Stumpy, your turn again." He tossed the cowboy a second, longer rope from his saddlebag. "Tie it around our friends here. Get 'em bunched up nice and close so we get it good and tight. Wrap it around a few times. There you go, now tie it off. Cinch it up good. Okay, now get on the ground."

Once the wounded man was lying down, Brock dismounted, tied the man's hands and feet, and then mounted Lightning again. All the while, his former friends were cussing him out.

"Now, it may take you a while to get yourselves free, but when you do, you can get yourselves that gun. Your horses will be farther down the road here on the way to Brela. I suspect you boys can use the walk to do yourselves some thinking. It has been a pleasure riding with you men. We had some good times. It's too bad it had to end like this." He gave Lightning a slap, and the horse bolted, with the others following.

Brick rode as fast as he could with four horses in tow. He knew he wouldn't have much time before the men were free, and he believed Pretty Boy when he said that they would come for him.

He came upon another cottonwood and tied the four

horses to it. He then gave Lightning a kick and said, "We gotta go, boy."

He headed for Brela as fast as he could. Lightning was anxious and kept pulling at the bit, so Brick let him have his way. They left a trail of dust behind them as they sped across the prairie, headed for town.

Brick's thoughts were on Ruby. He had to get to her before Troy and the gang did. The men's fight was with him, but he wouldn't put it past Troy to use Ruby to get to him. They had been friends for a while now, but Troy had always had a hard side that Brick was wary of.

He came into town like a bat out of hell and went straight to the saloon. He jumped off Lightning and blew through the doors. "Ruby! Ruby! Where are you?" He looked frantically for her but did not see her.

A young brunette came up to him and put her hand on his shoulder. "Calm down, Brick. What's all the commotion? Come over to the bar and get yourself a drink."

"Not now, Simone. Where's Ruby?"

"She's upstairs, of course. Where else? What's going on?"

Brick pushed past Simone and went upstairs, yelling for Ruby. He kicked open her bedroom door with his gun drawn. A startled cowboy jumped up off the bed. Ruby was standing half-dressed in the middle of the room.

"Brick! What are you doing here?'

"Get dressed. We gotta go. Now."

The cowboy butted in. "Look, mister, I don't know who you are, but I paid to spend some time with this little lady, and I'm gonna do just that."

Brick smashed the cowboy's nose with the barrel of his gun. The man fell to the floor, screaming, blood gushing from his face. "This here is my girl, so shut your mouth or be prepared to draw."

"Brick! You know what I do; you've never had a problem before."

"It's not about that right now, honey. Please get dressed. We gotta go."

"Go where?"

"Listen, mister," the man on the floor moaned, "I didn't know she was your girl. I was just . . ."

"Shut up." Brick turned his attention to Ruby again. "Quickly, darlin', please!" He went to the dresser by the window and opened the drawers. "You gotta pack. Where's your suitcase?"

"I'm not leaving until you tell me where we're going and why we're leaving so fast." Ruby sat down on the bed.

Brick was getting frustrated. "I did it, okay? I left The Brotherhood."

Ruby jumped up with excitement. "You mean it? You really did it?" She wrapped her arms around him.

Brick tried to pry her off. "Yes, I really did it, and the boys aren't too happy about the way I left. We really need to leave. Please, darlin', pack your things."

Ruby started to pack as fast as she could. The cowboy on the floor spoke again. "You were in The Brotherhood?" he said. His voice was shaky.

"In it? He ran the Brotherhood," Ruby offered as she packed.

The cowboy's eyes grew wide with fear.

Brick looked out the window. He could see a cloud of dust in the distance. That would be Troy and the boys coming for him. By the size of the cloud, they were coming hard.

"Look, mister, I . . . I didn't know that you were running

The Brotherhood. My apologies. Let me make it up to you. Please. Don't kill me."

"Jesus, you're still here?" Brick stared at the cowboy. He was about to hit him again just for being stupid when an idea crossed his mind. "You want to make it up to me?"

"Yes, sir, I surely do," the cowboy pleaded.

Brick grabbed him by the collar and dragged him to the window. "You got a horse? Which one?"

The cowboy pointed. "The little chestnut sorrel tied up right there."

"That horse is mine now, understand? Saddle too. Then you can call us even."

"But I need my horse. How am I gonna leave town when I need to?"

Brick raised his gun ever so slightly.

The cowboy swallowed hard. "She's yours. I suppose this here is a nice enough place. I can stay for a few more days."

Brick grabbed Ruby by the wrist. "We gotta go, darlin'. Say thanks to the nice man for your new horse."

"Thank you!" Ruby yelled through a smile as she was pulled from the room.

They left the saloon, and Brick helped Ruby up onto the sorrel before mounting Lightning. He took a look; the dust cloud was a lot closer. "Hang on, darlin'. We're gonna have to ride hard for a bit and put some ground between us and this place."

"Where are we going to go?"

"I don't know yet. For now, away." He slapped the sorrel and gave Lightning a kick. The duo left town and headed into the prairie, not knowing where.

THE MEMBERS of The Brotherhood rode into Brela and went looking for Brick. The man Brick had wounded headed for the town doctor while Troy, Tank, and a third member made their way to the saloon. If they couldn't find Brick, maybe they could find Ruby, and that would be enough to draw Brick out.

Troy burst through the saloon doors in a fighting mood. He couldn't believe that Brick had had the nerve to do what he did, and he was ready to kill him himself, history or no history. "Where the hell is Brick Warner or Ruby Munchin?"

The force with which he yelled the words made all the saloon activity come to a stop as everyone froze and stared at the doorway.

"I want Warner, and I want him now!" Troy bellowed again.

Simone approached Troy as she had Brick moments earlier. "Troy, why don't you sit down and have a drink?"

"Where's Brick, Simone?"

"He ain't here. I ain't seen him all night," Simone lied.

Troy raised his right hand and brought the back of it down across Simone's cheek, knocking her to the floor. "Don't lie to me. I know he was coming here. Where's his whore?"

A cowboy stood and tried to come to Simone's defense. Troy drew his gun and fired a bullet into the man's chest before he even knew what was happening. Simone crawled over to his sprawled body. "He's dead!" she yelled at Troy. "Dead! And for what? They ain't here! I told you that, you bastard!"

"Where were they headed?"

"I don't know. Nobody does. I doubt they know where

they're going. They blew out of here a few minutes before you showed up. Now get the hell out of here, you son of a bitch!"

Troy was about to hit her again for her insolence when there was a thunderous report from across the room, and the door frame above his head spit splinters everywhere. He looked in the direction the shot had come from and saw the bartender staring at him from behind a double-barreled shotgun. "Don't you hit her again, Troy. She still has to work. She told you to leave, and I think you should go. I got one barrel left, and this gun is getting heavy. Maybe next time, I can't aim as high as I did."

Troy and his gang backed out of the saloon. Once outside, Troy spoke to the third cowboy. "Curly, you stay here with Bill. Once he's out of the doc's, you guys hunker down here and keep your eyes open in case they double back. Tank and I are going after Brick. We're gonna finish this right."

Troy and Tank rode out of town in the direction they thought Brick must have gone. It was hard to see in the growing darkness, but they tracked as well as they could. With every mile they covered, Troy's anger grew wilder.

BRICK AND RUBY were still riding hard. Brick wasn't sure if Troy would try to follow them in the dark, but he didn't want to take any chances. Troy was motivated by anger, and Brick guessed that the whole situation had given him enough fuel for a good while.

The ride was taking a toll on Ruby; she was getting tired. They rode until Brick found a place where he thought they could make camp and still keep watch for anyone trailing them.

It was a small hill with some cottonwoods on the left end and some small bushes on the right. Tall grass around the area provided additional cover.

There was an abandoned fox den in the side of the hill. Using his hands and some sharp stones he found, Brick dug at the den until he had enlarged it enough for Ruby to lie in and get some sleep. He built a small fire to offer a little additional heat and, following advice Jim had given them, cut some branches from the cottonwood and built a sort of lean-to or teepee above the flames to hide them from view and dissipate the smoke, making it harder to see than one thick plume, especially in the dark. Brick knew it wouldn't keep them hidden forever, but Troy and the gang would be slowed in the dark, and maybe this would buy enough time for Ruby and the horses to rest. He sat with his back against the hill, off in the shadows, staring out into the darkness, careful not to stare directly at the flames of his fire.

Another lesson from Jim. He told them that if they were staring into the flames and then they heard something in the darkness, it would take time for their eyes to adjust to seeing in the black again, and those few seconds could be the difference between life and death.

Sitting there in the dark, thinking about Jim, Brick felt incredibly lonely. Even with Ruby sleeping just a few feet away, the loneliness felt so large that it almost physically hurt. It was overwhelming.

He was deep inside his head when he heard rustling in the dark. He spit quietly onto the ground as he stared into the blackness. Troy had found them faster than he thought he would.

He held his breath and listened intently. He heard what he thought was quiet whispering, and he carefully raised his gun, slowly exhaled, and fired in the general direction of the whispers. There was a loud cry of "Jesus Christ!" followed by frantic rustling.

Brick rolled quickly to his left. The shot had startled Ruby, and she had awakened with a scream. Brick put his hand across her mouth and motioned for her to move to the shadows on the right. The cry hadn't been one of pain, so he knew he hadn't hit anyone, but he was close enough that it had startled them. Brick had no idea how many were out there, but he guessed at most three since the man whose hand he had shot would have required medical attention.

"Brick!" The yell came out of the blackness. "Brick! I told you we were coming for you!" It was Pretty Boy. "That was a pretty good shot right there, almost parted Tank's hair for him. I'll make you a deal, Brick. You give up right now, and we'll leave Ruby alone. She can go back to Brela, and we won't bother her none."

Ruby squeezed Brick's arm and stared at him with eyes as big as saucers. She shook her head *no* in a panic. Brick reassured her and made sure she stayed sitting quietly where she was. The men had scrambled when Brick had fired, and that meant they had taken their eyes off him and currently were not sure where he and Ruby were.

Troy yelled again. "Come on, Brick. It's a good deal. You're not getting out of this one. Come out now, and it'll be quick. Make me wait, and I promise it will be much, much worse."

There was a gunshot, and a bullet hit the side of the hill about four feet to the right of them. Ruby jumped a little, and Brick restrained her. He knew the shot was just a test; the men had no idea where they were yet. He also knew that there could be another test shot coming, and if they chose to move to their left instead of their right, they would hit either Ruby or himself.

Brick looked around, trying to find a way out. Their horses were hitched on the other side of the den and were starting to get antsy with all the gunplay. In order to reach them, they would have to run directly across the mouth of the den and through the light of the fire, making themselves easy targets.

Brick removed a handful of bullets from his gun belt and threw them into the fire. The wait for the fire to heat the bullets up enough to set them off seemed to take forever. Troy kept yelling, and another shot hit the hill, but closer to the horses. They had chosen the wrong direction, and Brick was grateful.

Suddenly, the bullets reached the desired heat and began firing from inside the fire. Hoping the men in the dark would be scrambling for cover, Brick yelled, "Run!" and pushed Ruby towards the horses. He fired into the dark as they crossed the mouth of the den. Only one shot came back from the men; it slammed into the hill directly behind Brick. He quickly untied the horses, and they rode off with Brick firing back into the dark, trying to keep their pursuers at bay.

Angry screams and gunshots sounded behind them as they rode away at a gallop. Little plumes of dust kicked up as random bullets hit the ground around them.

Then a bullet slammed into Brick's left shoulder, throwing him over his saddle horn. He grabbed the horn tightly with his right hand to keep from falling off the speeding horse. Ruby let out a yell as she, too, caught a bullet in the left calf. Brick yelled at her to hold on as they kept galloping across the prairie.

The moon, full and bright and high in the sky, gave them some light to see their path. Brick didn't know where they were going, but he knew they had to keep riding. Riding at such a pace across unknown land in the dark was a good way to get yourself or your horse injured or killed, but Brick knew that if they stopped, Troy and the gang would be on them in no time, and that meant certain death.

Both he and Ruby were injured and needed some attention before they went much farther, but they couldn't slow down. Brick turned the horses toward a group of hills he knew to be east of them. Like the hills that concealed The Brotherhood's hideout, these hills were small but held a maze-like series of canyons. The gang knew of the hills as well, of course, but Brick figured they might be able to lose them in the canyons long enough to tend to their wounds and rest the horses.

They entered the hills and made a series of quick, zig-zagging turns through different passes to disguise their trail. After a few minutes, they came to a box canyon with a sheer rock wall on one side. With only one way in, it provided them a place to rest where they could monitor any activity at the entrance. Unfortunately, one way in also meant one way out. If they were discovered, they would have to shoot their way out, and he only had one good arm.

They dismounted, and Brick looked at Ruby. She was young, a child really, just like him, but she was tough. She had lived a hard life, and it had given her grit, something other women didn't have. It was one of the things that had attracted him. If some of the girls he had gone to school with were in this situation, on the run with a bullet in their leg, they would have folded long ago, but Ruby hadn't said a word. She was with him until the end, no matter what that end might be, and she always had been. He was determined to get her out of this and not let her down.

"Darlin', we gotta get that bullet out of you, and I'm afraid it's not going to be easy," Brick said.

"I've seen it done in the bar a hundred times over. I'm not worried about easy."

"We need something to use as a bandage when we're done." Brick began looking in their saddlebags.

"Here." Ruby lifted her dress and pulled her slip down from under her skirt. "Use this."

Brick ripped a strip from the slip and had Ruby lie on her belly on the ground. He took his pocketknife out of his pants and stared at the hole in her calf, leaking blood down her leg. He grabbed the reins from the chestnut sorrel and handed them to Ruby. "Bite down on this, darlin'. This is gonna hurt. I'm gonna need you to stay as still as possible. I'm sorry, Ruby."

"Save your sorry and get on with it before those bastards show up." She bit down hard on the reins.

Brick dug the knife blade into the wound, trying to find the bullet. Ruby groaned loudly and bit harder on the reins. Removing the bullet would have been hard with two good hands, but with his left arm all but useless thanks to the bullet lodged in his own shoulder and the only light coming from the moon, it was even more difficult. He wasn't able to provide enough pressure to hold Ruby's leg still, and she squirmed under the pain of the knife digging into her flesh.

After a minute, Brick finally felt the blade scrape against the bullet. "Found it, baby. Just hold on one more minute." Brick pried with the knife, and Ruby groaned louder, clenching the reins in her teeth.

The bullet came to the surface, and Brick grabbed it. "Got it." Ruby relaxed and let the reins fall from her mouth. She was breathing hard. "We need something to sterilize this wound," Brick said.

"There's a flask in my bag," Ruby said between gasps. "Use that."

Brick was proud of her. He had known full-grown men in the Brotherhood who hadn't handled having a bullet removed as well as she had. He pulled the flask from the bag and prepared to pour some of the alcohol over Ruby's wound. "This is gonna sting a little. You might need those reins again."

"Just do it already."

Brick poured the alcohol and cleaned the wound. Ruby let out a little yell when the liquid touched her skin, but that was it. Brick wrapped her leg in the makeshift bandage he'd made from her slip. "That's it, all done. Okay, now you have to pull the bullet out of my shoulder."

"What? Brick, I can't."

"Yes, you can, darlin'. You're about the strongest girl I know. You can do anything you set your mind to. You're gonna do it just like I did with you." He handed Ruby the knife and flask and took off his shirt.

"I can't. I don't know how."

"You said yourself that you've seen it done a hundred times in the bar, and you just saw me do it to you. You can do this, darlin'. Now, work fast before those boys find us."

Brick put the reins between his teeth while Ruby took a deep breath. She was nervous and clumsy with the knife. Brick bit down so hard on the leather that he could feel pieces of it in his mouth. She pushed the knife down farther, and Brick was slammed with pain.

"I think I feel it," Ruby said. She pried the knife a little under his skin. "Yes! There it is, I got it!" Ruby grabbed the bullet and showed it to Brick.

Brick felt his energy drain, and his body felt tired. "Great job, darlin'. I knew you could do it. Now get some of that alcohol on there, and then help me get my shirt back on, please."

Once his shirt was on, Brick used the rest of the slip to make a sling for his arm. "We better get moving," he said. "Troy can't be too far off."

"I haven't heard them in a while. Maybe they gave up for the night?" Ruby asked hopefully.

"Doubt it," Brick replied. "Troy's too angry for that."

As if on cue, they suddenly heard the voices of Troy and Tank echoing from somewhere in the maze of canyons. Brick looked around at their surroundings. The voices sounded close to their only way out, and with his arm tied up, Brick had no chance of outshooting two men. The wall behind them was sheer rock, too steep for the horses to climb, but off to one end, it looked like there might be a trail.

He walked the horses over for a closer look. It was a thin trail that followed a slight ridge in the wall. It wasn't much, and it was still steep, but it was their only hope to escape. "Okay, darlin', this is where we're gonna go. This is our way out."

"Where? I don't see anything."

"The trail is there. The horses will follow it; we're just gonna have to move slow and steady, that's all."

He started Lightning up the trail. Holding the reins was difficult with his bad arm, but he needed the good hand free in case he had to shoot. The horse moved gingerly but kept pressing forward.

Ruby's horse followed Lightning up the trail. They were about halfway up when they saw the men enter the canyon below them, dim figures in the moonlight. Brick slowed the horses as he watched Troy and Tank mill around. The dark provided some cover as they gradually made their way to the top of the canyon. There was confusion below; Brick's former friends couldn't understand how they had lost their two enemies, especially when they were wounded.

Then Ruby's horse slipped on the trail and knocked some loose rocks down the slope. The noise caught the attention of Troy, who looked up and saw the pair making their escape. He let out a yell, and he and Tank both opened fire. Ruby's horse let out a loud whinny as a bullet entered its stomach. Then it fell to its left, Ruby just managing to jump clear before the weight of the animal fell on her leg and trapped her.

"Ruby!" Brick yelled, stopping Lightning. He reached his good hand out for her. It was hard to balance in the saddle as he tried to hold on with his wounded arm while she grabbed his hand, but he managed to pull her up behind them. Then he took a chance and dug in his heels to move Lightning up the narrow trail faster. Lightning once more proved that he came from superior stock, navigating the narrow trail at speed with ease. It wasn't long until they were out of the canyon and galloping at full pace across the prairie again.

Even as tired as he was, Lightning was willing to run and carried on through the dark of night. Unless they were willing to risk the same trail that they had just used, it was going to take Troy and Tank some time to work their way out of the maze and pick up their tracks again.

Brick slowed Lightning to a trot after some time, and they relaxed in the saddle, finally having a chance to breathe and think about what their next move might be. Ruby, arms around Brick, started to cry softly, squeezing him tightly.

"It's okay, darlin'," he said. "We're gonna be all right."

"I know. I trust you."

"Are you hurt?"

"No. Nothing but my leg."

Brick was confused; he had never seen Ruby cry. "Why the tears, then?"

Ruby wiped her eyes with her sleeve. "I've never owned a horse before. I can't believe he's gone already."

Brick laughed. Ruby hit him in his ribs for laughing at her and then started to chuckle herself. "We'll get you another one, darlin'," Brick said. "That much I can promise you."

"Where are we gonna go, Brick? Troy's just gonna keep coming."

"We're going to the only place where you can be safe, and we can get some help."

"Where's that?"

"We're going to the Whistlestop. We're going to see Colt."

Chapter 22

Colt sat astride Thunder on the crest of the ridge, staring down at the Whistlestop. He couldn't believe he was returning without Jim but with his body in tow. He paused and thought about all the work he and Jim had done to build the ranch. His eyes prickled, but before tears could well up, Thunder, anxious to get home and knowing he was almost there, moved restlessly, snapping Colt back to the moment. "All right, boy, I get it. Let's go home and break the news to everyone."

They rode down the hill and into the yard. Sadie, emerging from the house and excited to see Colt returning, started to run toward him but stopped when she saw the body draped across Pete.

Ridge joined her in the yard. "That Borden?" he asked.

Colt nodded.

"Oh, Colt." Sadie's eyes filled with tears.

"Where's James?" Colt asked, looking past her at the house.

Sadie wiped her eyes with her apron. "Sound asleep. He'll be so excited you're home!"

"How'd it happen?" Ridge asked.

Colt glanced back at the body. "Shot in the back by a lousy no-good dry-gulcher."

"Damn. That's a shame. Jim was a good man; he deserved a fair fight, at least. Any idea who it was?"

Colt nodded again. "Jessie Mitchell."

"Jessie?" Sadie's eyes were wide with shock. "He's not like that, Colt. Jessie was gentle, almost timid. I don't believe it."

"Believe it, Sadie. I was there. It was Jessie."

By this time, the rest of the ranch hands had joined them, and Colt relayed the entire story, from Brela and Webb Logan to Bullard and the bank robbery.

"That's it," Colt said as he finished. "Brick is still with The Brotherhood, and Jim is dead, so it was a complete failure. I should never have gone; I should have just stayed and dealt with the ranch."

Sadie wrapped her arms around him. "Oh, Colt, it's not your fault," she said. "You were trying to help Brick, and Jim was trying to help you. He loved you both."

Colt looked at the group. "We'll bury Jim tomorrow. Lanky, can you get into town and bring Drake out? He'd want to be here for this. Bring Reverend Sullivan, too."

"On my way, Colt."

"Ridge, what did you find out about that other matter you were looking into?"

"It wasn't the Modocs' fault, Colt. Someone else got them all riled up first."

"Who?"

Ridge shuffled his feet and looked at Sadie before he answered.

"It's all right, Ridge," Colt said. "She's a partner in this. She needs to know what's going on."

"It was Sterling Walcott," Ridge said. "He told the Indians that you were coming for them. That you wanted whatever land they still had for yourself and that you had a strict shoot-on-sight rule for all your ranch hands. If they saw an Indian, they were to put them down, and you'd pay five dollars for every dead Indian they showed you."

"Daddy?" Sadie was shocked again. "Why would Daddy say something as awful as that? That's just not true."

"It's true, Sadie," Ridge continued. "You're not going to have to worry about a war with the Indians, though, Colt. I spoke to some of the Modoc, and that chief that came to visit you that morning was impressed with the way you treated their dead with the same respect as your own. He figured any man that would do that couldn't be the way Walcott described. He told his braves to stay away from here. You won't have to worry about them."

"Well, that's something, anyway," Colt responded. "Still have to worry about damn Walcott, though."

"Why, Colt? Why do we have to worry about Daddy?" Sadie asked.

"He wants the Whistlestop, Sadie. He wants our land and our cattle and wants me off it."

"But I'm his daughter! I can't believe that he would want to do something that would hurt me so deeply."

"I'm afraid it's true, Sadie," Alex interjected. "I was with Colt and Jim in town when your father offered to buy the Whistlestop from Colt and then threatened him when he wouldn't sell."

Ridge turned to watch Lanky as he rode out of the yard. "You're gonna have to worry about Walcott sooner rather than later, Colt. After his Indian plan failed, Walcott was fit to be tied. You can bet that he's coming and that he's coming with an army."

"Hopefully, he waits until I get Jim buried. Deal with one problem at a time. Ridge, can you and Lane take Jim to the barn until tomorrow and get the grave dug so we can lower him into it tomorrow? Oh, and get poor Pete here looked after? He ain't been right the whole trip back. He knows something's wrong. I gotta get Thunder taken care of, and then I think I need some time to myself for a bit."

"Sure thing, Colt."

The group dispersed, but Alex grabbed Colt by the arm as he started to walk away. Colt sighed and faced him. "What is it, Alex?"

"Colt, I just wanted to say how sorry I am about Jim. I know what he meant to you. If you need to talk sometime, any time at all, you know where to find me."

"Thanks, Alex. I'll be all right. Just need some time."

Colt took Thunder to the corral, removed his saddle, and gave him a rub-down and a helping of oats. Then he went back to the house, gave Sadie a hug, kissed his sleeping son on the cheek, and headed out on a walk. He eventually made his way up the mountain to his cave and stood at the mouth of it, staring out over the Whistlestop laid out below him. The ranch was everything he had ever wanted and everything he had worked for, but he could feel it slowly slipping away. What could he do? He had done everything the right way, worked hard, paid attention, learned his lessons, and it still wasn't enough. Brick was still gone, Jim was dead, and his ranch was on its last legs with the vultures circling and ready to pounce. He was at the bottom and couldn't see a way to get out.

Maybe he should just give the ranch to Walcott. The man had said that he would let Sadie and James live with him, that they would be taken care of. If he was going down, he didn't want to take his family with him. They deserved better. He could find work elsewhere, maybe with Shep again. Maybe save up enough to start another ranch in time. But then what? Start the same fight all over with Walcott because he had land again?

He stood on the ledge, staring for a long time, until, suddenly, he snapped back to reality. The land he was staring at was his. He'd worked for it, he owned it, and he wasn't about to let anybody take it away from him. This was where Jim would be buried, and nobody would keep that from him.

Colt could feel the fight brewing inside him. He was going to stand up for his family and for himself. If they were all he had, then he was going to hold on to them with all he could muster.

A thought came to him, one he needed to discuss with Alex. He was headed back down the mountain when he saw the bulky silhouette of a rider appear on the ridge. As the horse headed down the slope, he realized it wasn't one rider but two on one horse, a man, and a woman.

He looked closer. And then, he started to run.

The pair were met in the yard by Lane Trotter. "What can we help you folks with?" Lane asked cautiously.

"I'm looking for Colt Warner," The man said.

"Yeah? Who's asking?"

"We are. Me and the lady."

"And just who the hell are you?" Lane's hand was moving slowly toward his hip.

"Brick!" Sadie yelled from the porch. She ran down the

steps toward the pair. "Brick! My goodness, it's been so long. How have you been? Oh, the two of you are hurt. Are you okay?"

"Hello, Sadie. A little worse for wear, but we're okay."

"You know these folks, Sadie?" asked Lane.

"Well, of course I do. I mean, one of them, anyway. This is Brick. He's Colt's brother. Brick Warner, are you gonna introduce us to your friend like a proper gentleman or not?"

Brick chuckled as he dismounted Lightning and helped Ruby down. "Okay, Sadie, just give me a minute. Miss Sadie Walco—excuse me, Miss Sadie Warner, this here is Miss Ruby Munchin. She's my girl."

"Well, it's a real pleasure to meet you, Ruby."

"Same for me. You have a real lovely ranch, Sadie. It's beautiful."

"Why, thank you, Ruby. These boys here do a real good job of keeping it that way."

"What are you doing here, Brick?" Colt's voice came from behind the group.

The others fell silent as the two brothers stared at one another.

Brick spoke first. "Hey, Colt."

"I asked what you're doing here?"

"I did it, Colt. I left The Brotherhood."

Sadie was excited. "Really? Oh, Brick, that's wonderful."

"Just like that?" Colt's voice was steely.

"Just like that. I didn't want what happened to Jim. After he was shot, I couldn't get your voice out of my head. About family and all that. You were right, Colt. So, I left."

"They just let you go?"

"Not exactly. Pretty Boy and Tank are still on our tail."

"What about Jessie?"

"Jessie's dead, Colt. I shot him when I left. I was hoping that your offer was still good, and that Ruby and I might be able to stay here. At the Whistlestop. With you."

"Well, of course, you're welcome to stay. Right, Colt?" Sadie looked at Colt with a smile in her eyes.

Colt took a step toward Brick. The two brothers stood eye to eye for a long moment. Then Colt took a deep breath and said. "Of course, you can stay, Brick. Welcome home." The two shared a quick embrace. Colt straightened again and cleared his throat. "The corral is over there; you can get Lightning put away. Sadie will show Ruby the house and where you can put your stuff."

"Where's Lanky at?" asked Brick. "I haven't seen that cowpuncher in a coon's age. Thought for sure I'd see him here."

"Lanky went to get Drake. We're having Jim's service tomorrow."

"Drake! Haven't seen that one-eyed gambler in forever, either. Damn shame it's happening like this, but it will be good to see him."

"I'd introduce you to the crew here at the Whistlestop, but I think the only one you don't know is Lane. You met Ridge at Shep's, and you already know Alex and Lanky." Seeing Alex reminded Colt of the idea he had had on the mountain. "Alex, you remember that paper you gave me after we first met? That one from the steel company?"

"The shares in R.B. Higgs Steel Company. Sure. Why?"

"Didn't you say that it might be worth more if I held onto it longer?"

"As long as steel is in demand, it should grow in value. That's correct."

"Can you find out what it might be worth now? It's just

been sitting in that box in the bank, but it might be just what we need to get this place back on its feet again."

"Absolutely. I'll have to go into town, so I'll do that the day after tomorrow. That's a great idea, Colt. With the way they've been building railroads, those shares should be worth a small fortune now. I can't believe you held onto them this long."

"My advisor told me I should, so I did." Colt smiled as he put his hand on Alex's shoulder.

"How much do you need, Colt?" Brick asked.

"One thing about ranching, Brick, you can always use more."

"Well, if I'm living here now and it really is our place, then I'd like to buy in. You know, be a partner. After I watched you buy my horse, the one thing I did learn from watching you scrimp all those years was how to save. I put away some from every job we did. I thought Ruby and I might use it for our future one day. I guess our future is in ranching now. There's probably around one thousand, maybe one thousand five hundred. It's yours if you need it."

Colt thought about the conversation he'd had with Alex. Could he be all right with taking ill-gotten money to keep the Whistlestop alive? He decided that since Brick was done with The Brotherhood, and it would be a one-time thing, he could live with it. Besides, there was no way he was letting Sterling Walcott have the ranch without a fight.

"You sure you want to do that? You haven't been here long. What if you hate it? What if it's too much like life with Pa for you?"

"A man's gotta find a place to call his at some point and since I don't think I'm welcome back at my old place, that point might as well be now." Brick grinned. "Besides, if my brother can do it, how hard can it be?"

Colt laughed. "Thanks, Brick. Glad to have you on board. It's appreciated. Lane, show Brick and Ruby around, will ya? Show them everything, including the cave up the mountain. They may need to use it at some point."

"It'll take a couple of days to collect," Brick said. "I've got it stashed in a few different places, but I'll get it."

HIGH ATOP THE RIDGE, Troy Benton and Tank Jepson lay in the long grass, looking down onto the ranch. "That's him, all right," Troy whispered to Tank. "Him and his girl. I knew he'd head for his brother. Still can't handle his business by himself after all this time. Coward."

"Let's go down there and get him, Troy. Get this over with. I want to head back to our place."

"Not yet, Tank. One Warner with a gun is bad enough, but two? You've heard about Colt and his shooting. The way people talk, he may be even faster than Brick. I've sent word back. The boys will join us here tomorrow, and then we'll go get him. Get our revenge for Jessie."

The two cowboys backed slowly away from the ridge, then headed off to build their camp for the night. Troy smiled to himself, a slick, evil smile, as he thought about what tomorrow would bring, how he would finally best Brick Warner and take over The Brotherhood for himself.

"Tomorrow is your day of judgment, Brick Warner," he said out loud. "And I will be your judge and jury."

He and Tank laughed as they tended their fire.

CHAPTER 23

The next morning dawned gloomy and overcast, with a chill in the air. It was as if God and Nature both knew what the Warners' task was for the day and the burden it brought and had provided the appropriate atmosphere. Colt sat at the table, staring into his coffee cup between sips. His heart was heavy. He still found it hard to fathom that they were going to bury Jim today.

Brick and Ruby joined him at the table. Colt couldn't believe that Brick was there. It had been so long since they had shared breakfast together. "Morning, brother," said Brick.

"Morning, Brick. Ruby." Colt raised his cup to acknowledge their presence.

"Looking a little sullen outside. Could get some weather later today. You reckon it'll hold off until we get Jim buried?"

"Hope so. Depends on how long Drake and Lanky take getting here, I suppose."

No sooner had Colt said the words than there was the sound of a wagon and horses coming down the hill into the yard.

"You wait inside, Ruby," Brick said. The brothers grabbed their guns and stepped out onto the porch.

It was Lanky and Drake. They'd returned and had brought company with them: Reverend Sullivan was riding in the back of the wagon, and Shep Broxton and Ed Waters were riding their own mounts beside them.

"Damn, Lanky!" Colt called. "I expected you to be a little longer yet."

"Drake wouldn't let me linger, Colt," Lanky said. "We drove all night. I ain't slept yet."

"I wanted to get out here as soon as I heard the news, Colt," Drake said. "Couldn't believe it, and I wasn't about to let Jim Borden hit the ground without me being there to pay my respects. I found some other fellows that wanted to pay their respects, too."

Colt and Brick each said their hellos to everybody and thanked them for coming out, and Brick called out Ruby and introduced her around.

"Where's your lady, Colt?" Shep asked.

"Still asleep with James," Colt said. "You'll see her later."

Drake spoke again. "You boys popped out here with guns in hand. Expecting trouble, Colt?"

"It's possible. Brick has made a few enemies, and I hear Sterling Walcott is none too happy with me."

Drake glanced back up the hill. "Well, then," he said, "you should know that last night, we saw a couple of fellas camped off the trail a little way, back in behind some bushes. They were keeping their fire low like they were trying not to be seen. You're the only place out here for a few miles. I was just wondering if they might be headed this way."

"Troy Benton was one of them, Colt," Lanky said. "I recognized his horse."

"That's my trouble," said Brick. "They're looking for me."

"Well, I'm glad you fellows showed up early." Colt glanced up at the sky. "Maybe we can get Jim laid to rest before the weather changes for the worse."

"What do you wanna do about Pretty Boy?" asked Lanky.

"Nothing. There are only two of them. They'd have to be half crazy to try anything with all of us here today. Let's have some coffee, maybe a little breakfast for you guys, give Jim our respects, and worry about Troy and Tank later."

By the time they all got into the house, Sadie was up, and James was toddling around, getting underfoot and greeting everyone. Sadie and Ruby served up some food while everyone sat and talked, swapping their best Jim Borden stories and laughing fondly as they remembered their fallen friend.

After breakfast, Colt changed his clothes and rejoined the group wearing all black. He had combed his hair, and he cut an impressive figure standing there in front of everyone.

"Whooeee, Colt. You've grown into a full-on man," Drake said. "Jim would be so proud of you."

Sadie wrapped her arms around Colt's waist. "You definitely are a handsome man, Mr. Warner."

Colt could feel himself blushing from Sadie's comment in front of all his friends. "All right, well, let's get the service underway before the rain hits."

Alex entered the room with a look of shock on his face. "Colt, you need to see this."

Colt walked out the door with the others following him. Once in the yard, Alex pointed up towards the ridge.

A group of riders had gathered there. Trying to count silhouettes, Colt guessed thirteen or fourteen. They were just sitting atop their horses, staring into the yard.

"Troy and the gang?" asked Brick.

"Nope." Ridge was using his spyglass to see the riders on the ridge. "Looks like Sterling Walcott and some of his men. I count fifteen in total, including Walcott."

"What do you wanna do, Colt?"

"We're gonna put Jim to rest like we planned. If they wanna sit and watch us do it, that's just fine with me. Maybe if the rain shows up, that'll change their minds, and they'll go home."

Up on the ridge, Sterling Walcott was having a debate of his own. Word of Borden's death had spread around Monroe. He had only brought a handful of men with him, expecting to see four men occupying the ranch. The additional men down there had drastically altered the odds, even if they were a one-eyed gambler, a rancher, and a livery owner. They still had trigger fingers, and they could still point guns. The incoming weather could pose a problem.

Sterling had to decide if it was worth the risk to try to take the ranch today or if they should retreat, regroup, and come back with more men at a later date. Not having Jim Borden down there was a blessing, to be sure, but that damn Colt Warner was pretty handy with his pistols. Walcott hadn't forgotten the standoff the last time he was at the ranch. Warner had had his pistol drawn before he had even seen him make a move.

"What do you wanna do, Boss?" asked one of Walcott's men.

"We'll let them have their funeral. Jim Borden deserves at least that much. We'll make a decision after the service."

"I think we can take them now. I don't think they know we're here. We can surprise 'em."

"That's why I pay you to watch cattle and not to think. They know we're here, all right. They're waiting to see what our next move will be."

While he himself considered his next move, Walcott heard riders coming up behind him and turned in his saddle to see a group of about ten riders emerging from the bushes. As they got closer, Walcott thought he recognized the leader. "Aren't you that Benton boy? Henry Benton's son?"

"Yes, sir, Mr. Walcott. Name's Troy."

"Right, Troy Benton. Friend of the Warners. Went to school with them." Walcott saw his chance of taking the ranch slipping away. An additional ten men put his group at a disadvantage. The odds had shifted greatly.

"Went to school with them, but I ain't no friend of the Warner family anymore, I can assure you."

Suddenly, Walcott's odds had shifted again. If he and this group of ten joined forces, that put the Warner group on the defensive once more. "Not a friend, you say? What's your business with the Warners, then?"

Troy gritted his teeth. "Brick and us have some unfinished business that we're aiming to finish."

"Brick Warner is down there, too?"

Walcott hadn't planned on that. He had heard that the younger Warner was almost as fast as Colt when it came to gunplay, although he had never seen it himself. Another experienced gunman could pose a problem. He was going to need all the help he could muster.

"Well, then, Mr. Benton. Let's you and I have a little chat. I believe that we have some business we can conduct together. I will make it worth your while for you and your men."

DOWN ON THE RANCH, the service was taking place. Ridge leaned over to Colt and whispered to him. "You been watching that ridge, Colt? Lot more men up there now."

Colt whispered back, "I've been watching. Looks like Pretty Boy and Tank have arrived with their men, too."

"That ain't good news, boss. Twenty men to nine is two-to-one odds."

"I like our nine, Ridge. And it looks closer to twenty-five, not twenty."

"That don't make me happier, Colt. I wasn't planning on ending up beside old Jim here today."

The service wrapped up, and Jim was lowered into the grave the boys had dug the day before. Each of the men took turns on the shovel, burying their friend and saying their last goodbyes. Just as they had finished filling in the grave, there was a large crack of thunder, and the sky opened up, pouring rain down on them. It came fast, and it came hard—no light drizzle but a strong downpour. It was hard to see anybody through the sheets of rain.

Sadie and Ruby took James and ran for the ranch house while the men gathered at the bunkhouse.

"They're still up there, Colt," Brick said.

"Hopefully, this rain changes their mind—but if I know Walcott, he's gonna see this as his best chance. He's not gonna want to wait. This is it, boys. Let's get a plan together and save the Whistlestop. Here's how we'll set things up. And Brick... I'm giving you the most important job of all."

ON THE RIDGE, Sterling Walcott decided that there was no time like the present. With the addition of Troy Benton's men, he felt he had a force large enough to accomplish his goal. The driving rain complicated matters, but he had already come this far and did not want to leave empty-handed. "Here we go, men. Let's take this ranch. Any man that shoots my daughter or grandson had best keep riding cuz if I catch you, you will suffer like nothing you can imagine. Mind your bullets; hit your targets. There's a handsome payday for all of you when this is over. Let's go!"

Walcott fired his rifle into the air, and the men started their stampede down the hill and into the ranch yard, weapons blazing.

Colt and his men were waiting for them and returned fire on the hard-charging band. As Wolcott's men and The Brotherhood entered the ranch yard, they split off in all directions.

At Colt's instructions, Ridge and Lanky had flipped the wagon in the yard onto its side before the attack began and squeezed off shot after shot toward the marauders. The air was thick with rain and smoke. The sound was deafening as lead crashed into wood, glass shattered, six-shooters belched, and thunder clapped.

Colt had positioned himself behind a water barrel at the side of the bunk house. He had both pistols drawn and was firing at the riders stampeding through the yard. Water splashed into his face as bullets slammed into the barrel, but it didn't make much difference in the rain. The rain didn't affect his aim, either: his revolver barked, and a rider lurched in his saddle and then fell from his horse to the mud below.

Splinters spewed from the wall above Colt's head as a bullet struck the building. Colt fired another shot, and another rider was knocked from his horse to the ground below.

As the attack began, Brick ran into the ranch house to get Ruby, Sadie, and James to safety. He'd wanted to stay and fight, but Colt had begged him to take care of their women and the boy. "It won't matter if we save the ranch if anything happens to them," he'd said. Reluctantly, Brick had agreed.

Now he found them huddled in one of the bedrooms. Sadie had her hands over James's ears. "Come on, ladies, nephew, let's get you out of here. We'll go to the mountain cave; get you out of the line of fire."

As he helped Ruby to her feet, he heard a rustle behind him and wheeled with his weapon leveled. Staring back at him was the Reverend, whose hands shot into the air.

"Sorry, Preacher." Brick lowered his weapon. "Keep your head down. Don't want you meeting the Big Guy just yet." Sadie hadn't moved. "Come on, Sadie. We've got to go."

Sadie shook her head. "I'm not going anywhere, Brick. This is my home, and if my husband is staying, then so am I."

"Sadie, please. Colt will kill me if he finds out I left you here."

"I'm not leaving, Brick." She handed James to Ruby. "Take my son. Keep him safe."

Ruby took the child, who immediately began to cry and reach back for his mother. She stared wide-eyed at Brick.

"Okay. Let's go, darlin'." He looked at Sadie one last time. "Stay away from the walls, keep your head down. Stay low. You stay alive, you hear me?"

"I hear you. You keep my son safe."

Brick flung the front door open and fired out into the chaos. He grabbed Ruby's arm, and the two moved to the edge of the porch. Brick hopped the rail, took James from Ruby, and waited for her to jump the rail as well. As she struggled, her wounded leg still stiff and tender, a bullet slammed into the wall just inches from her head. Brick wheeled, firing as he did so. One of the members of The Brotherhood put a hand to his chest as blood spewed from his mouth. He fell to the ground.

Ruby hit the ground. Brick handed her the child and grabbed her hand, and together they ran as best they could for the path up the mountain behind Alex's house.

Alex had made it into his house when the shooting started. He saw Brick, Ruby, and James heading for the mountain, smashed out a window, and laid down covering fire for the pair, giving them time to get behind the house and have some shelter as they headed up toward the cave.

Alex's shooting practice had paid off. He wasn't fast on the draw yet but was a very accurate shot. Every bullet he fired hit its mark. Dead and wounded men lay all over the yard now.

Lane Trotter had chosen not to take cover, instead opting to stay free and keep moving. It was a strategy that had paid off to start with, as he was able to move through the chaos with relative ease, firing at will.

His luck finally ran out when he was cornered by two members of The Brotherhood. Lane took a bullet in his left thigh and fell to the muddy ground. Tank Jepson approached him while he lay there and stood over him, gun leveled at his chest. "Nothing against you, mister," Tank snarled. "You just chose the wrong side."

Suddenly, his chest exploded, spinning him around before he, too, fell. Mud, blood, and water splashed as the body hit the ground.

Lane rolled over to see Drake running toward him with his

pistol out, ready to fire again if needed. "C'mon, let's get you out of here," Drake said as he reached him. "Can you stand?"

Lane tried to get to his feet but fell back into the muck. "I don't think so."

Drake grabbed him by his collar and dragged him through the slop, but then took a bullet to his left shoulder and dropped to one knee. He fired back at his assailant, killing him instantly, and then forced himself to stand again. He continued to drag Lane with one good arm, and they both took cover behind the water trough.

"Thanks. I owe you my life," Lane said.

"Don't thank me yet," Drake responded. "We aren't out of this. I may have just delayed your departure a little bit." Both men tried to tend to their wounds while still firing at their invaders as best they could.

Pretty Boy Troy had been looking for Brick since the start of the attack. Visibility was poor in the rain, and he hadn't found him yet. The longer it took, the angrier he became.

A bullet whizzed by his waist and pierced his duster. Troy looked to see where the shot had come from and saw Shep Broxton with his gun pointed at him. In a fit of rage, Troy fired at Shep, hitting him in the right arm, then charged forward. He was on Shep before the man knew what had happened and brought the barrel of his gun down across the right side of Shep's head, knocking him to the ground unconscious.

As he looked for another enemy to shoot, Troy caught sight of Brick and Ruby heading up the mountain. He bared his teeth in a fierce grin. "Run all you want, Brick Warner!" he shouted into the rain. "Today is the day you die!" He, too, headed for the mountain.

Colt surveyed the yard. The fight was petering out as more and more men fell injured or dead. Ridge and Lanky were pinned down behind their overturned wagon, and Colt saw Lanky take a bullet and hit the ground. He leaped from his cover to run to them and help Ridge.

Suddenly, there was a crushing blow to his jaw and a blinding light in his head. Colt fell to the ground, losing his grip on his revolvers. As he wiped the mud from his eyes, he saw Sterling Walcott standing over him. Sterling might be a wealthy ranch owner, but he was still a tough man, and the punch he threw had landed square. Colt's head spun and his ears rang as Walcott yelled at him.

"Couldn't take the hint, could you, Warner? I told you to stay away from my daughter." He landed a kick to Colt's midsection. "I offered you an easy way out of this mess you call a ranch." Another kick. Colt was having trouble breathing. "All you had to do was say yes, and you could have walked away from here a rich man and started a life somewhere else."

Walcott tried to kick him again. Colt grabbed his foot and heaved, knocking Walcott to the ground. Walcott lost his revolver as he fell, and Colt jumped on top of him. They rolled around on the sloppy ground, each landing blows before they broke free of each other and scrambled to their feet, bleeding in the rain from various scrapes and cuts.

"The Whistlestop is mine. I'm not going anywhere," Colt managed to get out between labored breaths. "I love your daughter, and I'm not leaving her or my son, either!"

He shouted the last as he lunged at Walcott. The men traded blows again, with Colt landing several to the midsection of the older man, who was now having breathing troubles of his own.

Finally, Walcott grabbed Colt by the throat with his left hand and, with his right, landed a blow to the side of Colt's face that knocked him to the ground and almost knocked him unconscious.

As Colt lay in the mud, trying to regain his senses, Walcott bent down, pulled his revolver out of the sludge, and stood over Colt with the gun pointed at his head. "All you had to do was leave." His breathing was heavy. Even through the driving rain and the mud caking Walcott's face, Colt could see the hate in his father-in-law's eyes. "All you had to do was leave. You didn't belong here in the first place. Why didn't you just go back to whatever God-forsaken dust pit you came from?" He cocked the gun. "Goodbye, Mr. Warner. And good riddance."

A shot cut through the sound of the rain. Colt checked himself for wounds. There was nothing. He stared up at Sterling Walcott who had an anguished look on his face and a stain on his shirt that was growing larger by the second. Colt scrambled to grab one of his pistols from the mud and get to his feet while Walcott fell, first to his knees, staring at Colt with disbelief in his eyes, and then finally face down in the puddles that had formed on the ground.

Colt looked around, bewildered, straining to see where the shot had come from.

On the porch was Sadie, Colt's rifle in her hands, her eyes as big as saucers, and a look of shock on her face. Colt ran to her and gently removed the gun from her hands. "Sadie, are you all right?"

"He . . . he was going to kill you." Sadie's voice shook. "I didn't have a choice. I couldn't let him do it. Oh, Colt." She buried her head in Colt's chest and started sobbing.

The killing of Sterling Walcott ended the fight. His men weren't willing to continue if there wasn't going to be a payday. The only sounds now were the driving rain and the moans from the injured men.

Colt looked around the yard. His men were worse for wear, but he didn't think any had been killed. It was nothing short of a miracle.

He looked again, trying to see Brick. He couldn't find him anywhere. "Where's Brick? Why didn't he take you up to the cave like he promised?"

Sadie looked up at him. "He tried to, Colt. I wouldn't let him. He took Ruby, though. And they have our son with them."

"I don't care what you said, he shouldn't have left you!" Colt raged. "He promised me . . ."

Then Ridge yelled something that sent a chill down his spine.

"Colt, Troy Benton ain't here either."

CHAPTER 24

Colt searched the mud for his second revolver. "Ridge, stay here and look after Sadie," he said once he found it. "Make sure none of these guys get any second thoughts. I'm going to find Brick and my son." He ran toward the mountain.

Brick stood at the mouth of the hideaway, gun at the ready, listening to the commotion below. He had lit a small fire toward the back of the cave, and Ruby sat beside it with James in her lap. The boy was scared and crying.

"Darlin', I'm gonna need you to keep that boy quiet as best you can," Brick said without looking around. "No use hiding if we're gonna tell everyone where we are."

"I'm trying, Brick. He's scared. So am I. I don't know anything about kids."

"I know, Ruby. I'm sorry. Just do your best."

Brick kept peering through the rain, looking for anyone that might have followed them. The noise from down below suddenly stopped. "It's gone quiet down there," he told Ruby.

"What does that mean?" she asked.

"Not sure yet, hon. Either we have a place to go to after this, or we don't."

IN THE RAIN, Troy had lost sight of Brick and Ruby. He was now scouring the mountain, trying to find where they had gone, confused. How could two people just disappear into thin air?

He continued up the slope, becoming angrier with each step. He was out here getting cold and wet, and he couldn't find who he was looking for. Why didn't that damn Brick just come out and fight like a man? That son-of-a-bitch was going to pay for this. And for what he did to Jessie and The Brotherhood. He was going to make Brick suffer.

What was that he heard? Was that a child's cry? He strained to hear above the rain and kept climbing, looking for his prey, moving slowly and cautiously on the wet, slippery slope. At one point, his boot slipped, and he almost slid down the mountain. He caught himself, but some rocks and mud went tumbling down the side. "Godammit!" he said aloud. "You're gonna pay for this, Brick Warner. I'm a goddamn cowboy, not a mountain goat."

BRICK THOUGHT HE HEARD A NOISE, and then some rocks and mud slid down the mountain face just to the left of the cave opening. So, someone was above them, then? Troy? Tank? Some other member of the gang?

Troy, Brick decided. It had to be Troy. Troy was so angry with him that there was no way he would let anybody else have the privilege of killing him. He would want to do it himself.

Colt had found a great spot. The cave was hard to see at the best of times, and in this rain, it was almost invisible. Brick peered out from the mouth. No sign of Troy. He slowly moved to his left along the face of the mountain, trying to see above the cave.

There was a loud crack and then the high-pitched whine of a bullet ricocheting from the rock beside him. Brick dropped to one knee, trying to see where the shot had come from.

There was a yell from somewhere up the slope. "Almost got you right there, Brick! You know you got this coming for what you did. Stand up and take what's coming to you like a man!" Another shot, but it wasn't as close.

"Just leave it alone, Troy," Brick called back. "Nobody else has to die here today. Walk away and keep The Brotherhood. It's yours. Just let me and Ruby live our lives."

"Can't do it, Brick. You killed Jessie and disrespected everything The Brotherhood was supposed to stand for. Can't let you get away with that."

Brick needed Troy to keep talking until he could pinpoint his location. "Listen, Troy. Hear that silence? There's no more gunfire from down below. Whatever this was, it's over now." He squinted, fighting the rain, desperate for any sign of Troy.

"It was never about the fight, Brick," Troy yelled back. "Meeting Walcott and his men was just a happy coincidence. This is between you and me. We rode together; we robbed together. We were more than friends. We were brothers—and you turned your back on all of that. You don't do that to family."

Troy raised up a little, then, to get a better angle, and Brick spotted him at last. He fired two quick shots. Both missed, but Troy reacted by leaping back—and lost his footing. He fell hard on his back and started to slide down the mountain face. He slid right over the top of the cave and thudded down to Brick's right, still on his feet.

Brick swung toward him, and they squared off, guns in hand. "Jim *was* my family, Troy, him and Colt," Brick said. "They kept trying to keep me from what we were doing. Right up until the day Jim died, they were trying. That's family. You and the boys, we were friends. As long as I kept planning our jobs, kept making us money, then you kept me along. For a long time, that was enough. You boys filled a hole for me, too. But I was never gonna be as tight as you and Tank and Jessie. I was always going to be the outsider."

"You should have stayed that way." Troy snarled. "Should have beat your ass every day in that schoolyard. You and your brother. Two city boys turned sodbusters trying to fit in out here. Well, first, I'm gonna kill you, and then I'm gonna kill your girl and whoever's kid that is that's crying in there."

"Well, here's your chance, Troy," Brick said, desperate to keep Troy's attention on him instead of Ruby and James. "Let's put down the guns and settle this like men."

"Really? You wanna fight with a buggered arm? Are you crazy? You were barely tough enough in school. You got no chance now."

"You going to keep standing there getting soaked and flapping your yap, or are you gonna man up and throw hands?" Brick holstered his gun, then removed the sling from his arm and unbuckled his gun belt.

"Oh, I'm gonna enjoy this, huckleberry. You can count on that." A sick smile came across Troy's face as he holstered his own gun and removed the belt.

For a moment, they looked at each other, then, at the same time, they tossed the gun belts aside.

As soon as the guns hit the ground, Troy lunged. He grabbed Brick's waist and wrestled him to the ground. Both men landed punches as they rolled around in front of the cave opening, but Brick's left arm was in agony. With an almighty shove of his good arm, he managed to push Troy off him and scrambled to his feet before Troy managed to do the same. He stepped forward and landed a blow with his right hand to the side of Troy's head that knocked him flat on his back again, stunned.

Brick straddled his chest and started to land more punches. Troy's head jerked from side to side with every blow, blood splattering from his mouth and mixing with the rain on the ground.

Brick's left arm was screaming in pain. He had to let up in order to give it a rest. He stared down at Troy, who smiled back at him. It was that same sadistic smile that Brick had seen a hundred times, only this time, it featured missing teeth and bleeding lips.

"That all you got?" Troy asked. Then he drew back his arms and smashed both fists into Brick's chest, hurling him backward and knocking the breath from him. Brick rolled in the mud, trying to get back to his feet while he fought for air.

Troy was up and on him quickly, landing a boot to Brick's midsection that laid him out again and flung him over onto his stomach. "My turn now, gimp."

Troy put his boot on Brick's shoulder, covering his bullet wound. He pressed down with all his weight. Brick screamed. Benton laughed. "I thought you were something, that maybe we could build something together. We could have been famous! Could have been bigger than the James boys." He pressed down his foot again. "But I see now you were just a poser all along. You weren't fit to lead The Brotherhood."

Brick summoned up enough strength to roll quickly to his right. The movement knocked Troy off balance and sent him to the ground once more. Again, Brick jumped on top. This time, he concentrated on Troy's body and felt a satisfying snap as he broke some of Troy's ribs. Troy moaned.

As Brick drew back his arm for a final right cross to Troy's jaw, Troy jabbed a finger in his eye. Yowling, Brick rolled off, one hand clutched to his eye, trying to clear his vision.

Troy scrambled to the side and picked up his revolver. As Brick lowered his hand and blinked blearily up at him, he leveled the gun. "Enough is enough. Your time is through. Goodbye, Brick." Troy pulled the hammer back.

"Don't do it, Troy!" Colt's voice cut through the rain from behind Troy. "Put the gun down nice and slow and turn around."

Troy paused, and Brick scrambled to his feet. Troy lifted his hands out to his side a little but held onto the gun.

Colt walked toward the men, emerging from the rain with both guns drawn. "You all right, Brick?"

"I'm fine, Colt. Just a little bruised. And damn tired."

"It's over, Troy," Colt said, his voice flat and serious, guns at the ready. "You lose. Get back on your horse and get the hell out of here before you make me do something that I don't want to do."

Troy smiled again. "You know, I always wondered if what they said about you was true."

"What's that?"

"Are you really that fast on the draw? You don't look like much. I think I can take you."

"Don't do it, Troy," Brick tried to warn his former friend. "You'll lose."

"I don't think so." Without taking his eyes off Colt, Troy knelt, laid his gun on the rock, and then reached for his gun belt. He stood, buckled it on, bent over and picked up the gun, and then shoved it into its holster. "You ready, Warner?" He moved into a showdown stance.

Colt holstered his own pistols. "Don't, Troy."

"Shut up and draw you—" Troy went for his gun as he spoke.

Two shots rang out. Troy's bullet hit the ground a few feet in front of Colt. He stared, surprised, red blossoming on his chest as his gun fell from suddenly nerveless fingers. He'd barely started to raise his arm before Colt's bullet found its mark. "You weren't even ready," Troy muttered. "How'd you . . .?"

"I warned you, Troy."

Pretty Boy fell to the ground, let out one last breath, and was gone.

Ruby emerged from the cave with James in her arms. "Are you all right, Brick?"

"I'm fine, darlin'. Everything's okay now. Troy's gone."

Colt took his son from Ruby and then turned his attention to Brick. "You left my wife down there in the middle of that mess. What the hell is wrong with you?"

"She wouldn't come, Colt. I tried to take her like you told me to. She wouldn't leave. Damn stubborn woman, she is."

Colt was still angry. "I don't care if she threatened to shoot you. You should have dragged her out of there. I've half a mind to beat your ass myself."

The rain suddenly stopped, and Brick was about to argue

back when they heard a voice from behind them. "Just turn around easy, boys. Don't fire them weapons."

Tired of the fighting and not ready for another round, Colt and Brick slowly turned to face Sheriff Van Atten.

"What are you doing here, Sheriff?" Colt asked.

"I was on my way out here to pay my respects to Borden and bring you some news. Storm slowed me down. By the looks of things, I may have gotten here a little late."

"It was justified, Sheriff. They attacked the ranch. We weren't about to let 'em have it without a fight."

"That's what your friend Alex said down below. I don't doubt it for a second, boys. Look, there's another reason I'm here. I heard some scuttlebutt that the leader of The Brotherhood might be out here at this ranch as well. Know anything about that?"

Colt and Brick stared at each other. Brick wasn't sure what was going to happen next. Colt spoke first, never taking his gaze off Brick. "He sure is, Sheriff. He's right in front of you."

Brick sucked in a startled breath. His own brother had sold him out!

But Colt wasn't done. He switched his attention from Brick to the sheriff. "Unfortunately, I already killed him. Troy Benton was the leader of the gang."

The sheriff stared at the boys apprehensively. "You mean to tell me that Troy Benton ran The Brotherhood?" The sheriff gave Brick a narrow look. "I don't recall Benton having a hitch in his step, and witnesses say the leader walked a little different."

"Aw, come on, now, Sheriff," Colt said. "That was one witness account from one robbery. Who's to say Troy didn't get kicked by a horse? Or fall off the sidewalk drunk? Any number of reasons why he could have had an issue walking."

The sheriff kept his eyes on Brick as he thought for a few seconds. Finally, he turned his attention back to Colt. "Well, I guess that does make a might bit of sense. I suppose that could be the case. That Benton boy always was a bit of trouble."

The brothers looked at one another with relief.

"I guess as long as there won't be no more trouble from The Brotherhood, then case closed."

Brick spoke up for the first time. "There won't be, Sheriff."

Van Atten smiled a little. "No, I'm guessing there won't be. I'll send a deputy back with a wagon to help collect the bodies."

"Wait a minute, Sheriff." Colt was curious. "You said you were bringing some news?"

"Right, right," said the sheriff. "I almost forgot. Webb Logan is dead, Colt. I thought you'd want to know since he and Borden were friends and all."

Colt felt stunned. "What? When? I was just with him."

"I just got the news from the sheriff down in Brela. Way I hear it, Logan was at the bar, all broken up about Borden, getting drunk and shooting his mouth off about some business in Bullard and how the no-good lily-livered cowards of The Brotherhood shot the man in the back. Couple of members of the gang were there and didn't take too kindly to old Webb's drunken mutterings. They waited for him outside the bar and jumped him when he came out. Webb didn't stand a chance."

Colt couldn't believe what he was hearing. "Sheriff, can you have his body brought out here? I'd like to bury him next to Jim."

"Webb didn't have no family that I'm aware of, and I'm sure he'd appreciate the gesture. I'll talk to the sheriff in Brela and see if we can arrange that."

Chapter 25

—————————

The sun broke the horizon the morning after the battle, and the men of the Whistlestop started to rise. All were worse for wear and bore the wounds of the previous day. Drake, Shep, Reverend Sullivan, and Ed Waters loaded the wagon and were ready to head back to town when Drake pulled Colt aside for a discussion. "Colt, I know you're going to miss Jim, but I want you to know that you're ready for this. You can do it. Jim taught you well, and you listened to everything he said. He was so proud of you. You're going to be okay, you and your family."

"Thanks Drake, that means a lot." Colt gave the man a hug.

Drake reached into his pocket and pulled out a roll of bills. "You remember that two hundred dollars you gave me? How I told you that I would hold on to it for you for a later time? Well, I did a little more than take care of it." He handed the money to Colt. "I had a good run at the card table. There's a thousand dollars there, Colt. Use it for the Whistlestop."

Colt couldn't believe what he was seeing. "I can't take that, Drake. It's too much."

"It's your money, Colt. I was just caretaking it." Drake chuckled. "Besides, this place could use some work now."

"Thank you, Drake." Colt put the money in his pocket. He gave a wave as the four men drove off in the wagon with their horses in tow. He was glad they had come. If it weren't for them, he might have lost the ranch in the altercation. He couldn't believe how lucky he was to call those men friends.

He looked around at the remaining men and was thankful for their friendship, as well. Lanky was nursing a serious shoulder injury, and Lane and Ridge were caring for their own injuries. Alex was the only man who had emerged unscathed from the skirmish. Jim and Drake had been right all along. A few good friends were all a man needed.

The day was spent cleaning up the wreckage and putting together a plan for the future of the Whistlestop. With the money from Drake and Brick (once he retrieved it), plus whatever Alex could get for Colt's steel-company stock, the Whistlestop was suddenly ripe with capital to invest, and with Walcott and The Brotherhood no longer an issue, there were no obstacles in the way of their success. He and Brick were about to achieve the life that his father had envisioned when he had put them on that train all those years ago. He was sure that his parents would be proud of them.

The following day, Sterling Walcott was laid to rest beside Jim. In spite of all the trouble the man had caused Colt, he was still Sadie's father. Besides, without Walcott, Colt probably wouldn't have everything that was most important to him in the world. Without Walcott, there would be no Sadie, without Sadie, no James. It was even partly his desire to show Walcott that he could be something that had led Colt to purchase the

Whistlestop. He had been intimidating and hostile, but there was no doubt about the impression he had made on Colt's life.

Colt and the boys were standing in a group in the yard when Sadie and her mother approached them. "Colt, I would like you to meet my mother."

Lydia Walcott was a proper western woman who had always listened to the wishes of her husband. Although Sadie had managed to sneak a visit or two with her mother over the years, Lydia had never been to the Whistlestop or introduced to the man her daughter had married. Now, she extended her hand. "Mr. Warner."

"Colt is fine, Mrs. Walcott." Colt shook her hand.

"Colt it is, then. Please, call me Lydia."

"Mama has something she wants to ask you, Colt." Sadie's eyes were filled with excitement.

"Please, go ahead and ask, ma'am. Whatever I can do for you."

"Very well, then. Colt, my husband was a hard man, no question about it, but he also cared very deeply for his family and worked to make sure that we were taken care of. I'm not excusing his methods, mind you, just giving you some insight as to why those decisions were made."

"I never doubted your husband's love for Sadie or for you, ma'am."

"Well, good, then, that's settled. What I wanted to ask, Colt, was this: my husband built a very successful ranch, one that is both very large and very lucrative, which I have now inherited. I never paid any attention to the business myself, and since it would legally go to Sadie if I were to pass anyway, I was wondering if there might be a chance that you would consider taking over the ranch yourself?"

Colt couldn't believe what he was hearing. Him running

Sterling Walcott's ranch? "I already have the Whistlestop, Ms. Walcott, and I've fought long and hard to keep it. I don't want to give it up."

"I'm not asking you to give it up, Colt. I'm asking if you think you could run them both."

Colt didn't know what to say. Taking on both would make him and Brick the largest ranchers in the area.

He looked at Alex. "Think you can handle the business affairs for two operations?"

Alex smiled. "I believe I can, yes."

Colt turned to Ridge. "The Walcott spread is a damn sight larger than here. I'm gonna need a good foreman to keep things in line over there. Are you up for the job? There'll be a pay raise, of course."

Now Ridge looked stunned. "Me? I got a job right here, Colt. Who would look after things here?"

"I'll need my best over there, Ridge." He turned to Lanky. "Besides, I think we've got someone here who can handle the foreman duties."

"Me?" Lanky's voice squeaked a little.

"Why not? You've been watching Ridge and learning what he was doing. You're my best friend, Lanky. Who else would I want running the show?"

Lanky and Ridge, looking stunned, both nodded in agreement.

Colt turned to his brother next. "What do you say, Brick? Want to be a cattle baron?"

"You know, Colt, I believe I do. I think ranching life will suit us just fine." He put his arm around Ruby.

Colt turned back to his mother-in-law and smiled. "Well, Mrs. Walcott—uh—Lydia, looks like we're gonna run your ranch for you." He put out his hand again to shake on the deal.

Lydia Walcott accepted his hand and shook it. "Glad to hear it, Colt, but it's not my ranch; it's yours now. I want nothing to do with the place. You just make sure my daughter and my grandkids come to visit me regularly and that she takes care of me."

"It's a promise."

The rest of the day was filled with celebrating the good fortune that had fallen on everyone.

Later, Colt and Brick sat out on the porch looking out over the yard as the sun went down behind them, and the shadows crept farther and farther over the ground in front of them. They listened to the sounds of the people they loved the most, talking happily in the house.

With a smile on his face, Colt said, "Well, Brick. Now that you're a successful cattle rancher, what's the first thing you're gonna do?"

Brick smiled back. "Well, I promised Ruby she could have a horse."

The two brothers laughed.

For the Warner brothers, the future looked bright.

ACKNOWLEDGMENTS

I would like to take this opportunity to thank some of the people who have helped this story come to life with their invaluable contributions. Those people are: Devlin Plesniewicz, Jocelyn Smith, Karlie Kowalchuk, Curtis Turner, Andy Melvin, Dawn Ferguson, Melina Tallentire, and Jess McKenzie. Without you, the story wouldn't be what it is today. I thank you.

About the Author

The Brand of Brotherhood is the second novel for T.D. Zummack, who is also the author of the thriller *Amazing Grace*. He is a member of the Saskatchewan Writers' Guild and spent his adolescence reading authors such as Agatha Christie and Louis L' Amour and his adulthood reading true crime.

He is a true crime and mystery nerd and when not writing can be found lounging around his house with his family and their pets.

You can find any and all author-related information at his website, tdzummack.com, as well as short stories he's written on the platform page vocal.media/authors/t-d-zummack.

About Endless Sky Books

Founded by award-winning author Edward Willett, Endless Sky Books assists authors with publishing all kinds of books, from children's books to poetry to novels to nonfiction. Select titles, like this one, are released under the Endless Sky Books imprint.

Find out more about Endless Sky Books on our website, endless-sky-books.com, and visit our sister publisher, Shadowpaw Press, at shadowpawpress.com.